PARKER

CHARLIE TEAM 5

ANNA BLAKELY

PARKER

Charlie Team Series 5

Anna Blakely

Parker

Charlie Team Series 5

First Edition
Copyright © 2023 Saje Publishing
All rights reserved.
All cover art and logo Copyright © 2022
Publisher: Saje Publishing
Cover by: Lori Jackson
Edited by: Tracy Roelle
Proofreading by: Angelia Springs, Judy Wagner, and Kim Ruiz

❀ Created with Vellum

ABOUT THE BOOK

He's a billionaire with an attitude and a secret government job. She's a hacker on the run from her past. Together they must fight to keep her alive or lose their chance at happiness forever.

To the world, Parker Collins is little more than an entitled rich boy. He has a reputation for spending his days playing games and his nights in the arms of the next in a long line of willing women. But what you see isn't always what you get, and for Parker, there's only one woman consuming his every thought. One he's starting to fall for...and he doesn't even know her real name.

Quinn "Jinx" Wilder is a woman hiding from her past. She's tried changing her name, using an encrypted phone, cutting herself off from the rest of the world... Everything a person with her skills is capable of. But it doesn't matter. The man taunting her is still there. A faceless, nameless creature lurking in shadows. And when things escalate into a life-or-death situation, there's only one person Quinn knows to turn to... A man she's never actually met.

After a whirlwind rescue—and slightly awkward meet-cute —Parker and Quinn's online friendship soon turns into something more. But just as these two computer geniuses begin considering they might have a future together, the unthinkable happens and Quinn is taken. Desperate to find the woman he loves before it's too late, Parker turns to the one group he knows he can count on... The men of Charlie Team.

With five highly trained operatives by his side, Parker finds himself in a race against time and a greedy fugitive hell-bent on revenge. And failure is not an option. Not when it comes to the woman he loves.

To my Grandma Billie. You've been the mom Dad never had, the best mother-in-law Mom could ask for, and the very best grandma a girl could be blessed to have.

From my earliest memories of standing at the window waiting to see your car pull into the drive (and the more embarrassing ones where I stood at that same window crying as you drove away), you've always been there to love, support, and cheer me on. Your kindness knows no bounds, and your heart is as big as any I've ever known. Thank you for everything. For always being there for us when you didn't have to, for loving us as if we were your own, and for being a shining example to all of what unconditional truly means.

I'll love you forever ~
Anna

AUTHOR'S NOTE

It's hard to believe that Parker and Quinn's story has brought the RISC Charlie Team series to an end. Fun fact, I hadn't initially planned on furthering the RISC world past Bravo Team. But after receiving several reader requests during my completion of the Alpha and Bravo series, here we are! And I can't tell you how much I've enjoyed writing these characters.

As for Parker, I couldn't think of a better hero to wrap things up than a sexy billionaire who's every bit as alpha as the guys on the team. Of course, it takes a special kind of woman to keep a man like Parker Collins grounded...and Quinn Wilder is the perfect gal for the job.

What starts out as an unconventional friendship leads to inextinguishable flames. To the discovery of self-love and the acceptance of being loved. And of course, what Charlie Team story would be complete without, well...Charlie Team?

Oh, and did I mention you'll also get a sneak peek at a couple of the guys from RISC's new Delta Team? No?

Hmm...I guess you'll just have to take my word for it. Or better yet...keep reading ;)

Until next time...

Hugs and Happy Reading!
  ~ Anna

PROLOGUE

CHICAGO, Illinois
Six years ago...

QUINN WILDER STOOD IN THE ALLEY UNDER THE BUILDING'S narrow overhang, a curtain of rain filling her vision as it poured from the gutters above. It was late—nearly midnight —and she was at the back of the yards near Forty-Seventh Street in Chicago.

It was all she could do to keep her wild imagination from taking a dark and twisted turn.

Using her mitten-clad hands, she pulled the collar of her plush winter coat tight, bringing it to her chin in search of the slightest respite from the bone-deep chill of the night. The rhinestone belted backer boy hat offering little protection from the late winter weather.

Damn it, Justin. Where are you?

Fifteen minutes had passed since her boyfriend was supposed to meet her. Fifteen minutes of standing outside in the freezing cold, waiting for Justin to finally decide to grace her with his presence.

Of all nights to be late...

Keeping her movements subtle, Quinn slid a sideways glance to her right. Her chest grew tight, the palpitations of her heart increasing in both speed and force when she spotted a black car with tinted windows. It was parked across from the alley's entrance, its tires snuggled up to the curb on that side of the street.

The men who'd followed her were there, sitting in the sedan's front two seats. She couldn't see them, but they were there.

Watching.

Waiting.

Nausea churned as she began to second-guess her decision. This wasn't how things were supposed to go. This wasn't how things were supposed to end.

They will, you know. Once you do this, that'll be the end.

The urge to flee was so damn tempting, but she didn't dare. As much as she hated everything about this plan, it was still the better option.

For her. For Justin.

This is for him, Quinn. Remember, you're doing this for him.

She felt that truth down to her bones.

Every single decision she'd made over the course of this last year had been for Justin. The reckless abandon with which she loved him...the stupid, crazy things they'd done together...even her heartbreaking betrayal...

It had all been for him.

Blinking away the stinging moisture collecting in the corners of her eyes, Quinn shivered from the cold as she slid her frozen hand into her coat pocket and pulled out her phone. Using her teeth, she removed one of her wool mittens.

With a few trembling taps, she put the phone to her ear and waited. Justin answered on the second ring.

"Keep your panties on, sweet cheeks. I'm almost there."

He sounded happy. Normal. As if he didn't have a care in the world. As if he wasn't about to commit a crime that could send them both to prison for the next twenty years.

That isn't going to happen, Quinn. You made sure of that, remember?

Forcing the second-guesses away, she ignored the newest wave of shivers and stuttered out, "Y-you're late."

"No shit," her boyfriend of eleven months quipped. "Traffic was nuts, and this weather didn't help."

Right on cue, a giant explosion of spider lightning appeared above them. The powerful force of nature illuminated the night sky, its deadly tendrils spreading wide beneath the clouds before dissipating into nothing.

Seconds later, the air in the lightning's path expanded from the sudden discharge of heat, sending a loud clap of thunder rolling past.

Quinn jumped, her already heightened anxiety leaving her back teeth grinding together. "Is it bad out? I hadn't noticed." She did nothing to hide her sarcasm. "I mean, I've only been standing out in this crap for nearly twenty minutes waiting for you to show up."

"It's only been fifteen." Justin appeared from around the building's corner. "And I'm here."

Beneath the protection of his dark gray hoodie, a flash of near-perfect teeth appeared with the twenty-six-year-old's boyish smile. With the jeans and a faded denim jacket he always wore, Quinn thought—and not for the first time—

the guy could totally be related to the famous Hemsworth brothers.

And the way his handsome face lit up when he saw her...

Sometimes he looks at me as if I'm his everything.

Quinn's worried heart filled as Justin joined her beneath the narrow overhang, but the moment of serenity was over as quickly as it came. As she stared up into those crystal blue eyes that had stolen her young heart months before, she could almost *feel* the shift in her universe begin.

"Hey, babe." Justin leaned in for a quick, chaste kiss. "You ready to do this?"

Am I?

Her gaze flittered to that black car again before bouncing back to him. Quinn swallowed her apprehension and smiled. "Yep."

"That's my girl." He kissed her again.

Reaching around her, Justin unlocked the padlock on the plain metal door next to where she stood. With a quick glance at their immediate surroundings, he yanked the metal lock free, pulled the door open, and ducked inside.

Quinn risked a hidden glance to her right. The heavy downpour all but concealed the black car now, which explained how he'd missed seeing it.

Giving the invisible men inside a final look, she followed her boyfriend through the back door of what had been a small deli. But like most business in this area of the city, the local establishment hadn't lasted.

It was there one day, and plywood boards and newspapers covered the windows the next. An unfortunate turn of events for the owners...a struck of luck for Justin. The perfect spot, he'd called it.

Perfect. Right.

Guilt assaulted her as she moved cautiously into the unlit space. Walking past the stainless-steel counters, sink, and commercial-grade stove, the two made their way through the empty kitchen and into the open space at the front of the unoccupied business.

"Wait here," Justin ordered, not waiting to see if she'd obeyed before shifting directions.

As instructed, Quinn stayed put, watching his shadowed form move toward the blackened corner of the wide-open space to their right. Her lips parted in surprise when a light came on and the reality of the situation sank in.

The small lamp's warm glow revealed a long table fitted with four large, curved computer monitors, two wireless keyboards, a state-of-the-art desktop, and a laptop she didn't recognize. Resting to the side was a small, portable machine she recognized as an instant issuer credit card embosser.

Praying her acting skills were up to par, Quinn lifted a stunned gaze from the tech-filled table to him. "Justin... When did you get all of this?" The better question to ask was, "*Where* did you get it? You don't have the money for this sort of set-up."

"Correction." His lips curved into an arrogant smirk. "I didn't have the money."

"But you do now?" Quinn frowned.

Like her, Justin had come from nothing. It was the first of many connections they'd made along the way, and the driving force behind his plan. Also like her, he still jumped from job-to-job. Always part-time and rarely over minimum wage.

That's how she knew there was no way Justin had the savings to cover something like this. Not without help.

"Where did you get the equipment, Justin?" she asked again.

Quinn knew full-well where it had come from, but she needed him to say the words aloud.

Their original plan had been to use a refurbished PC he'd bought from a guy at the big box store where he currently worked. They'd scrimped and saved, pooling their cash together to cover the cost.

When they finally had enough, Justin brought the computer home, to their run-down apartment, and she immediately went to work taking it apart. Rebuilding the computer from scratch, Quinn had used all new parts, each purchased as soon as they could afford them.

It took several weeks, but by the time she was finished, they were the proud owners of a custom-made PC with enough power and speed to pull off the biggest hack they'd ever attempted.

Biggest and most dangerous.

"I did a dry run a couple days ago." Justin kept his focus on his current task. "It worked okay with the system you built, but a job this big needs the best." His eyes found hers. "Go big or go home, right?"

Quinn's stomach dropped. "I thought you agreed to wait until tonight. You *promised* we'd do this together."

If he'd messed up a single step during his practice run...

He could have ruined everything I've been trying to do. If he'd gotten caught somehow...we'd both be sitting in a jail cell right now, instead of sneaking around in this shitty building in the middle of an even shittier night.

"Relax, babe." Those blue eyes rolled the way they always did when she got worried. "I didn't fuck anything up. I can do a simple hack. Besides, now we know for sure it's gonna work."

"Well, then." Quinn crossed her arms at her chest and stared. "As long as we know..."

No acting was required at the moment, her anger and frustration most definitely real. How could he risk himself like that? Risk *her?*

"Don't be like that."

"Like what?" She scowled. "There's a reason I didn't want you messing with any of it without me, Justin. Did you stop for even a second to think about what would've happened if you'd gotten caught?"

Lips tight, she struggled to control the conflicting emotions filtering through her veins. Anger and fear. Uncertainty and dread. The war raging inside her was strong.

Stronger than the actual one currently filling the skies right now.

"I wasn't going to get caught, babe. I also wasn't going to risk trying to pull off the whole job without you behind the keyboard. I need what's locked in here"—a light tap of his finger to her temple—"to do that."

"Then how—"

"I picked the day manager's wallet from his pocket when I was leaving work that morning. Took no time to hack into the guy's online credit card account. Once I was in, I changed the email on file to a dummy one I'd set up before. That way, he wouldn't get alerted to the activity taking place. After that, I reported the card lost."

Quinn stared back at him. "If you canceled the guy's card, then how—"

"Some of the bigger card companies have started issuing e-cards instantly after reporting a card lost or stolen. The poor bastard's new numbers popped up right there on the screen." Justin smiled proudly. "By the time he realizes what happened, it'll be too late. The available credit will have already been spent. I get that we're not messing with the whole lost or stolen card scheme for the big job, but I

wanted to see if it would work, and it did. Now come on."
Justin pulled out one of the two folding chairs butted up to
the table and sat. "With you at the helm, it'll go a helluva lot
faster, but we need to be out of this place before dawn, and
we have all of these to get through."

From his jacket pocket, he revealed a stack of crisp, clean
credit cards. No customer names or numbers, just a plain
front with their target's name and logo, and a back with a
black electronic strip and the usual small-print gibberish on
the backs of all credit cards.

Quinn swallowed hard, her eyes zeroed in on the cards.
This was it. The point of no return.

You can do this. For him, remember?

She lifted her schooled gaze to his, praying he wouldn't
see the truth behind her casual façade. "You get those from
that guy you told me about?" She asked. "What was his
name...Matt...Mark..."

"Monty." Justin set the stack down and shrugged his
denim jacket off his shoulders. "Yeah. That's the guy." Laying
it sloppily on the back of his chair, he removed the thick,
blue rubber band from the stack.

"That's right. What was his last name again?" Quinn
went to the empty chair. Working to control her breathing—
and racing heart—she licked her dry lips and took a seat.
"Or maybe I never asked you. I can't remember." She forced
a light chuckle. "And how did you even find someone who
knows how to make fake credit cards?" She reached for the
stack to get a better look but was stopped with a firm, almost
painful grip around her wrist.

Her eyes flew to Justin's, his expression unreadable
despite his close proximity.

"Careful, babe. These things cost me a pretty penny.

Don't want to risk scratching the electronic strips and ruining them."

A condescending tone squeezed her heart a little. It was something she'd come to notice more and more in recent weeks, along with the eye rolls and head shakes. All things she'd brushed off, excusing it as a byproduct of the stress he'd been under.

Hacking into a major credit card company can do that to a fella.

With another nervous lick of her lips, Quinn scooted in close and placed a hand on his denim-clad thigh. "I know they had to have cost a lot." *More than you know.* "I bet they set you back, what? A grand? And that's not including the other stuff."

"Gotta spend money to make money."

"Right, but how do we even know this Monty guy can be trusted?" She continued her attempts at getting him to keep talking. "I mean, what if he goes to the cops?"

"Jesus, Quinn," Justin snapped. Shoulders rising with a calming breath, he turned to face her, cupping her cheeks and softening his annoyed expression. "Look, Monty is *the* guy to go to for this sort of thing, okay? The man makes his living on this shit. Hell, he has a whole team of guys working for him."

"A team?" She blinked. "Really?"

He nodded. "They steal the goods, bring them to Monty, and then he either sells the stuff or makes a trade. So no, the guy sure as hell ain't turning us in to the fucking cops."

Almost there, Quinn. Just need a little more...

"What about the money?" She needed to know. "You never said how you were able to buy all of this."

Justin's eyelids twitched, his gaze flickering away a fraction of a second before zeroing back in on hers. "Let's just say Monty and I came to an agreement."

"An agreement." Quinn kept her tone even despite her thundering heart. "How much?"

"Babe, you have to understand—"

"How big is Monty's cut, Justin?"

Come on...tell me.

His Adam's apple bobbed with an audible swallow. "Thirty percent."

"Thirty?" The air in her lungs escaped with a harsh huff.

He'd offered up thirty percent of their cut without so much as a word about it until she asked? And if she *hadn't* asked, what then?

They tried telling you this would happen, but you didn't listen.

Angry—both at Justin and herself—Quinn shot to her feet before pacing the open area nearby. "You agreed to give away fifteen percent of *my* cut, and you didn't think to, I don't know, include me in that decision?"

"Of course, I was going to tell you." He turned away as if her concern meant nothing. "In case you hadn't noticed, I've been a little busy getting things ready."

He was *going* to tell her, but he hadn't. Not about any of it.

Not the decision to buy the new equipment...not the deal he'd made in order to *get* those things... Justin also hadn't told her he was planning to test the program without her.

Quinn stopped pacing and looked at him. Though she tried to ignore it, she also couldn't help but wonder...

What else haven't you told me?

The hypocrisy of the unspoken question wasn't lost on

her. She was fully aware of her own secrets. A massive, glaring, gut-knotting one in particular.

But that was different. The secrets she held were for his benefit as much as they were hers, and despite his own recently revealed deceptions, Quinn still felt the need to protect him.

Justin was the first man to actually give a damn about her. He'd befriended her. Loved her. And once she'd proven he had no reason not to, Justin had finally come to trust her.

From day one, he'd had her back. Now it was time to return the favor.

He was becoming impulsive. Reckless, even. And given some of the things he'd spouted off in recent weeks—like threatening to find someone else to do the job every time she started to question the sanity of his plan—Quinn knew...

If I don't step in right now, he's going to end up spending the rest of his life in prison. Or worse.

She pushed away the guilt and jutted her chin. Adjusting her hat, she straightened her shoulders and went back to where he was sitting. "Sorry." She offered him a smile. "I didn't mean to freak out. I guess I'm just nervous."

Major understatement, Quinn.

"No need to be nervous, babe. Come on." Justin tapped the chair's metal seat. "Let's get this party started, yeah?" When she removed her coat and sat down beside him, he framed her face once more before pressing his lips against hers. "In case I forget to say it...thank you."

"For what?"

"For being my partner in all of this." When she opened her mouth to dispute the undeserved title, he cut her off with a finger to her lips. "I get that this whole thing is my brainchild. But what started as a fleeting thought turned into a doable plan, and that's all thanks to you. Well, you and your mad hacking skills, that is." He tapped the tip of her nose before returning his attention to the equipment in front of them.

Quinn had admittedly used her God-given talent with all-things tech to break the law on numerous occasions. But it was always to help those who'd been wronged.

People...animals... It didn't matter. If she saw a clear-cut need, she did whatever she could to help. And she never, *ever* kept anything for herself.

It was how she justified what she did. Everything Quinn had done was for the greater good. But this was different. What Justin had pressured her into agreeing to...

"For once, we're making this about helping ourselves and taking what *we* deserve." Justin spared her a pointed glance. "What *you* deserve."

When he'd first broached the subject, he'd told her he wanted to make a point. To teach the big credit card companies a lesson on preying on the weak and desperate.

Soon, what started as a fantastical idea somehow morphed into something real. A reachable goal with a tangible reward...and some very real, very *serious* risks.

She looked over at Justin, the knowledge of what needed to be done warring with the thick blanket of dread weighing heavily on her soul. In a moment of weakness, Quinn's fear of losing the only person to ever find her worthy of love overtook everything else.

"I think we should wait," she blurted before thinking.

Justin's incredulous laugh echoed throughout the empty space. "Wait? Hell no, we're not waiting. The time is now, babe. We'll start with this first mark, and if everything goes smoothly, we'll move on to the next. And the next." His lips spread into a wide, toothy smile. "Just think. In a few short hours, we'll have access to more money than we can spend. We'll be able to go anywhere...do anything. *Buy* anything." Justin shook his head as if he didn't believe his own words. "We're going to be so fucking rich."

Excitement poured over him in waves. His cheeks became flushed; the blues in his eyes darkening. And if Quinn didn't know any better, she'd almost think he was almost becoming aroused at the thought of what they were about to do.

It's the pre-hacking rush.

Though she'd never experienced it herself, she'd heard about the oversized dose of adrenaline some hackers got before a job. A massive rush brought on by one thing, and one thing only...

Power.

That blanket grew heavier, the churning of emotions becoming stronger inside her gut.

"I thought this was about showing these big companies how wrong it was to prey on the weak and desperate." Quinn frowned. "To pay them back for dragging your parents into bankruptcy."

"Yeah...about that." He licked his lips before flashing his signature *I'm so innocent* smile. "I may have embellished that whole backstory about my parents a bit."

She gave a slight tilt of her head, her throat working to swallow the knot forming there. "Define a bit."

I need him to say it. I need him to look me in the eyes and tell me the truth.

Hesitating in his answer, Justin drew in a breath before rambling off what he almost certainly believed was a justifiable explanation for having lied.

"Okay, listen." He gave his lips a nervous swipe of his tongue. "Don't get mad, but my parents never actually filed for bankruptcy when I was ten. Or...ever." A crooked smirk lifted one corner of his lips. "I just told you that because I knew you'd never agree to this if I'd shared the real motive behind it."

Quinn stared into the eyes of a man she no longer recognized. Despite having already been told the same by others, she'd tried so hard to ignore the truth.

But there was no denying it now. Not when Justin, himself, had just laid the whole ugly truth right out there for her to see.

This grand plan of his wasn't about teaching the companies a lesson. Not like he'd first claimed it was.

No, Justin's so-called crusade to rid the world of heartless, soulless companies was nothing more than a quest to obtain power. To be able to sit behind the safety of a keyboard and change countless lives—for better or worse—with little more than the click of a few buttons.

Quinn had come across others like him before. Men and women who delved into the deep, dark hacking world armed with little more than a sweet set-up and a massive ego trip. And from what she, herself had witnessed in those incidents, it was a combination that almost always ended badly.

For everyone involved.

"You ready?"

Quinn looked at Justin again. She hated herself for what she was about to do. To him. To herself.

But she didn't have a choice. Not really. Not when their entire future was on the line.

Filling her lungs, she let the air out in a slow, steady stream before offering him a small smile. "Yeah." She nodded. "I'm ready."

Justin grinned, smacking his hands together in anticipation. "You realize, we're about to change our lives forever, right?"

You have no idea.

Pulling the keyboard close, Quinn drew in another steeling breath and began to type. A few minutes and clicks of the keyboard later, the screen directly in front of her lit up with a spreadsheet filled with account holder information.

Names, account numbers...

"I'm in."

"Hot damn!" Justin slapped his palms onto the table, the unexpected noise making her jump. When she didn't make a move to proceed, he turned to her and frowned. "Well? What are you waiting for? Click that shit so we can get the ball rolling."

Quinn's fingertips hovered over the mouse. This was it. Once she opened that first account, there was no going back.

She moved the curser up the screen to the first group of blue numbers. With a slight tremble in her hand, she held her breath and closed her eyes...and clicked. "There." Her lids lifted, her chest tight from the unstoppable events she'd just put into place. "It's done."

"Oh, nothing's done, babe." Justin began entering his own name into the card printer he'd gotten from Monty. After that, he began typing in their first unsuspecting account holder's credit card number, expiration date, and three-digit security code.

The new card—the one with Justin's name on it—was completed and activated in less than two minutes.

"You did it!" Looking more like a kid at Christmas than a twenty-six-year old man, he grabbed her face and brought her in for a hard, rough kiss. "You fucking did it!"

Oh, she'd done it all right. Quinn just prayed he'd somehow find a way to forgive her.

"Well." Justin's stare turned expectant. "What are you waiting for? Let's hit the next one on the list."

She turned her attention back onto the screen in front of her and waited. When nothing happened, Quinn had no other option but to continue on with his plan.

She opened the next account and repeated the process, her pulse throbbing painfully with each terrified beat of her heart. A stretch of silence passed between her and Justin as they each continued with their assigned tasks.

One-by-one, they worked together. She accessed the individual accounts, and he transferred the information on the screen to the physical cards. And with each new account Quinn clicked open, the more overwhelming her fear and doubt became.

It should be over by now. Why isn't it over?

The cryptic thoughts had just passed through her racing mind when the front door to the closed-down deli burst open, and all hell broke loose around her.

"FBI! Step away from the table with your hands up!"

Quinn's entire body jolted as she jumped to her feet. Throwing her hands high into the air, her lungs froze as five men and two women—each wearing matching coats with bright yellow lettering announcing they were with the Federal Bureau of Investigations—moved toward them with swift, purposeful steps.

"Get down on the ground!" one of the women yelled. Like her co-workers, she had her arms outstretched in front of her, a black pistol pointed directly at her and Justin.

"Don't shoot!" Quinn shouted back, her quivering legs folding beneath her as she dropped to her knees.

Justin followed her lead, shock and fear leaving his eyes wide and his mouth slack jawed. Confusion twisted his face as he swung his stunned gaze to hers. "How the fuck did they know we were here?"

"I—"

"Stop talking and lace your fingers behind your heads!" One of the male FBI agents ordered, cutting off her confession.

Clamping her mouth shut, Quinn did exactly as she was told. With her next heartbeat, she found herself being pushed chest-first to the floor, her left cheek pressing against the cool tile as one of the agents brought her arms down behind her back before slapping a pair of metal cuffs around her wrists.

Stay calm, Quinn. You knew this was how it would play out. Remember, it's all part of the plan.

The mental reminder was desperately needed. Forcing herself to listen, she slowed her breathing and did her best to remember why she'd agreed to this in the first place.

Justin.

Quinn looked across from where she lay to find him staring right back at her. His expression had changed, the fear that was there before replaced by a cool, calculating stare.

"Sorry, babe." He attempted to shrug a shoulder while being cuffed. "I have no choice."

No choice? "Justin, what are you—"

"This whole thing was her idea!" His shouted voice cut her off. "I want to make a deal!"

The blatant lie left her momentarily speechless.

"You have the right to remain silent..." The agent who'd secured Justin's wrists began reciting their Miranda rights, reading the words from a small white card in his hand. "Anything you say can and will be used against you in a court of law. You have the right to an attorney. If you cannot afford an attorney, one will be provided for you. Do you understand these rights I have just read to you?"

"Yeah, I understand, and I don't need a lawyer." Justin was pulled to his feet. "That's what I was trying to tell you...I didn't do anything wrong. It was her." He nodded toward where she was being carefully guided to her feet. "Quinn planned the whole thing. If you don't believe me, you can look at her notebook." He tipped his head toward the table where her personal notebook lay. "It's all in there. She did it all. The planning, the hacking... In fact, I was trying to get her to stop when you guys barged in here!"

Quinn couldn't believe what she was hearing. Her lips parted, but the crushing betrayal spewing from Justin's mouth stole her ability to formulate a single sound.

He said he loved me. How could he do this to me?

Time stood still, the bustling activity around her momentarily ceasing to exist. Quinn no longer saw the federal agents swarming about. She paid no attention to the equipment being seized and carried away.

All she could do was stand there, listening to the man who'd once claimed to be her soul mate spill lie after lie about her.

You were made for me, babe. Did you know that? We're soul mates, you and me. And together...we're going to do remarkable things.

Those were the words Justin spoke the night Quinn fell in love with him. He'd said others that same night, words that made her believe he loved her, too.

But now, as she was led out the door and into one of two awaiting vehicles, she realized all the guilt and indecision she'd been harboring the last few days had been for not.

Justin didn't love her. Probably didn't care about her at all. He'd simply used her.

He's been using me this entire time.

The door to her right slammed shut, snapping her attention back to the moment at hand. While waiting for the agent who'd arrested her to make her way to the driver's seat, Quinn watched through the tinted glass as Justin was put into the car in front of her.

His heartbreaking lies still littered the damp night air.

"I'm telling you; you've got the wrong guy! It was her! It was all Quinn!"

A tear fell from the corner of one eye as Justin disappeared inside the other SUV. Her arresting agent slid behind the wheel as Quinn used her shoulder to wipe the tear from her cheek.

The vehicle she was in rumbled to life but made no forward movement. Through the windshield, she watched as Justin's transport drove away with him in it, its shining red taillights growing smaller and smaller with each second that passed.

The door to her left opened, and a familiar face slid onto the seat beside her.

"Good job in there, Quinn." Special Agent Kimberly Manning looked pleased. "You got us exactly what we needed."

"Great." She didn't bother faking a smile. "Now can you please take these off me?"

Shifting in her seat, she turned her back to the woman who'd approached her days earlier with an offer Quinn couldn't refuse...

Get Justin to admit he got the equipment and cards from Monty Dunne—the FBI's main target—and also, that the plan to hack the credit card company was his. She'd get immunity for her role in designing the code to make it happen.

How the Feds knew anything about any of it was still a mystery, the answer to which Agent Manning had continually refused to divulge. Until now.

The metal bracelets loosened, and her wrists were freed. Settling back into the seat, Quinn rubbed her reddened skin as she stared at the woman beside her. "You said once the sting operation was successfully completed you'd tell me how you knew about all of this."

A set of pretty blue eyes stared back into hers, their shimmer the perfect complement to the long, blonde hair framing Agent Manning's flawless face. "I did say that didn't I?" Her sharp features softened. "Well, I suppose a deal's a deal, so here it is. Like I told you before, we've suspected Monty of playing an active role in a lot of recent, high-stakes cybercrimes. But until now, we could never get close enough to prove it."

"What changed?"

"We were able to turn one of Monty's crew. He was low-man on the Totem pole, though, so he couldn't get us any hard and fast evidence. But what he did do was feed us intel on jobs he heard whispers about. If it piqued our interest, we'd begin an investigation. Unfortunately, nothing ever panned out. That is, until your boyfriend ran his mouth to the wrong person...which also happened to be our source."

"*Ex*-boyfriend," Quinn corrected swiftly.

She removed her hat and handed the other woman the camera before reaching up under her shirt and yanking the taped wire free. In an awkward move, she then reached around to the small of her back and pulled the tiny recorder free.

Quinn handed the items to Manning, who already had an evidence bag waiting. Gathering the thin wire into a ball, she slid it, the camera, and the recorder inside.

"Good choice." The agent smiled. "You can do a whole lot better than that guy."

There was no choice. Not really.

She'd literally been losing sleep over her part in the takedown. Had sold her soul to a three-piece with her future clasped tightly in her fist in exchange for their promise to go easy on Justin.

Sorry, babe. I don't have a choice.

Quinn rubbed the spot over her heart, desperate to ease the ache there as she pictured his emotionless expression when he'd said those words to her. She'd given him all she had to offer. It wasn't much, she knew. But to her, it had meant everything.

And the big jerk had tossed her aside without so much as a second's hesitation.

Should've known better, Quinn. You're a jinx when it comes to love, remember?

That's what her addict of a mom had told her on count-less occasions, and it was true. The people in her life who'd claimed to love her had all been pretending.

Her mom. Her dad. The handful of men who'd come in and out of her adult life... They'd all "loved" her until she'd outlived her usefulness. Then they left.

Why Quinn thought Justin was any different was beyond her.

See? Jinx.

"We did you a favor, you know." Agent Manning's blue gaze locked onto hers. "You're far too smart to get mixed up with a guy like that. So smart, in fact, my boss wanted me to give you this." She reached into her jacket pocket before offering Quinn a simple white business card.

Quinn made no move to take it. "What's that?"

"See for yourself."

Begrudgingly, she took the card and scanned it. Her breath stuttered when she saw the name printed in black lettering...

Quinn Wilder, Technical Analyst
Cybe Crimes Unit
Federal Bureau of Investigations
2111 W. Roosevelt Road
Chicago, IL 60608

HER EYES FLEW UP TO THE OTHER WOMAN'S. "SO THIS IS real."

It was a statement, rather than a question.

"Oh, yeah." The pretty blonde smiled. "It's real. It's also a one-time offer. Flip it over."

When she did, Quinn found a date and time scribbled in blue ink across the heavy paper.

"That's when you report for work. If you're so much as a minute late, the deal's off. Boss's terms, not mine. And he means it."

Quinn licked her lips but said nothing. For the next several seconds, she found herself unable to do *anything* other than stare at the handwritten date.

Two days. That's how long she was being given. Two days from now, she was to report for duty as the Federal Cyber Crime Unit's newest tech analyst.

If she didn't, the woman beside her would obtain a warrant with her name on it. Quinn would be arrested with little—if any—chance of avoiding prison.

"Guess there's not much of a choice, is there?" she mumbled low.

"There's always a choice, Quinn. I really hope you make the right one here."

Her heart gave a hard thump. She looked at the front of the card again, the pad of her thumb brushing over her embossed name. The longer she stared, the less disparaged she began to feel.

And suddenly, Quinn found herself feeling something else. Something she hadn't felt in so long she almost didn't recognize it...

Hope.

She may not have been destined for love, but deep-down, Quinn had always known she had a purpose, and it wasn't committing petty, Robin Hood-esque crimes. It also wasn't helping a parasite of a boyfriend steal from innocent, hard-working people.

This, Quinn. Maybe this is it. Maybe this *is your purpose.*

There was no way to know for sure, but it definitely beat prison, so...

Quinn felt the SUV slow to a stop. Looking away from the card, she took a quick glimpse through the window, surprised to see they were already at her apartment building.

"Don't worry." Agent Manning spoke softly. "He won't be getting out. Not for a while."

"And after that?" She kept her saddened and angry gaze locked on the run-down brick building where she and Justin lived.

"After depends on Justin. If he cooperates, a deal will be made, and he'll start his sentence immediately. If he doesn't, the charges will be changed to fit the crimes we know he's committed, and he'll likely stand trial. Either way, you have some time to get yourself out of there. Which reminds me..." Agent Manning pulled an envelope from her other jacket pocket and handed it to her. "There's a list of several available apartments in the city. Nothing super fancy, mind you. But they're a damn sight better than this place. My boss also approved a sign-on bonus for you, which is enough to cover the first and last month's deposit for any one of the apartments on the list."

Quinn frowned as she took the weighted envelope. Lifting the thin paper flap, her gasp was audible.

"There has to be like three thousand dollars in here." Her thumbnail fanned through the stack of hundreds, twenties, and tens.

"Twenty-six hundred, to be exact."

She huffed out a breath, her brows arching with surprise.

Oh, yeah. You're definitely making the right choice.

Refusing to give Justin—or the other users from her past —another second of her time, Quinn gave her head a solemn nod. "Don't worry, Agent Manning. I'll be there."

The blonde smiled wide as she raised her outstretched hand. "Welcome to the team, Quinn. And since we'll be working together, I suppose you should start calling me Holly."

Sliding her palm against *Holly's*, she gave it a solid shake. "See you in two days."

With that, she opened the door and stepped out onto the curb, watching as the SUV disappeared into the night. Making her way up the half-crumbled steps, Quinn couldn't shake the feeling that her entire world had just shifted.

For better or worse remained to be seen, but one thing was for sure, she was chasing an impossible dream.

From now on, Quinn was going to put all her talent and energy into making a difference. A *real* difference by working with the FBI.

She opened the door to her soon-to-be former apartment, her mom's voice from long ago ringing through her mind as she stepped inside.

You're a jinx when it comes to love, Quinny. You and me, we aren't worthy of a good man's love, so we have to settle for what we can get. It's harsh, but true. Best to face facts now, rather than spend your life being disappointed time and time again.

They were the truest words her mother had ever spoken. Tonight being the prime example.

When it came to men, Quinn was one hundred percent, without a doubt, a complete and utter jinx. She knew it. Her mother had known it...so why keep putting herself through that kind of pain?

Justin's face flashed before her again, but this time, she pushed it and any hopes of a happily ever after away for good.

She was done being disappointed. Finished putting herself in a position to get hurt.

And most importantly, Quinn was done being a jinx.

1

————————

RICHMOND, *Virginia*
  Present day...

PARKER COLLINS LOOKED OUT THE LARGE WINDOW TO HIS right but saw nothing. Not the illuminated streetlights or the cars passing by. Even the people walking past were a blur, their images smudged by the distracting thoughts filling his brilliant mind.

Thoughts of a woman he'd never met in person but who, in many ways, knew him better than anyone else. A woman who went by Jinx—her gaming username—and who's raspy voice made him think of sex.

But more than the erotic fantasies his healthy, thirty-year-old brain had conjured starring the nameless, faceless woman, Parker cherished their purely platonic—albeit sometimes a tad flirty—conversations.

What had started as gaming opponents turned into a two-person, online alliance. Before he knew it, an honest-to-goodness friendship had developed.

And then she'd vanished.

Damn it, Jinx. Where are you?

It had been a month since Parker had last spoken to his online friend. The spunky, mysterious woman had called him, just to chat. As with all their shared phone calls, the two had talked about nothing important, teasing and laughing as they filled the time with each other's company.

He could still hear her sweet voice from that night...

"You give anymore thought to my proposal?"

"To meet IRL?" She'd sounded so hesitant. *"I don't think it's a good idea."*

Parker could still feel the disappointment her answer had brought with it. When he'd pushed for an explanation as to why, Jinx had kept her answers vague.

"I just don't think it's the right time. Maybe...maybe later?"

"How much later?"

"I don't know. Maybe like..."

But Jinx hadn't finished the thought. Parked could still hear the audible gasp that had cut her words off at the pass. She'd gasped and then...

"What the...shit. I have to go."

Parker remembered the chills that had raced down his spine when he heard the panic in her words. He'd asked her what was wrong. Was ready to spin his car around and go to her...no matter where in the world she was.

But Jinx never told him. All she'd given was...

"Can't talk right now. I'll call back when I can."

Her tone had become hushed. Parker distinctly remembered thinking maybe Jinx was scared of someone else hearing her. Someone who meant her harm.

"Jinx, wait!" He'd practically yelled those words. *"Tell me what's going on!"*

"I can't," she'd whispered back. *"I'm sorry."*

He'd hollered for her again, but she'd already ended the call.

Worried for his friend—and regardless of the unconventionality of it all, they *were* friends—Parker had immediately tried calling Jinx back. The first couple tries it just rang and rang. And on the third, he'd gotten the automated voice telling him the number was no longer in service.

Though the evidence was all highly circumstantial, Parker's gut told him Jinx was in danger. And he'd give every penny he had to find her and make sure she was safe.

"Helloooo..." A female voice tore through his spaced-off mind. "Earth to Parker..."

He blinked, his focus brought back to the present—and the woman currently sitting across from him. "Sorry, what?"

"Are you okay?" Dr. Sydnee Blake frowned. With her brows scrunched together, she ran her dark, assessing gaze over him as she spoke. "That's the third time in the last ten minutes you've drifted off mid-conversation."

Really? Well, shit.

"Sorry, Syd." Parker offered his childhood friend an apologetic smile. "Guess I just have a lot on my mind."

"I'd say so. What's going on? You never lose focus like that."

No, he typically didn't.

Shrugging it off, Parker picked up his iced tea and took a sip. With a quick swallow, he answered with a casual, "Nothing."

He should have known the too-smart-for-her-own-good woman wasn't letting him off the hook that easily.

Syd's blue eyes narrowed. "Try again."

It's no use, Collins. You know she's like a dog with a bone when she's worried about you.

Parker sighed. "You're not going to let this go, are you?"

"Nope."

Didn't think so.

Taking another sip, he put his glass down onto his usual table at the one restaurant in town he could dine in peace. "Okay, fine. But you have to promise not to laugh."

Her rosy lips curved as her head began to shake. "You know I can't make that promise."

"I mean it, Syd." Parker rested his elbows on the crisp white tablecloth. "This is...serious."

All signs of humor vanished as a deeper concern marred the sweet woman's pretty face. "Okay, now you're really scaring me. What's going on, Park?"

The worry in her voice warmed his heart. He and Syd had known each other since he was ten, and she was eight, and in spite of her gorgeous looks, impressive smarts, and amazingly sweet personality, he'd never seen her as anything more than the little sister he'd never had.

"I'm good. Honest." *Sort of.* "But there's this woman—"

"Oooh...now I get it." Sydnee sat back in her seat and chuckled. "There's always a woman with you, Park. So what is it this time? Your newest conquest trying to pressure you into marriage or having a baby? Or both?" Her dark curls swayed with a shake of her head. "I swear, Park. One of these days, you're going to meet a woman who looks at you and sees more than just dollar signs. You just need to quit wasting time with those gold diggers, always sniffing around and hold out for the right woman to come along. Because she's out there, you know?"

She wasn't wrong. In all his adult years, Parker had never had an actual serious relationship with a woman. An unfortunate side effect of being a billionaire bachelor, he supposed.

But he also wasn't as generous with his affection—or his

bed—as the press had led the public to believe. Not even close.

But this wasn't about that. This was different.

Jinx was different.

Was there a natural chemistry between the two of them? Sure. Had he pictured a gorgeous woman staring back at him when he heard that raspy voice of hers in his ears during their online chats and phone calls? Absolutely.

But the physical wasn't what drew Parker to Jinx. How could it be, when he'd never seen more than Jinx's fictional avatar?

No, the connection he shared with her ran much deeper than the flesh. When they spoke, it was as if she reached him on a whole other level. One built from intelligence, a sweet and sassy disposition, and a shared love for all things tech.

And as Sydnee had so bluntly pointed out, the other women who'd come in and out of his life—present company, excluded—looked at him and saw nothing more than a chance to gain money, fame, and a fortune.

They were always more than happy to use him to elevate their own social status. Of course, the second he broke things off—for their benefit as well as his own—those same women would turn on him the first chance they got.

It's why he'd sworn off relationships—casual or otherwise—a few months back. The only exceptions were Sydnee and Jinx.

Sydnee was his dearest friend, so no way he was going to fuck that up. And Jinx...

Despite knowing next to nothing about the woman, Parker had an innate feeling the intriguing woman was nothing like the others he'd met. A fact that drew him to her like a moth to a flame.

I need to find her.

"Okay, so here's the deal." He filled his lungs before releasing a slow exhale. "This woman...she's different."

"Different, how?"

This was where he expected the laughter to erupt.

"She doesn't know who I am," Parker finally admitted. "Not really."

Sydnee's dark brows arched high. "What do you mean, she doesn't know you?"

"I mean...we've never met. Not in person, anyway."

"If you've never met, then how—"

"We play the same MMO."

There. He'd said it.

"MMO?"

Parker nodded. "Technically it's an MMORPG, or massive multi-player online role-playing game. Sometimes when I can't sleep, I'll log onto the OG version of a game that came out like twelve years ago. That's where I met Jinx."

"Wait." His childhood friend put a hand up to stop him from furthering his explanation, a tiny smirk lifting one corner of her mouth. "Let me see if I've got this right. You, the most successful video game designer in the world, spend your evenings playing an online game that came out over ten *years* ago to pass the time?"

Parker nodded but remained silent.

"Okay...but why?"

"I don't know." *Yes, you do.* "I guess maybe because when I'm on there, I'm not Parker Collins, America's Most Eligible Bachelor." A pointless, shallow-as-fuck title he'd been awarded the last two years in a row. "When I'm playing that game, I can talk to people from all over the world without worrying about what I'm wearing or how my hair looks. I can joke around and have honest conversations without the fear that something I've said getting twisted into something ugly and plastered all over tomorrow's top headlines."

As if by design, a giant flash of white blinded them from the other side of the window at that exact moment. Having spotted the intrusive photographer a half-a-second before, Sydnee was already in the process of swinging her head in the opposite direction, her hand flying up to keep her face hidden as the stranger snapped the picture.

Parker wanted to hide, too. No, what he *really* wanted was to jump to his feet, march outside, and beat the guy's inconsiderate ass for trying to take Syd's picture without her permission.

But he didn't. Because of Jinx.

If he beat the guy's ass, he'd most likely be arrested. Then he'd have to call his lawyer, wait for him to come to the police station to bail him out, and spend the next six weeks or more defending himself.

In court and in the press.

I can't find Jinx if my days are tied up with a senseless lawsuit and settlement negotiations.

So with that in mind, Parker forced his lips into a smile and offered the man with the camera a casual wave from his side of the glass. After a few additional flashes, the stranger turned and left as quickly as he'd appeared.

"He's gone."

"Thank goodness." Sydnee sat back up, brushing some hair from her face. "I swear, I don't know how you deal with that on a daily basis."

"Years of practice." He took a larger swig of his tea, the move helping to calm his bubbling frustration.

Parker understood how the whole rich and famous game was played. Hell, he'd spent most of his adult life in the winning spot. But that kind of money...it came at a hefty cost.

The constant recognition and occasional heckling by the paparazzi...the ridiculous lies plastered across the fronts of supermarket tabloids and streaming on all the major social media platforms...

Those were the things most people didn't consider when wishing for a giant windfall to come their way.

For Parker, it was different. Thanks to his parents' wealthy status, he'd learned to accept all aspects of the rich-and-famous lifestyle a long damn time ago. But that acceptance didn't come with an all-encompassing enjoyment, which was where the online gaming community came in.

"That guy... the one who just took our picture? He proves my point, exactly."

"Which is?"

How do I explain this without sounding like an arrogant ass?

Giving it a shot, he asked, "Do you ever wonder why I always bring you to this particular restaurant for lunch when I'm in town?"

Sydnee blinked her blue eyes a few times as she pondered the question. With a slight shrug, she guessed, "I just assumed it was because you really like their food."

"You'd be wrong." Parker exhaled slowly. "I bring you here because this place is known for its discretion. The cooks and servers here all know if they get caught Tweeting about me or any of the other well-known patrons who frequent here, they'd be fired on the spot. Same reason so many politicians and other higher-ups choose to carry out their business luncheons here as opposed to some of the more popular places in town. It's not because we can't get enough of their bland-as-fuck foie gras. We come here because it's safe from all the prying eyes we deal with out there." He motioned toward the window again. "Well, safe-*ish*, anyway."

"Makes sense, I suppose." The pretty brunette's expression softened. "In a really sad sort of way."

He shrugged a shoulder and swallowed another drink of the ice-cold beverage. "It's the reality of the life I've chosen to live. It's also why I enjoy spending time in the online gaming community I mentioned. When I'm in there, like most of the time when I'm here...I can just be myself. The *real* me, not the flashy man whore the press has made me out to be."

"Oh, Park..."

"We're getting way off track, here." A quick wave of his hand cut off Sydnee's well-intended pity. "My reasons for playing the game aren't important. Jinx is what's important. *She's* what matters."

She's all that matters.

"Jinx?"

"The woman I told you about. The one who plays the game with me. Jinx is her username. I don't..." Parker swallowed down a giant ball of regret before admitting, "I don't know her real name. We decided not to share those just yet. And before you ask, yes. I've tried like hell to find out what hers is."

At first, Parker had thought a simple hack into her in-game profile would do the trick. But when he'd tried accessing it, the system showed no account with the username Jinx existed.

It was at that very moment when he began to suspect the secretive woman was crazy skilled with the keys. Not only that, but given that he, of all people, still hadn't been able to uncover Jinx's true identity, he was left with only one plausible conclusion...

The faceless, nameless woman he'd come to care a great deal about was a hacker. And not your ordinary, run-of-the-mill techie, either.

Jinx was good. Like *really* fucking good.

"Maybe this Jinx woman doesn't want to be found."

Sydnee's soft-spoken words weren't anything Parker hadn't said to himself a dozen times in the last few weeks. And if there was even a small part of him that believed them to be true, he'd stop looking.

But that part of him didn't exist, and he damn sure wasn't about to give up. Not when, deep down, he knew something was wrong.

When he didn't respond, Sydnee prodded him with an insistent, "Tell me about her."

Staring across the table at his friend, Parker did just that.

He filled her in on everything. How he and Jinx first "met". Some of their more memorable conversations. And when he felt she had a more solid picture of what Jinx had come to mean to him, Parker shared how their last phone call had ended.

"Something happened that night, Syd." His chest tightened as he tried not to imagine the worst. "Something or someone had Jinx so terrified, she rushed off the phone, disconnected her number, and erased the only link that might have led me to her."

All within a matter of minutes.

"Maybe she's a criminal on the run from the law." Sydnee hypothesized. "If she can do the things you're claiming, maybe she used those skills to commit some sort of cybercrime. Maybe the authorities finally caught up with her, so she cut ties with everyone she knew and split town."

Another possible explanation for Jinx's sudden disappearing act. One Parker had already considered.

"I have a system that's been running since the day after I last spoke with Jinx," he told Sydnee. "I entered the basics I managed to piece together from our conversations...female, approximately late twenties, early thirties, slight mid-western accent...extremely tech savvy...that sort of thing. After that, I built a program to cross reference the types of crimes she'd most likely commit—statistically speaking, of course."

"And? Did you get a match?"

He shook his head. "According to every federal law enforcement agency in the country, in the last four weeks, no woman matching Jinx's description is or has been wanted for any sort of cybercrime."

"Not even one?"

"Nope.

"Huh." Sydnee finished off her lemon water. "That's interesting."

"No, not interesting," he disagreed with his friend. "It's fucking frustrating."

Sydnee's lips twitched, and it was obvious the woman was fighting a smile. "Listen, Park... You and I, we both grew up with silver spoons in our mouths. And while I'm no bigshot game designer like you, I've done okay in the adulting department, too. But you...you're used to getting everything you want, pretty much at the drop of a hat. That's not a bad thing, mind you. Just an observation."

Sure didn't sound like a *good* thing, but okay. He'd bite. "What's your point?"

"Just that..." She sighed. "Do you think it's possible that this obsession with finding Jinx is more about the challenge of it all rather than the woman, herself?"

"No." Parker's answer was swift and definitive. "I can see why you might think that, but that's not what this is about."

And just so he'd made himself clear, Parker added a reassuring, "It's *not*."

"Okay." The sweet doctor's nod held no judgement. "So what's the plan? Do you want me to have Ash talk to the team? Maybe you'd have better luck tracking Jinx down with their help."

Asher Cross was Sydnee's fiancé and an operative for RISC'S Charlie Team.

RISC—which stood for Rescue, Intel, Security, and Capture—was an elite private security firm based out of Richmond. RISC headquarters was in Dallas, Texas along with the firm's Alpha and Bravo Teams.

From what Parker had been told, there was also a fourth team—Delta—which worked out of Chicago. He hadn't heard whether an Echo Team was in the works yet, although with the volatile state of the world, he wouldn't be surprised.

"I thought about giving Ash a call," he confirmed. "But those guys have more important things on their plates than helping me on my quest to chase down a ghost."

"You know they'd do whatever they could. In fact, I have it on good authority that Ash still feels indebted to you for helping when I was in trouble."

"In trouble." Parker scoffed. "Pretty mild description for getting kidnapped *twice* and almost getting yourself killed."

That shit still gave him nightmares on occasion.

The first time Sydnee was taken, Parker hadn't even learned about it until after her rescue. She'd been in Abu Dhabi doing volunteer medical work when a group of insurgents had kidnapped and held her captive.

Luckily, Charlie Team had been the ones sent in for the rescue, which was how Syd and Asher first met. But the craziest part of their story happened a couple weeks later, after Sydnee was back on American soil.

A man who turned out to be a friend of Sydnee's family blamed her father for his own dad's suicide. He stalked and kidnapped Sydnee with a plan to kill her as payback.

Thankfully—with Parker's help—Charlie Team was able to locate and save Sydnee before it was too late.

So yeah. Asher and the other three men on his team were the toughest sons of bitches Parker had ever known. Even so...

"Your fiancé doesn't owe me a damn thing." None of those guys did. "Besides, there isn't anything Charlie Team can do that I haven't already done. But I appreciate the offer."

"Well, if you change your mind, you have his number."

"I do." Parker nodded. "Thank you."

Waiting a beat, Sydnee flashed him an adorable smile before returning to their previous conversation. "What you said earlier, about that game and this restaurant being the only two places you feel as though you can be yourself... that's not true." She shook her head. "You can be yourself with me, Park. Always."

The ache in his heart lessened slightly. "I know that, Syd." He reached across the table and covered her hand with his. "I really do."

"You'd better." She raised a single brow. "And don't forget, you have an open invitation at the new house. You don't even have to call first."

With a quick squeeze of her hand, Parker pulled his free and settled his back against the cushioned seat. "Careful what you're offering, darlin'. You and that fiancé of yours might end up with a permanent houseguest."

"Gladly." The pretty brunette smiled wide.

He held Sydnee's ocean-blue gaze a moment longer. She was sweet, smart, put him in his place when no one else would, and gorgeous as hell. On top of all that, Syd didn't give two shits about the available balance in his checking account.

On paper, she was his perfect match in every way. Except one...

She isn't Jinx.

The uninvited thought tore his focus away. Unwilling to let himself go down the insanity of that rabbit hole—he didn't even really know the woman, for fuck's sake—Parker picked up the bill their server had discretely placed on the table beside him earlier.

"I'm guessing it probably won't do any good, but I can cover my half."

"You're right." He slid a credit card out of his wallet and laid it on the silver tray with the thin strip showing what he owed. "It won't do you any good."

Minutes later, the bill was paid, and Parker and Sydnee were saying their goodbyes.

"Promise you won't do anything crazy looking for this girl, Park." Her big eyes pleaded with his as they stood by her valeted car. "If anything happened to you..."

"You kiddin'?" He pulled her in for a tight hug before separating them enough to see her face. "I'm invincible, baby." A quick wink. "Like Superman."

"Even Superman could be taken down by Kryptonite, Park. I'd hate for this Jinx woman to be yours."

With another hug and a promise not to do anything reckless, Parker watched as Sydnee left for her new home. A home she shared with the man she loved.

I want that, too.

It was the second pause-inducing thought he'd had in less than twenty minutes. It was also the truth.

Parker did want what Syd and Ash had. And the other men on Charlie Team, for that matter. Trace, Kellan, Greyson, Rhys... if those guys could find their happily ever after, why the hell couldn't he?

You can. You just have to know where to look.

And wasn't that the crux of his whole fucking problem?

Grinding his back teeth together, Parker waited as the valet pulled up in his 2005 Bugatti Veyron. A kid who barely looked sixteen climbed out from behind the wheel, his eyes widening with excitement as he handed Parker the keys.

"Here are your keys, Mr. Collins. And..." He glanced around and lowered his voice as if to keep from being over-heard. "I know we're not supposed to act like we know the customers, or even talk to them, really...but I have to tell you...I am a *huge* fan of your work. I have every game you've ever designed, and I've beat all the levels multiple times."

In a seamless transition, Parker donned the image his public expected to see. "That's cool, man." Parker shook the kid's trembling hand. "Thanks."

"Oh, no. Thank *you*." The kid made no move to let go of his hand. "Seriously. I know it sounds stupid, but your games got me through high school. I wasn't very popular." He chuckled nervously. "Sports were never really my thing. I'm clearly not the biggest guy out there, so...yeah. I got picked on a lot."

"I'm sorry to hear that. Hey, what's your name?"

"Trent." The kid shook his hand again. "Trent Shipman."

"Good to meet you, Trent. And hey...you're not the only one who got picked on as a kid."

Trent's brown eyes grew even wider. "You? Really?"

"True story." It really was.

"Oh, shit...sorry." Trent *finally* let go of his hand. "But wait, I thought I read where you'd gone to some fancy private school somewhere."

"I did." Parker nodded. "Money doesn't make people nice, Trent. In fact, it usually has the opposite effect."

"So the kids at your school were assholes, too, huh?" Trent smirked.

Parker matched it with one of his own. "Massive assholes."

A look was shared that only guys like them—nerdy kids who were constantly picked on by the bigger ones who thought they were tough shit back in the day—would understand.

"Well." Trent stepped out of Parker's way. "I'm sure you have important places to be. I just wanted to let you know the amazing worlds you created gave me a safe place where I could escape. So thank you."

And just when I was starting to think about giving up the whole game designer gig.

It was something he'd considered on more than one occasion during the last few months but had kept to himself. The last thing he needed to deal with was the massive jump in paparazzi news like that would cause.

"Thanks, man." Parker offered the kid a parting shake of his hand. "It was great meeting you."

"You, too, Mr. Collins." Trent returned the gesture with gusto.

"Call me Parker."

"Really?"

He nodded with grin. "Tell you what. You got a phone, Trent?"

"Uh...y-yeah." The phone appeared almost instantly. "Why?"

"Let's take a selfie together. Post them on your socials and tag me in them. Might take me a bit, but I promise I'll respond. And who knows? Maybe some of those dickheads you went to school with will see it and realize you're a hell of a lot cooler than they'll ever be."

"Dude!" The poor kid looked like he was about to burst from his excitement. "That would be freaking awesome!"

After a few quick snaps, Trent had his pictures and what Parker hoped was a great memory to hold onto. For Parker, the unexpected exchange was a well-timed distraction.

Unfortunately, the small respite from his worries didn't last long.

Pulling away from the curb, Parker began the two-hour drive—or with him behind the wheel, more like an hour-and-a-half—from Richmond to his beach house in Chesapeake Beach, Maryland. As he passed familiar landmarks and crossed over bridges, he was reminded of the phone call he'd received the last time he'd made this same drive...and the woman who had made it.

Come on, Jinx. Let me know you're okay, sweetheart. Just pick up the phone and let me hear that sexy voice of yours.

Even as he thought it, Parker feared he'd never hear the enticing rasp of Jinx's voice again. And suddenly, that scared him more than the thought of waking up tomorrow without a penny to his name.

I'd give it all away if it meant finding you and knowing you're safe.

It was crazy. Certifuckingfiable, even. Because honestly, Sydnee could be right. Jinx could be a criminal. A scammer who used innocent people to make a quick buck. Or worse...

Maybe Jinx had known who he was all along.

He'd taken every known precaution to keep that from happening, but very few things in life were a true impossibility. She'd sure been able to outsmart him when it came to trying to track her down.

Parker's gut tightened as he thought back to that last conversation...

You give anymore thought to my proposal?

"To meet IRL, you mean? I don't think it's a good idea."

Was that it? It made sense, in a way. After all, things had been going just fine until he brought up the idea of meeting face-to-face. Had he scared her off because doing so would ruin her plan?

He let that roll through his head for the next handful of miles. But the more ground his expensive-as-fuck tires crossed, the guiltier Parker felt.

Jinx wasn't a criminal. She wasn't a scammer. She was a sweet, sassy woman with a shit ton of secrets who needed his help. But unless she reached out, Parker feared she'd be lost to him forever.

Come on, sweetheart. Whatever it is, I can help you. All you have to do is ask.

2

———

"Have a nice day."

Quinn blinked and found the bored-looking teenager behind the register staring at her expectantly. It took a few seconds for her to realize that *look* was because the young girl was still waiting for her to take the receipt from her outstretched hand.

"Oh." She took possession of the outlandishly long receipt. "Sorry."

A half-nod was the girl's only response before she turned her attention to the next customer in line. Not that Quinn could blame her.

It wasn't the first time she'd been caught daydreaming lately.

Heat crawled up her neck as she snatched up the four plastic sacks holding her groceries and headed for the automatic door. Truth be told, it was the *subject* of those daytime fantasies that left her pale skin flushed, rather than embarrassment from appearing flighty.

You have bigger things to worry about than some guy you've never met.

The voice in her head was right. The last thing she should be thinking about was a man she hadn't spoken to in over a month. A man she didn't know.

You know him. The most important parts, anyway.

That time, her subconscious was wrong. Quinn knew very little about the man whose player name was "ByteMe69".

He was smart. Funny. Knew code and could tech-talk with the best of them. But the thing that had drawn her to him more than anything was his ability to make her laugh.

In her whole life, Quinn couldn't remember ever laughing as much as she did when she and ByteMe69 talked. Or as hard.

The man could seriously make her laugh harder than anyone else she'd ever met. Only she *hadn't* met him. Not really.

He wanted to, though. He wanted to meet in 3D, but you were too scared.

And just like that, her subconscious was back in the lead.

It was true, she *had* been scared. Of a lot of things, really.

Quinn was afraid they'd meet, and he'd turn out to be a giant disappointment. A preppy, pretty boy who cared more about the products in his hair than her.

Or worse, they'd meet up, and she'd find herself face-to-face with an overweight, sixty-five-year-old man with a massive pot belly and a pull-out couch in his eighty-six-year-old mother's basement.

She'd done her best to avoid picturing that last one, although the sneaky bastard still tried to pop through every now and then.

The most terrifying scenario of all, though—the one that had kept Quinn up at night just thinking about it—was if her nameless, faceless friend turned out to be every bit as sweet and funny as he was on the phone.

And as sexy as that deep, rumbly voice of his made him seem.

More than anything else, it was *that* fear that was the driving force behind her rejection of ByteMe69's offer to meet in real life. Because a man like that would have no use for someone like her, so why waste either of their time?

You're a jinx when it comes to love, baby girl. Just like me.

Quinn had ignored her mother's wise words once before, and it had come back to bite her in the ass. Of course, that didn't keep her traitorous mind from imagining her anonymous gaming partner as the quintessential perfect man...

Tall. Fit. Eyes she could get lost in. A smile that made her heart melt. A heart of his own that wasn't tainted by greed.

Those were traits she pictured ByteMe69 possessing. When she allowed herself those few, stolen moments to remember a man she'd never met but knew she could fall for...that was always how she saw him.

His facial features and hair color would often change, as did his height and build. But the important stuff—those things that could only be found on the inside—always stayed the same.

And when she thought of a life filled with all the things she wanted but was never meant to have, it was his shadowed image Quinn saw standing by her side.

It's been a month, Q. Pretty sure that ship has already sailed.

The nagging voice had a point, but that didn't make it sting any less. Especially when Quinn thought of the last trait on her imaginary list.

A heart of his own that wasn't tainted by greed.

ByteMe69 most definitely had a heart. It wasn't something her fantastical imagination had conjured up. It was as real as the one beating inside her own chest.

And for reasons Quinn would never understand, his had been filled with concern...for her.

It was there, echoing its way through the phone's speakers as he'd pleaded with her to tell him what was going on. The guy knew nothing about her, yet he'd done everything he could to keep her from hanging up.

Not because he wanted something from her, but because he'd been worried.

A single tear fell from the corner of one eye, but she used a shoulder to swipe it away. This was stupid. *She* was stupid.

She never should have started a relationship with the guy in the first place. Sure, it was an anonymous one that only took place either online or with the occasional phone call. And apart from a few flirtatious moments over the course of their last few weeks of contact, they'd pretty much kept things well within the friend zone boundaries.

Quinn also never should have ghosted the poor man the way she had. But she'd been so scared that night, and while the moment of terror was short lived, it had sent her straight into survival mode.

Thinking you're going to die can do that to a girl.

As it turned out, she wasn't in any sort of imminent danger, after all. The scratching coming from the patio door located on her living room's north wall wasn't her ex making good on his many threats. No, no.

It was a cat.

A scrawny black and white cat, to be more precise. And the only things the poor girl was guilty of was being hungry and seeking shelter from the cold night air.

At the time, however, Quinn was *certain* someone had been trying to break into her townhome. So she'd hung up on ByteMe69 and immediately implemented her go-plan.

With a system already in place—and her high-end, encrypted-out-the-wazoo tablet within reach—it had taken less than a minute to disconnect her phone service and erase her gaming account.

The only two points of contact ByteMe69 had.

It wasn't until Quinn ducked down and carefully made her way to the small coat closet near her front door that Quinn got her first glimpse of the would-be intruder.

After calming her racing heart—and releasing several under-the-breath curses directed toward the furry feline— she'd gone to the door, slid it open, and greeted the cat with a cautious hand.

A few licks and the sweetest purr later, and Quinn was the proud owner of a cat she'd affectionately named Oreo.

The furry feline was a godsend those first few days. Oreo had snuggled and purred, keeping her company when the one person she wanted to couldn't.

Well, he *could* have. If she'd let him.

And there were many, *many* times over the last few weeks when she'd considered making that call. But in the end, she'd decided against it.

Not because she didn't want to. Nothing could be further from the truth.

The reason Quinn hadn't called her only true friend—a sad fact she refused to give much thought to—was because the shockwave of fear that had rolled through her system that night had left a mark.

It was a stark reminder of a promise she'd made herself six years ago. One that had remained unbroken...until him.

She'd learned the hard way that life was much less

painful when she kept the deepest parts of herself closed off from everyone else. And for the first five years following Justin's arrest, that was exactly what she'd done.

But then, one day several months ago, Quinn had gotten bored and decided to log into a game she'd played back in high school. It wasn't long before she stumbled upon a cocky, smart-assed gamer with a voice that made her think of sex, and the uncanny ability to make her laugh when she needed it most.

In a moment of weakness, Quinn had let her guard down. Not fully, mind you. She'd never, ever do that again. But with ByteMe69—God, she wished she'd at least gotten his first name—Quinn felt different.

Almost...happy.

He'd done that for her, and what had she given in return? A broken promise to call when she could and a vanishing act that could rival even the best of magicians.

What's wrong?

Tell me what's going on.

Jinx!

A wave of the same heartbreaking regret she'd felt that night came crashing down on Quinn, but she pushed it aside and focused on the present. Picking up the pace, she quickly covered the final stretch of asphalt to where her car was parked.

Out of habit, she waited to press the button on her fob that would unlock the doors until she was almost there. After securing the groceries on the car's back seat, she slammed that door shut before climbing behind the wheel and buckling herself in.

Quinn gave the small, built-in screen on her dash a quick glance and sighed. It was already after eight...and she still hadn't had supper.

At this rate, it'll be midnight before you get around to eating.

Making a legal U-turn at the next light, she hit the nearest fast-food drive-thru and ate her dinner as she drove. By the time she was pulling into her garage, Quinn's grilled chicken sandwich—and the small bag of fries—were little more than a memory.

Pressing the button to close the garage door, she retrieved her phone from the passenger seat and slid it into her pocket. Turning the ignition off and freeing her keys, she unfolded herself out of the car.

Quinn reached back inside and grabbed the paper sack from her impromptu meal. Cleared from the car once again, she gave a practiced flip of her wrist, the trash from her less-than-satisfying meal landing in the large can by the door with ease.

Getting the sacks of groceries from the back seat, she used her hip to shut the car door before making her way up the two concrete steps and into her home.

The two-bedroom townhouse was a rental, but with areas of exposed brick, tons of natural light, gorgeous hardwood floors throughout, and a kitchen that made her want to cook, it was one she was damn proud of.

Given some of the dives she'd called home in the past, this place was like living in the lap of luxury. It was also a symbol of how far she'd come.

And a reminder of what she stood to lose.

"Here, kitty, kitty," Quinn called out for Oreo. She set the bags down onto the spacious island's pristine, granite countertop with a sigh. "I brought you a surprise."

Shaking the small bag of cat treats, she attempted to entice the sweet animal to join her while also toeing off her slip-on canvas shoes.

When Oreo didn't show, Quinn put the treats away. "Fine, be that way."

With the assumption that her recently acquired pet was either napping or simply disinterested, she began emptying the bags one-at-a-time, putting everything exactly where it went.

She didn't used to be so particular with her things, but after taking a job with the FBI, Quinn had finally been able to afford a decent place to live and a nice, reliable car. The job she had now—freelance cybersecurity work from home —paid even more, which provided Quinn with the opportunity to upgrade a few things...

Desktop, laptop, tablet...and even the occasional mid-level wine as a treat.

It was more than some and much less than most. But she woke up every day feeling grateful as hell for her change of luck, and she never, ever took any of it for granted.

Too bad you can't change your luck in the romance department, eh, Quinnie?

Jawbones clamped tightly together, she ignored her mother's imagined quip and marched back to the table. Grabbing the empty plastic bags, she quickly checked them each for holes before nesting them one inside the other and shoving them in their designated basket under the sink.

She exhaled slowly, ready for a relaxing shower and some quality time with her DVR. But first...

Quinn walked over to the refrigerator and opened the door. Enveloped in a rush of cool air, she reached inside and pulled out a half-full bottle of wine. A recent, albeit accidental, discovery was such that two small glasses before bed tended to dull the details of her dreams.

And since she was doing everything in her power not to think about how much she missed talking with ByteMe69...

Don't mind if I do.

Quinn pulled the cork free with a loud *pop*. Grabbing the glass she'd used last night from the wooden drying rack to her left, she turned it over and began to pour.

The first sip had her eyes closing and her shoulders relaxing. *This* was what she needed. A moment to herself with nothing on her mind but the sweet taste rolling over her tongue.

She opened her eyes and took another sip before turning to leave. She barely made it a full step when a dark figure appeared before her.

Several things caught her attention at once, but Quinn could see and understand them all clearly. Almost as if time had been altered, and everything had begun to move in slow motion.

The glass fell from her hand. Sharp shards of cheap crystal burst across the floor around her, the crimson liquid that had been inside splattering into a puddle at her feet.

Though she was aware of those things happening, Quinn hadn't seen any of it with her own eyes. She was too busy studying the person staring back at her.

Dressed in head-to-toe black, the intruder was close to six feet in height and obviously male. There was something clasped in one of his gloved fists, but she couldn't tell what it was.

He moved toward her, the motion fast-forwarding Quinn back into real time. Her heart pounded against her ribs when the man came even closer. First one booted step, and then another.

Think, Quinn! You can make it out of this, if you just think!

Even though it was damn hard to do, she fought the urge to run. Using skills she'd learned during a brief stint living on the streets, back in the day, Quinn took a calming breath and a few seconds she didn't have to consider her options.

It didn't take long for her to realize only one offered her any real chance of escaping.

Her fingers twitched as the man began closing in on her. The timing had to be perfect. A second too soon or too late could make the difference between survival and death.

And she hadn't come this far just to let some sick bastard kill her in her own kitchen.

Muscles tensed and her posture grew rigid as Quinn's heartbeat thrashed inside her ears. Tendrils of fear wrapped their meaty claws around her heart and squeezed, but she didn't dare give in.

Not yet...not yet...just a few more inches, and...
Now!

In one fluid motion, she raised her right arm, twisted it palm-out, and grabbed the wine bottle by its neck. With her next breath, Quinn swung the makeshift weapon around as hard as she could.

A dull, sickening thud filled the otherwise silent space as the bottle's thick glass connected with the man's head. He grunted in pain, the force of the unexpected blow sending him stumbling to the side.

Though he fought against it, the man's flailing arms did nothing to prevent his legs from crumbling beneath him. Eyes rolling in the back of his head, the man fell to the floor, taking a barstool down with him in the process.

From where she stood, Quinn couldn't tell if he was still breathing. And unlike the lead characters in those cheesy, cozy mystery movies she secretly loved to watch, she wasn't about to endanger herself further by moving in closer to check for a pulse.

What she *did* do was run.

3

As FAST AS her quivering legs would take her, she ran past the fallen man, out the kitchen and into the small entryway before racing through the door leading to her garage. Skipping the bottom step, Quinn pulled the keys from her jeans pocket and flung open her car door.

Locking herself inside, she slapped her hand against the remote clipped to her visor. The garage door's motor hummed to life as she inserted the key into her car's ignition.

With a hard twist, the engine's roar consumed the enclosed space. At the same time, the door to her left burst open, splinters of wood flying in all directions as her attacker reappeared.

Standing a bit unbalanced, he raised his right hand. And this time, the item in his fist was clear to see.

Gun!

A few slivers of wood skidded across the hood of Quinn's car, but she was too busy shoving the vehicle into reverse— and slamming her socked foot down onto the gas pedal—to notice. She also didn't care that the garage door was less than halfway up.

With her foot planted firmly on the gas, she squeezed the steering wheel with both fists and prepared for impact. The car jolted, her upper body flinging back against her seat as its rear end smashed against the half-raised metal door.

A loud banging and the sound of metal bending and scraping surrounded her. Quinn flinched, but she didn't dare stop.

Knuckles white and heart racing, she forced her way through the half-hanging door. The space around her darkened as she slid beneath the broken and twisted barrier, and when the front bumper cleared those final few inches, Quinn bolted down the paved driveway and into the street.

She pushed the gearshift into drive, her tires squealing with the sudden change in direction. Risking a quick glance through the passenger window, she looked up in time to see the masked man staring back at her from the shadows.

He made no move to give chase or raise his weapon, but rather stood there. Watching with an eerie, almost ominous look in his cold, emotionless eyes.

He could have killed you.

Quinn sped down the road with no particular destination in mind. With her fight-or-flight responses still at the helm, she blew out several long, forceful breaths to keep from hyperventilating.

What. The. Hell?

Her gaze bounced between the street in front of her and her rearview mirror. Relieved to see no one was following her, she caught a glimpse of her reflection...nearly gasping at what she saw.

Pale skin and nostrils flaring, a look of pure and utter

fear stared back at her through a set of wild green eyes. The terrified look reminded her of another time. Another life.

And it pissed her the hell off.

Fury exploded from somewhere deep inside as Quinn continued driving aimlessly. Damn it, this was *exactly* the kind of thing she was afraid of.

This was the exact reason she never should have let her guard down.

But she had. Over the last six years, Quinn had gotten complacent in her day-to-day routine. Comfortable.

It was a comfort she couldn't afford.

She should call someone. She should call nine-one-one...or Holly...or...

ByteMe69

The unexpected thought had her flinching, yet she found herself giving it serious consideration as she ran through all her options.

If she called the cops, they'd send units to her house. She'd have to turn back around and meet them there, and spend the next two hours walking them through what had happened, knowing that entire time they wouldn't find anything.

With the exception of his eyes and mouth, the man's entire body had been covered. Including his hands.

Gloves meant no fingerprints, and though she'd literally been running for her life, Quinn hadn't noticed a single drop of blood on her kitchen floor where the man had been laying. So the likelihood of the police making a positive I.D. from DNA or prints was zilch.

This wasn't some random home invasion, Quinn. That man was no amateur.

No, he was a professional who'd sought her out for a

reason. And while it made absolutely no sense, Quinn's gut was screaming that Justin was somehow involved.

He's still in jail, remember? That man couldn't have been him.

As far as she was concerned, those were moot points. She'd dealt with enough criminals—both before and during her stint with the FBI—she understood all too well how resourceful prisoners could be.

Guards or other prisoners, it didn't matter. If the motivation was strong enough, those on the inside could reach pretty much anyone out here.

The occasional notes she'd recently started receiving had all been left in random locations at different times of day, their deliverer's face always hidden from any nearby cameras.

And Quinn had accessed them all.

CCTV, grocery store parking lots, her own home-security system... None of the security footage she'd looked through had caught enough features for facial rec. Just a tall man dressed in black, just like her intruder. The only difference was, in the footage, he wore a black baseball cap instead of the ski mask.

Although she'd bet her entire savings it was the same exact man.

It definitely wasn't Justin. She would have recognized his eyes behind the mask. But despite him currently being behind bars, Quinn would have to be a fool to think they'd come from anyone else.

Miss me?

You're not as smart as you think you are.

You can't hide from me.

I'm coming for you.

You're going to pay for what you did.

The tone behind the messages grew more and more

threatening with each subsequent note. The scribbled handwriting was one she didn't recognize, but it didn't matter.

Justin may not have physically written the words, but they were his. She was sure of it.

Her convict of an ex had been keeping tabs on her. Quinn felt the truth of that to her bones. But for the life of her, she couldn't figure out how.

The answer was there, she just had to find it. And once she did...

He'll be the one to pay.

Several turns and one secluded underpass later, Quinn was parked beneath a bridge, her car concealed by its dark shadow. She fell back against her seat, the air in her lungs expelling loudly.

Pinpricks of tears stung the corners of her eyes, but she refused to let them fall. Now wasn't the time for a breakdown. That could come later.

Right now, she needed to figure out what the hell she was going to do. And where the hell she was going to go.

Doing her best to ignore the tiny needles poking the tips of her fingers and toes, and the quivering in every muscle in her body, Quinn breathed through the aftershocks of a massive adrenaline rush and did her best to think.

Where can I go?

The townhouse was out. Statistically speaking, it was probably the safest place in town since most home invaders never hit the same location twice. But Quinn knew better than most that statistics could be skewed to fit their creator's needs.

And since this wasn't your average break-in...

Her scattered thoughts had her abandoning her quest for a safe haven and turning in her seat. Quinn's thumping heart sank as she reached for the passenger seat only to discover her tablet wasn't there.

Damnit!

It was back at her house. The same house she couldn't return to. Along with everything else.

"Ahhh!" She shouted at the universe, giving her steering wheel a white-knuckled shake in the process.

Everything she needed was still back at the house. Her tablet and laptop. Her purse and wallet. Her driver's license and cash.

How'd that go-bag work for ya, huh?

The sarcastic thought sparked a low, frustrated growl. Everything had happened so fast, she hadn't had time to grab it without risking her chances of getting away.

You also didn't have time to put your shoes back on.

Quinn froze a fraction of a second before glancing down. She closed her eyes, a hysterical bubble of laughter escaping from the sight of her wine-stained socks.

"Perfect." She shook her head at herself. "That's just perfect."

With a groan, she bent forward and rested her forehead on the steering wheel's padded center, careful not to activate the horn and give herself away.

She needed the tablet to check Justin's status as an inmate. The program she'd designed was supposed to alert her of any change to the contrary. It hadn't pinged her, but technology wasn't perfect.

Not even her own.

One of the first things Quinn had learned during her good-Samaritan hacker years was no matter how sophisticated the code, there was always a chance for a glitch.

That's why checking on Justin's status was the first thing she did every morning, and the last thing she did before falling asleep. It was a sucky way to live, for sure, but at least she'd been living.

Have you, though? Or have you simply been existing?

Ignoring the ill-timed questions, she cleared her rambling thoughts and focused on her most urgent issue at hand.

Someone had broken into her house tonight. He'd been in the one place she should have been safe. Or as safe as someone like her could feel, anyway. And he'd had a gun.

I'm coming for you.

You're going to pay for what you did.

The foreboding words from the last notes she'd received rang through her ears at a deafening level. A flash of black filling her vision, the memory of seeing that man standing in her kitchen appearing suddenly in her mind's eye.

Whether the asshole's goal was to kill, kidnap—or worse —Quinn didn't know. But she sure as heck wasn't about to stick around while a bunch of overworked and underpaid cops work tirelessly to figure it out.

Which brought her back to the question of who to call for help.

Since calling the cops would only hinder her ability to go dark until she could figure out her next steps, she moved to the next option: Holly.

Her handler-turned-co-worker had been nice enough to work with, and she and Quinn had even shared a few meals back in the day. But the driven woman had accepted a transfer to the FBI office in Denver less than a year after Quinn started, and the two lost touch almost immediately.

She didn't even have Holly's new number.

If she had her tablet, she could find it no problem. But since she didn't...

Next option.

She could call someone else at the Bureau. But it had been four years since she left that job to work for herself, and last she'd checked, everyone from her old unit had moved on to other offices. Other cities.

What if Justin knows you used to work for the FBI? What if he found out, and that's how he was able to find you?

Roots of past paranoia began to dig deep. The logical part of her brain knew the chances of him having access to that kind of information were slim, but she'd had enough experience with determined criminals to know there's always a way.

A loose-lipped agent. The wrong person overhearing something they shouldn't. A bribed guard who knows someone who knows someone...

Quinn had witnessed it herself a half a dozen times during her three years with the FBI. If an inmate was determined and had the right motivation, there wasn't anything that would keep them from getting what they want.

Especially ones as smooth and charismatic as Justin Reynolds.

And if there was even a chance he'd somehow discovered her professional connections to the Agency, she couldn't risk trusting anyone else there. Which meant that option was a no-go, as well.

You trusted him, *Quinn. He's the one you need to call.*

She opened her eyes and lifted her head, slowly sitting back against her seat. It was crazy to even consider calling ByteMe69, right?

Of course, it was crazy. For a whole slew of reasons.

One, she didn't know him, either. Not really. Two, she hadn't talked to the guy in a month. And three, for all she knew, he could be married with six kids and a batshit crazy wife who'd kill her just for talking to her husband.

He's not married, Quinn. You asked him that, remember?

Her chest tightened from the memory. That's right. She *had* asked him. Well, sort of.

It was during one of their most recent phone conversations, and actually, *he'd* been the one to broach the subject.

They'd been talking about their latest online quest—joking about how one of the other opposing players had been whining like a little baby when his team lost—when ByteMe69 had grown quiet.

At first, it seemed as if the call had been dropped, so she'd asked, *"You still there?"*

"I'm here."

"Everything okay? You got really quiet for a second, there."

"I'm good. I just...I had something I wanted to ask, but I don't know quite know how to word it."

"Well, in case you haven't figured it out by now, it takes a lot to offend me. So whatever it is, just ask."

"All right. I was wondering if you were seeing anyone."

Quinn could still feel the way her heart had nearly stopped when he'd asked.

Up to that point in their newly-formed friendship, they'd only shared a few inconsequential details of their lives. Never anything as personal as what he'd just asked. But she hadn't wanted to lie, so...

"I don't really date."

"Ever?"

"I mean, of course, I've dated. Just not recently. What about you?"

In spite of her vow to never get close to anyone again—to not let herself care about a man in that way again—

Quinn had found it impossible to breathe as she'd waited for his answer...

"Wouldn't be talking to you if I was."

A silent exhale and then...

"You think our team's ready for the next level?"

The question's intent had been to change the subject, which it had. But that was also when the flirting had officially started.

An insinuating comment here, a harmless tease there.

Quinn knew as well as anyone how easily lies could fall from someone's lips. But somehow, she knew in her heart— she *knew*—the man she'd gotten to know this past year was telling her the truth about being single.

And it had been so easy to let her guard down with him. Probably because she'd known it would never go anywhere.

They'd never know each other's names. Never see the other's face. And with such a low risk of getting hurt again, Quinn had convinced herself that allowing herself the anonymous connection was okay. That she deserved at least *that* much.

But now...

She looked at her phone again sighed. Even if she *did* call him, there was no guarantee ByteMe69 would answer. Not that she could blame him if he didn't. Not when she'd dropped him out of her life like a hot potato.

A fitting metaphor, since you were trying to avoid getting burned.

"You can't call him." Quinn spoke aloud to herself again. "Even if he does answer, he's probably pissed as hell at you. And if he's not, the guy could still live a world away."

And then what? Did she honestly expect him to be some sort of white knight who would appear at a moment's notice, ready and willing to wisk her to safety on his trusted steed?

A sarcastic huff left her shoulders shaking. Of course, that wouldn't happen.

There'd be no white knight. No romantic gesture or daring rescue. Because those things didn't exist. Not for women like her.

What do you have to lose?

Nothing, really. Not anymore.

Tonight had been the cold, hard slap of reality she'd clearly needed. The neighborhood and new name, encrypted phones and computers... It was never enough.

And until she figured out a way to stop Justin—or whoever was after her—it never would be. Which left Quinn with only one choice.

I have to disappear.

It was exactly what she needed to do. She needed to go someplace else, far away from Chicago, and start a whole new life. But she couldn't do it on her own. And certainly not without money or shoes.

Call him.

Quinn pulled the phone from her pocket and tapped the screen. Her hand trembled as she paused, the fear of rejection so strong she could taste its bitterness inside her mouth.

If he doesn't answer or refuses to help, you'll find another way. You always do.

The voice in her head was right. She'd been in worse situations...or at least, other bad ones she preferred to forget. If this call was a dead end, that didn't mean she gave up.

If she did that, Justin would win. And Quinn refused to let that happen.

She opened the app she used to make her phone number appear as the sequence of her choice. Another added layer of protection she'd added after receiving that first note. Just in case.

Typing in the phone number she prayed he'd still recognize, Quinn tapped the next screen and dialed the number she knew by heart on the illuminated keypad.

She pressed the green button and brought her phone to her ear, praying he hadn't blocked her or changed his own number.

The air in her lungs became static, her heart slamming against her ribs so hard she felt as though it would burst free any minute. It started to ring.

Once. Twice. Three times. Four...

Quinn's shoulders fell as she moved to end the call. She'd try back in a bit, not trusting a voicemail to reach him in time.

With the ringing still traveling through the phone's speaker, she started for the button to end the call. The tip of her index finger was a centimeter away from the screen when a deep male voice came on the line.

"Jinx?" The familiar rumble brought tears to Quinn's eyes. "Jesus, is that you?"

Her nostrils burned, and her throat became clogged, and for a second she couldn't speak.

"Sweetheart, talk to me." A slight pause. "Jinx?"

After another hard swallow, she forced the knot down, choking out a broken, "H-hey."

"Oh, thank God." A forceful exhale filled her ear a heartbeat before a clipped, "Christ, woman. Where the hell have you been? Actually, scratch that. Doesn't matter." Tone softening with what sounded like unfeigned concern, he switched to, "Are you okay?"

The man's show of relief from simply hearing her voice again—along with the fact that he still cared enough to sound worried—brought a fresh round of welled tears to Quinn's eyes. Her chin quivered, but she bit her lip to keep her face from crumbling into a bawling mess.

Blinking the moisture from her eyes, she finally found her voice again. "Yes," she lied out of reflex. Almost immediately, however, Quinn added a quiet, more truthful, "No. I-I don't know."

You're not okay, Quinn. You need help.

"Okay, let's start with physically." He waited a beat. "Are you injured?"

"No."

Another breathy exhale was followed by the rough clearing of his throat. "Good. That's really good, Jinx." He drew in a breath and let it out slowly. "Next question, and I need the truth. Are you safe?"

Quinn squeezed her eyes shut, a tight roll of her lips preventing an audible cry from escaping as she searched for a calm her body fought to accept.

"Jinx?" ByteMe69 spoke sternly that time. "Sweetheart, I need an answer. Are. You. Safe?"

The unexpected bite in his words made her flinch. A forceful blink sent a collection of trapped tears streaming down her cheeks, but Quinn used her free hand to wipe them dry.

Her voice quivered with the whispered, "N-no."

Everything changed with that simple, two-letter answer.

One minute, she was talking to the same sweet, worried friend she'd desperately missed. The same ByteMe69 who listened with a caring ear and made her laugh when she needed it most.

But with the very next beat of her anxious heart, a

different man took his place. Physically, Quinn knew it was the same person. But there was a change to his voice. An edge she'd never heard before.

"Where are you?" His tone was serious, its pitch impossibly deeper.

More than that, the clipped delivery of his no-rebuttal demand, the typically laid-back man sounded almost... *Deadly.*

"It's okay, Jinx." A rumbled vow. "You can trust me."

Quinn's face did crumble then. God, how she wanted that to be true. More than anything.

But the same old fears and insecurities from her past battled with the overwhelming desire to let this man in. To trust *him.*

"Sweetheart, please." ByteMe69's heartfelt plea cut through her indecision to reach her. "I'm right here. You just have to talk to me."

She opened her mouth to respond, but closed it again, unable to let go of that last bit of control.

"What do you need, Jinx? Name it, and it's yours."

The confidence in his open-ended offer was unyielding, as if he believed he had the power to make her wildest dreams come true. But there was only one dream. One thing she needed above all else....

"You," she whispered before she could talk herself out of it. Just to make sure he understood, Quinn added a stronger, steadier, "I need you."

And then she held her breath and waited.

4

ONE HOUR, forty-three minutes later...

PARKER STARED AT THE BLACK ABYSS THROUGH THE SMALL oval window to his left, those three little words filling his head for the millionth time.

What do you need? Name it, and it's yours.

You. I need...you.

Jinx had sounded so small. So vulnerable.

And so very un-Jinx-like.

He had no idea what kind of trouble she was in or why she felt unsafe. Those were all things they'd get into later. Right now, the only thing that mattered was his friend was alive.

She was alive and, according to her, uninjured. And she was fucking terrified.

Are you safe?

No.

The second he heard what he'd already suspected, Parker's decision was made. It hadn't mattered that, in that moment, he still hadn't a clue where she was calling him from. He hadn't cared.

Jinx could have told him she was in Timbuktu, and his answer would have been the same...

I need...you.

Done. It hadn't even been a question. *Where are you?*

Chicago.

So much closer than he'd expected.

Give me two hours, and I'll be there.

Two hours? W-where are you?

Doesn't matter. You just keep yourself safe until I get there. Can you do that, Jinx?

Yes.

Good girl. Now, listen...I need to put some things in motion so I can get to you. Text me the address where you'll be. And if something happens, and you need to change locations, let me know ASAP. Got it?

Got it.

Hang in there, sweetheart. I'm on my way.

Parker had added that last part as an afterthought. His need to reassure her—to protect her—almost primal. Which made zero sense, given that they'd never met. Except...

It somehow did.

Jinx was a friend, and she needed his help. Period.

"Just a heads-up, Sir. We'll be landing in five." A male voice filled the private jet's speakers.

Thoughts interrupted, Parker pressed one of the smooth buttons on his armrest and responded. "Thanks, Mase."

Mason Walters was a retired Air Force fighter pilot, and one of the few people in the world Parker truly trusted.

Guess Jinx isn't the only one with trust issues, is she?

No, no she wasn't. Although something told him the origins of their skepticism were very different.

I need you.

The hesitant woman's whispered admission carried with it a sense of duty Parker found both confusing and, oddly enough, somehow right. Like Jinx was his responsibility.

His to rescue. His to protect. His to...

Nope. Not going there. Jinx is a friend. Period.

The mental reminder was one he needed to hear.

He and Jinx may have connected on a deeper level than anyone else he'd ever gamed with, but that didn't mean there was anything else to it. And yes, he was the one she'd reached out to when she was in trouble.

But that's what friends were for, right? To be there for one another and lend a helping hand when one was needed? That's all Parker was doing for Jinx.

He was lending a helping hand to a friend in need. Nothing more.

Keep telling yourself that, dipshit.

Okay, fine. He *may* have imagined their first in-person meeting a time or two. *Or a thousand.* And maybe during those times when Parker would let himself go there, his mind's eye would always capture the very moment their eyes met.

He'd look at her...Jinx would stare back at...and bam! That's when it would happen.

They'd both be struck with the same, mind-altering connection Sydnee and Ash had felt when they'd first met. Like a jolt of electricity, she'd once told him.

It was a nice dream. A fantasy, really. One he needed to put out of his mind so he could focus on what was important...

Get to Jinx and get her to safety.

Everything else would have to wait.

The jet's wheels hit the runway with ease, the slight jostle cutting through Parker's wandering thoughts. Minutes later, they were stopped, and Mason was waiting in his usual place at the front of the cabin, next to the extended staircase.

"Your ride is waiting outside, Mr. Collins." The other man informed him. "Although, I'd feel much better if I was going with you. Just in case."

Once again, Parker was reminded of Mason's unwavering dedication and loyalty.

"I appreciate that, Mase. But I'll be covered. Besides, I need you and the jet ready to go." He arched a brow before adding a parroted, "Just in case."

"You're the boss."

Aware of Mason's disapproval, Parker stepped in front of the awaiting exit and looked outside. His scanning gaze finding the blacked-out GMC Yukon Denali Asher said would be here.

A cool Chicago breeze blew past, the sudden chill a reminder that he'd left his jacket at home.

Damn.

He'd been sitting on one of six wooden sun loungers strategically positioned around the pool built into the lower level of his expansive back deck when Jinx had finally called. With temps in the low seventies, his plain, olive-green T, worn jeans, and mocha suede and leather boots had been perfectly fine.

Of course, once the same sweet voice he'd longed to hear came through his phone, all logical thoughts went out the fucking window. There was only one thought then. And only one thought now...

Jinx needs me.

"I'll call with an update as soon as I can." Parker looked at a man he considered a friend.

Consummate professional that he was, Mason gave him a curt nod and a no-nonsense, "I'll have the jet re-fueled and ready to go."

"Thanks, Mason." Parker slapped his trusted employee's bulging bicep. Taking that first step, Parker stopped to give the other man a parting reminder. "I don't have a lot of details yet, so keep your phone close."

"Yes, Sir."

"Parker, Mase." He shook his head with a smirk. "I swear, one of these days, I *will* get you to call me Parker."

"If you say so, Sir."

Parker's smile started to grow, but as he made his way down the steep staircase, his lips fell back to the same worried line he'd worn the entire flight here.

Because he *was* worried. And the concern he felt for Jinx would continue until he could see with his own eyes that she really was okay.

I'm here, sweetheart. Just a little longer and you'll be safe.

Making his way to the slick-looking SUV, Parker felt a little punch to his steps. Not because he expected his fantasy to come true, but because—possible physical attraction aside—he cared about her.

And she needed him.

Full fucking stop.

The driver's side door opened and a tall, obviously fit man with tattoos covering the full length of his left arm climbed out. Parker recognized him from one of the files Asher had emailed just before take-off.

Christian Hunt.

Thirty-four- year-old former Navy corpsman and

current leader of RISC's new Delta Team. A man Asher Cross had vouched for without hesitation.

Having used the emailed files as a distraction, Parker had read through each one carefully. There were six in total —one for each member of RISC's Delta Team.

If he'd had the choice, he would have rather had Asher's team watching his and Jinx's backs. But when he'd called Ash to cash in one of many owed favors, the sniper had regrettably been forced to decline.

Apparently, Charlie Team had been called up unexpectedly for a gig overseas. From what Asher had shared during their short conversation, it was slated to be an in-and-out job, and he and the others planned to be back in a couple of days.

Max.

Since Jinx couldn't wait that long—and since she was in the same city as Hunt's team—Asher had put a call into Delta. Thankfully, the newest RISC operatives had been more than willing to step up.

"Collins, I presume."

"And you must be Hunt." Parker came to a stop in front of the other man. With a mutual shake of hands, he added a sincere, "Thanks for coming."

"No problem." A set of dark eyes wiser than their years met his.

The front passenger door opened, and a second man appeared. Parker recognized him as one of Delta Team's two former SEALS.

Brody King.

At thirty-eight, King stood at least a few inches over six feet. His short brown hair was several shades darker than Hunt's, and a thick, well-trimmed beard covered the man's stoic, unmoving jaw.

A set of cool, unreadable eyes stared into his, giving away nothing as the former Frogman joined the party.

"Parker Collins, this is Brody King. He's our—"

"Lead sniper." Parker greeted the other Delta Team member with a lift of his chin and an outstretched hand. "Cross told me all about you guys. Good to meet you."

Told...shared intel via emailing me copies of your personnel files...same difference.

King's bearded expression remained unreadable, his deep voice carrying with the brisk wind as he gripped Parker's hand tightly. "Likewise."

"In case I forget to mention it later, thank you." He shared a look with both men. "I really appreciate the help."

"Any friend of Charlie Team's..." Hunt let his voice trail off. With the introductions complete, he got right down to business. "I assume you also know about the other four guys on our team, as well?"

"I do."

"Good." He turned and headed for the top-of-the-line Yukon. "Saves me the time of telling you."

Parker grinned, appreciating the man's refreshing candor almost as much as his help. "Ash said you had a safe place for us to crash tonight?"

"Yep," Hunt confirmed. "It's not much, but it's clean, and there's food in the fridge."

"That'll work."

He didn't need fancy, just a place for Jinx to rest without fear of whatever—or whoever—had her running scared.

"I've got the address to where your girl's supposed to meet us." Delta's team leader opened his door and folded himself behind the wheel. "Store's near Humboldt Park, which is only a few blocks from here. Barring any major traffic jam, we'll have you there in less than fifteen."

With that, the other man pulled his door shut as King returned to his place in the front passenger seat. Meanwhile, Parker had barely managed to conceal his slightly faltering steps.

Fifteen minutes.

As a rule, he wasn't typically a nervous type of guy. But hearing Hunt say that...knowing he was *this* close to meeting the woman who'd consumed his every thought...

Hell yeah, he was nervous.

As. Fuck.

And the closer he got, the harder it was to hide.

He did his best to stay focused on the small talk-driven conversation between him and the other two men. But with every mile they crossed and every block they passed... the more Parker's symptoms worsened.

Sweaty palms. Trembling, fidgeting hands. A heart that felt like it was doing its damnedest to pound its way out of his chest. A fluttery, empty feeling swirling around inside his stomach.

Jesus, man. Get a fucking grip, already, would ya?

With a mental shake, Parker ran a hand down his face, the short stubble tickling his fingers making him wish he'd thought to shave on the jet. He glanced down at his rumpled shirt and faded jeans, adding a change of clothes to the pointless wish list.

This isn't about you, dickhead. Jinx isn't going to give two shits about what you're wearing.

"So." Hunt broke a block's worth of silence. "Cross said you pitched in on a few of their more recent ops. That's really cool, considering."

"Considering?" Parker forced his attention back to the other man's.

"Oh, I don't mean that bad, man. Quite the opposite, in

fact." Hunt flipped his blinker and took the next left. "I just meant it would be a hell of a lot easier to just sit back and enjoy your billions without giving anyone else a second thought. But you didn't. You volunteered your time and skills to help Cross and those guys when they needed it. Now, from what Cross passed along, it sounds like you're doing the same for this woman you barely know. As far as I'm concerned, that makes you as much a part of the RISC family as the rest of us."

King's low grunt of agreement came from the passenger seat.

Wasn't expecting that, but I'll take it.

"Appreciate it." He really did. "And just so you're aware, I know the press has made me out to be this cocky playboy who spends his days playing video games and his nights bedding every woman with a pulse. But that's not me." Not even close.

"Funny." Hunt flashed him a knowing smirk in the rearview. "Cross said the same thing when he called."

Asher had said that? "Really?"

The Delta operator nodded. "Said you weren't anything like the immature player the tabloids made you out to be, and that everything they printed about you was a lie." He huffed out a breath. "Other than the cocky part, that is. Ash said that was one hundred percent truth."

Parker grinned, his anxiety a little less on point than it had been a few minutes earlier. "I plead the fifth."

"I bet," Hunt replied.

Another, more comfortable silence fell over them once more. Before he knew it, Parker heard Hunt say...

"We're here."

Glancing through the windshield from the center of the vehicle's middle seat, he saw the grocery store's shining florescent sign. His nerves returned with a vengeance, the sudden urge to jump out of the moving vehicle and yell out her name much stronger than it should have been.

Chill out, Park. You don't even know she's here. This whole thing could be one big set-up.

But even as the thought formed, Parker knew that wasn't the case. Jinx was here, and the fear he'd heard in her voice when she'd called...

That shit was as real as it got.

He scanned the lot, noting several random spaces filled with various makes, models, and colors of cars. But he only had to find one.

"She drives a black Nissan Altima. Four-door."

"You got a plate?"

Parker shook his head. "She said I'd know it when I saw it."

The words had no more left his lips when he spotted a black sedan two rows over. "There! That might be it."

Lucky for him, they'd just reached the end of the row they'd been driving down, so Hunt was able to get them to the other car in nothing flat.

The car came into clear view, his heart leaping into his throat when he saw the silver, circular logo centered on the rear edge of the trunk.

A trunk that was dented all to hell.

What the...

"Holy shit." Hunt spotted the damage at almost the exact same time.

"She mention anything about getting into a wreck?" King finally decided to join the conversation.

"No." Parker zeroed in on the car's windows. From what he could tell, they were still intact, the car's rear bumper and trunk holding the majority of the damage.

His breathing picked up, his heart beating wildly as he tried like hell to catch a glimpse inside.

There!

"I see her!" Parker announced in a rush, pointing to the half-sitting, half-slouched figure in the Nissan's front seat.

Hunt slowed the SUV, pulling into an empty space a couple spots away. Not waiting for the wheels to come to a complete stop, Parker opened his door, his boots hitting the asphalt at the same time Hunt opened his door and hollered out for him to wait.

"Jesus, man." Delta's team leader shoved the gearshift into *park* before releasing his seatbelt. "Take a second and breathe."

"Thanks, but I didn't come all this way to fucking breathe." Parker shut his own door and turned away. He and King nearly collided when both men cleared the SUV's back bumper at the same time.

He moved to the right. So did King. Sliding to the left, he bit back an insulting curse when the other man followed his same movements again.

By the time King mirrored Parker's third attempt to continue on his current path, Parker knew it wasn't by accident.

"Get out of my way."

King did *not* get out of his way. In fact, the former SEAL didn't so much as blink.

"You have no idea who this woman really is or what she could be involved in." Hunt came to a stop at Parker's side. "Given who you are, it's not out of the realm of possibility that she could be working with someone else."

Parker shot the man a deep scowl. "Like who?"

"Could be anyone." Hunt shrugged. "Or no one. Which is exactly my point. This woman you're trying to play the hero for may very well be an innocent. Or, she could be a psychopath who'd love nothing more than to go down in history as the woman who ate the head of the world's Most Eligible Bachelor."

"Jesus, Hunt." Parker grimaced. "Jinx doesn't want to eat my goddamn head."

"Just sayin'." The other man shrugged again, his unapologetic expression grating on Parker's razor-thin nerves.

"Look. I get that you're only here as a favor to Ash, and I really do appreciate your willingness to help. And while I may not have the same military training you do, I can handle my own when the need arises. But most importantly, there's a woman sitting two spaces from where we're standing who's scared out of her mind. And she's waiting for me. So either you let me go to her, or the three of us are going to have a very big problem."

Parker stopped talking and waited, grateful as hell when Brody stepped aside enough to let him pass.

"Thank you."

With rushed steps, he made a bee line for Jinx's car. The closer he got, the clearer her silhouetted image became. And when he found himself standing beside her door, Parker suddenly found it impossible to breathe.

Jinx.

After nearly a year of wishing they could meet in person, there she was. Right there, within his reach...and he couldn't move a fucking muscle.

Couldn't breathe. Couldn't move. And for the life of him, he couldn't get his brilliant mind to think.

So for the next several seconds, he didn't even bother to try.

Instead, Parker gave himself that one, precious moment

in time to get his first real look at the sleeping beauty who'd become the star of his dreams.

And holy hell, what a beauty she was.

Thick, straight, shoulder-length hair the color of wheat partially covered the most angelic face he'd ever seen. Flawless skin, high cheekbones, a nose that was straight with just the right amount of lift right at the very end.

Parker's lips twitched when he spotted the tiny rhinestone adorning the slight dip at one side. Nose piercings weren't usually his thing, but from what he knew of her, this one fit Jinx's perfectly.

His gaze lowered, pausing over the woman's tempting mouth. Even from here, he could tell her bottom lip was slightly fuller than the top, and before he could keep from it, Parker was imagining what it would feel like to kiss her.

Not now, dickhead. You need to get her someplace safe and figure out what the hell's going on first.

With a mental shake of his head, Parker blinked, his focus drawn back to her eyes. They were still closed, so he couldn't tell their color, but it didn't matter.

This was Jinx. *His* Jinx.

After waiting for what felt like forever, she was right there, inches from where he stood. Jinx was here, and she was beautiful. She was also...

Waking up.

Every muscle in his body locked down as her lids slowly fluttered to life. Without so much as a sliver of breath in his lungs, Parker watched Jinx blink herself back to awareness.

As if suddenly realizing she'd fallen asleep, she shot straight up in her seat and swung her head wildly in both directions.

Parker opened his mouth with the intention of assuring her it was okay. That she was safe. But in that very same moment, the most beautiful, blue-green eyes he'd ever seen found his from behind the glass.

And just like that, everything else around him ceased to exist.

There was no longer a store full of food and patrons behind him. No other cars in the lot. Hunt and King had also vanished, along with every other living soul for as far as the eyes could see.

Everything around him was gone. Everything except...

Her.

A blanket of goosebumps fell around him, and this time it had nothing to do with the temperature. The unexplainable, exhilarating sensation filling his veins—filling his every fucking *cell*—was something else altogether.

Their gazes remained locked; the shared moment more powerful than any he'd ever experienced. So powerful, Parker felt as if he'd just been struck by a giant bolt of lightning.

What the hell was that?

Never, not once in his thirty years, had Parker been knocked on his ass by the mere glance from a beautiful woman. Until now.

And then it hit him.

This is it. That moment Sydnee told you about after she and Ash first met.

Before he could even begin to think about what that meant, Jinx blinked and parted her lips, the subtle movements breaking the entrancing spell Parker had been under.

Say something, dumbass. You're scaring her.

Realizing she was probably spooked by some strange man standing outside her car door, he threw both hands palms-up, praying she could see he meant her no harm.

"Jinx?" Parker purposely raised his voice so she could

hear through the glass and metal barrier separating them. "It's me. ByteMe69."

A snorting sound came from his right, where Hunt and King were standing guard, but he ignored it.

In fact, he ignored *everything* except the woman still staring up at him. The look on her face said she couldn't believe what she was seeing.

Tell me about it, sweetheart.

When Jinx made no move to exit her vehicle, he tried a second time to convince her she was safe.

"You're safe now, Jinx." Parker pointed to the other two men standing nearby. "I don't know if you can see them, but these are my friends, Christian and Brody. They're both former military, and they work for a nationally known private security firm. When you're ready, they're going to take us both to a safe house here in the city."

He waited patiently while Jinx tilted her head and leaned in closer, twisting her upper body in an effort to catch a glimpse of the two Delta men. When her trepidatious gaze returned to his, Parker felt the need to explain in greater detail.

"It'll just be the two of us inside the house," he promised. "But these guys will keep watch from the outside overnight. That way, you can relax and get a good night's sleep without worrying about...whatever it is you're worried about. We can worry about the rest in the morning. How does that sound?"

Jinx continued staring, those breathtaking eyes never leaving his. But still, she made no attempt to move.

A strong gust of wind flew past, and Parker instinctively began rubbing the exposed parts of his arms to stay warm. The apprehensive woman frowned, her light brown brows bunching together with obvious guilt.

Take your time, sweetheart. I'll wait.

And he would have, too. For as long as it took. But as luck would have it, Jinx finally began to move.

Reaching for the control panel built into the door's armrest, she pressed a button he couldn't see and disengaged the locks. Pushing her door open, she used slow, cautious movements when getting out of the car.

Jinx shut the door behind her and straightened her spine. The tip of her tongue peeked out; a nervous swipe of her lips that damn near made him groan.

For the next several seconds, the two of them stood just like that, each silently taking the other in for the very first time. Parker didn't dare look away for fear she'd disappear, and...

Lord, have mercy.

Standing about six inches below his six-two frame, the guarded blonde was taller than the average adult female. Dressed in a pair of snug, distressed jeans, a slightly loose white t-shirt, and a cropped, black leather jacket that fit her feisty personality to a T, Parker had no trouble imagining what was hidden underneath...

Long, toned legs. Curvy hips his fingers itched to reach for. A slightly tapered waist, leading what he just knew were two perfect, just-the-right-size breasts.

Physically, she was everything he loved in a woman and more. Add in the smart, funny, feisty personality he'd already known she possessed, and the woman was the whole package.

In a word, she was...

Fucking perfect.

Technically that was two words, but he didn't care. Jinx —God, he couldn't *wait* to learn her real name—was the perfect combination of cute, girl-next-door sweet and unapologetic badass.

And he was still staring.

Shit.

"Sorry." Parker finally got his head out of his ass. With an offered hand and a wide, cheesy smile he couldn't seem to control, he made their first official introduction. "Hey, Jinx. I'm Parker. Parker Collins. It's so damn good to finally meet you."

Jinx didn't respond immediately. Instead, her pretty eyes bounced from his, down to the offered hand, and back up. The mixture of disbelief and anger swirling around inside her pretty eyes was confusing, and Parker's mind whirled with a possible explanation.

What does she see when she looks at me?

Still standing there, hand out for a woman who clearly had no intentions of shaking it, Parker was so caught up in what she could be thinking, it took him a beat to notice the open-palmed hand flying forcefully toward his face.

And by the time he *did* see it...

Son of a—

...he was too late.

The unexpected blow had already landed.

5

QUINN GASPED, both hands flying up to her mouth in shock as she stared at the man whose head had just snapped to the side. A snap that had occurred because she'd just *hit* that same man.

In. The. Face.

Ohmygod! I can't believe I just did that.

She wasn't a violent person. Not even a little bit. Yet she'd just assaulted the one person she'd trusted enough to turn to when her life was in danger. And the worst part...

Quinn didn't even realize her arm was moving until it was too late.

Even now, she couldn't recall the exact moment it had happened. It was like she was having one of those out-of-body experiences or something.

One minute she was standing there, staring up into the most incredible eyes she'd ever seen. And the next...

Parker Collins. It's damn good to finally meet you.

His manifested greeting sparked her misplaced memory, the entire blocked-out scene replaying through her mind from beginning to end.

When she first saw him through her car window, Quinn had been terrified. Afraid the person who'd broken into her home had found her. But then she'd heard his voice—*that* voice—and she knew.

ByteMe69 had come for her, just as he'd promised.

So she'd gotten out of the car, stunned silent as she got her first full look at the sexiest, most mouthwatering man she'd ever laid eyes on. Quinn remembered standing there, doing everything she could not to break down into a puddle of tears for the relief from just knowing he was there when it had hit her.

I know him.

Not personally, of course. Although, she kind of did, given their ongoing online friendship. But that had been the moment when Quinn had first *recognized* him.

That face. Those eyes. That kissable mouth that made her think all kinds of naughty things.

She saw it all—and if she was lucky, sometimes a little more—practically every time she turned on the T.V. or flipped through a magazine while waiting in line at the grocery store.

That's when Quinn had finally put two and two together. And the only plausible answer was one that left her feeling thoroughly confused and more than a little hurt...

Parker Collins, billionaire playboy with an attitude, was ByteMe69.

Her online friend was the same rich and famous man she'd seen on all those magazine covers. The man she'd joked and laughed and teased with for the past year, the same one who'd portrayed himself as a regular Joe, actually had more money than God.

But the worst, most painful realization Quinn remembered was the man she'd come to know and care for—the one person she'd *trusted*—had spent the last eleven months feeding her nothing but lies.

And *that* was when she'd hit him.

"Have to admit, that's not exactly the way I'd imagined our first IRL meeting going." Parker lifted a hand to the reddened cheek, his rugged jaw stretching to work itself out. "Then again, you always have kept me on my toes, so..."

The crooked smirk curving his lips was the same, panty-dropping one she'd always imagined.

Damn it, Q. Focus!

"Parker Collins is ByteMe69," Quinn rasped, his name falling from her lips much too easily. "I did *not* see that coming."

It made a lot of sense, now that she thought about it.

The late-night gaming hours he kept. The occasional tech-speak. His cocky-yet-magnetic attitude that drove her mad and made her want him all at the same time.

The flirting.

"Guilty as charged." Parker's smile evened out as he shook his handsome head. "Damn, Jinx. It really is a pleasure to meet you. Although, something tells me the feeling isn't exactly mutual."

There it was. That same tempting combination of sweet and cocky she'd missed so much.

"I shouldn't have slapped you." Quinn hugged herself tightly. "I'm sorry."

He stared down at her, those hazel eyes of his searching hers as if they held the answers to life's greatest mysteries.

Joke's on you, buddy.

"Clearly I've done something to upset you." Parker's eyes remained locked with hers. "Although for the life of me, I don't have the faintest idea what that something is."

Not one to beat around the bush, Quinn decided to give

it to him straight. "You lied to me." She swallowed. "And I don't do lies."

Been there, done that, burned the damn t-shirt.

"I *lied?*" Parker's brows shot straight up half a beat before coming together with a frown. "When the hell did I lie to you?" Both arms stretched wide, his palms facing the sky as he pointed out, "I'm here, aren't I?"

Yes, he was here, but...

"That's not what I'm talking about."

His arms fell back to his sides, his handsome face looking more confused than ever. "Then wha—"

"You said you were an accountant!" The blurted accusation came out much harsher—and louder—than intended.

It also had the other two men's heads spinning in her direction.

With a simultaneous step, they started moving toward her. On instinct, Quinn's shoulders moved back, her spine stiffening with the first tingles of another fight-or-flight response. But Parker saw this and lifted a hand, the men's simultaneous steps halting mid-stride with the silent order.

Guess money really does equal power.

Clearing her throat, Quinn did her best to explain her volatile behavior. "Look, I know it sounds stupid, but...the ByteMe69 I know is an accountant for a Fortune 500 company. At least that's what he sai—" She shook her head and motioned toward him. "That's what *you*'ve been telling me for the past year. I mean, you said I could trust you, but if you lied about your job, how do I know you didn't lie about everything else?"

The stories about his neglective parents and being bullied in school for being a nerd. His business trip antics and the fact that he had no one special in his life...

"You're right." Parker shoved his hands into his jeans'

pockets. "I absolutely lied about my job, and I shouldn't have. Not with you."

"So why did you?"

"Wouldn't you, if you were me?" His intense gaze searched hers for more answers.

Quinn considered this a moment but shook her head. "If you were embarrassed about playing a game that's not up to par with the ones you make, why play it in the first place?"

"Nope. My turn." He gave her car a sideways glance and frowned. "What happened tonight, Jinx?"

The change of subject was an abrupt reminder of why he was here in the first place. It also made her feel like an ungrateful bitch.

Parker could have arrived with an entourage of personal assistants or some fake, too-skinny model to meet his pathetic, far-from-famous nerd of a friend. He could have shown up with a camera crew, or tipped off the paparazzi. Used her situation to put a shine on his popular but tarnished image.

Quinn could see the headlines now...

Parker Collins, Player or Protector?

That *could* have been how tonight played out, but he didn't do any of those things. Instead, he'd dropped everything to get to her.

White lies aside, this man—this super rich, seriously *famous* man—had traveled two hours on a moment's notice, not because he thought it would benefit him. He did it for her.

And he brought reinforcements.

Quinn looked over at the two men Parker had introduced as Christian and Brody. Standing several feet away, their stances were firm, eyes on their surroundings.

"Jinx?"

She swung her gaze back to his, heat warming her chilled cheeks. "Sorry." A small, nervous huff of a breath. "There was a man in my house tonight." The masked face appeared before her, but Quinn pushed the intrusive image away. "He, uh..." She licked her lips. "He was wearing a mask, and he had a gun."

"What?" Parker's alarmed tone grew lethal, his near-perfect features darkening with worry and anger. "Jesus. Are you okay?" His hands went to her shoulders, worry flashing through his assessing eyes. "Did he hurt you?"

Quinn's gasp was audible, the electric pulse from his firm but gentle touch stealing the air from her lungs. Mistaking the source of her reaction, he immediately dropped his hands and removed himself from her personal space.

"Shit." Parker shook his head with regret. "Sorry."

She opened her mouth to tell him he hadn't hurt or offended her but changed her mind last-second. This wasn't about that. Not that she'd have a chance with someone like him if it was.

Focus, Q.

"The man with the gun didn't hurt me," Quinn reassured him. "I never really gave him the chance."

"What do you mean?"

A cool breeze had her pulling the front halves of her jacket together. "He was in my kitchen, and there was a half-bottle of wine close by. I waited until he came within reach, and then I grabbed the bottle and hit him over the head. He went down, and I ran into my garage and got into my car. Luckily, I had my keys and phone in my pocket, but my purse, my wallet, my tablet and computers...they're all still back at the house." She looked down with an embarrassed chuckle. "I didn't even think about the fact that I wasn't wearing any shoes. I just smashed through the garage door and got the hell out of there."

Another inaudible curse traveled through the air. "I'll get you some shoes." Parker's gaze intensified as he added, "And anything else you need."

Her heart did that same pitter-patter thing it did when they'd be chatting, and he'd cross that line between friendly and flirty. Only he wasn't flirting with her now. He was being serious.

Which was even hotter than the flirting.

Handsome man, knows computers, loves gaming, acts like he cares... Sound familiar, anyone?

Quinn knew that story well, and it didn't come with a happy ending. She knew because she'd lived it, and there wasn't even the tiniest part of her that wanted to do it again.

Not even with a man who looked back at her as if he'd buy her the moon if she asked.

Probably could afford it with the money he has.

"Listen, I have more questions, and I'm sure you do, too." Parker's deep voice reigned in her scattered thoughts. "I promise I'll answer every single one of yours...*truthfully*... once we're at the safehouse." He glanced down at her feet. "What size do you wear?"

"Seven and a half."

The suddenly protective man gave her a curt dip of his chin, his eyes alert as he scanned the lot for possible threats. "Is there anything in your car that you need to take with you?"

She shook her head. "Like I said, it's all at home."

"Lock it." The order was stern. "We'll leave it here for a day or two in case you're being tracked."

"If I was being tracked, they would have found me by now."

He brought his stoic gaze back to hers. "Or they're regrouping and preparing for a second attack."

The man had a point.

Quinn reached into her pocket, pulled out her fob, and pressed the button to lock her car. "I'm ready."

"Let's go."

Warmth from Parker's hand spread across her lower back as they walked to where the other two men were waiting. Like when he'd touched her before, a pulse of electricity originated at the point of contact, and it was all she could do to hide the breath-stealing shock.

Refusing to acknowledge her body's inexplicable reaction to a man she barely knew, she focused on Parker's friends.

Dressed in jeans, boots, and t-shirts, they were both at least six feet, brunette, and fit. And more than a little attractive.

They don't hold a candle to Parker, though.

"Jinx, this is Christian Hunt." The star of her thoughts pointed to the man on the left. "He's a former Navy corpsman who heads up RISC's Delta Team. That's the local private security group I mentioned earlier."

Bulkier than the other man, Christian's shoulders were broader, his chest and biceps larger and more defined. The slicked-back hair on the top of his head was longer than the neatly trimmed sides and back, his matching scruff covering a chiseled jaw and slightly dimpled chin.

Her eyes fell to the ink covering his left arm from beneath his black t-shirt's short sleeve to his wrist. Peeking out from the sleeve's stretched hem was the head of a bald eagle.

Minus the bird's golden eye, the rest of the realistic lines and curves that had been permanently etched into his skin had all been done in black and gray. Feathers wrapped around the back of the top half of the arm, their tips morphing into the stripes of the American flag.

A saluting soldier whose bottom half was made from the infamous battle cross stood below.

Quinn couldn't see the back of his forearm from where she stood, but it didn't take a genius to guess whatever was there, it was patriotic in theme.

Someone with tattoos like that has to be a good guy, right?

Quinn knew that wasn't necessarily true but gave the man the benefit of the doubt and a guarded smile. "It's nice to meet you."

"Likewise." His expression was unreadable but not unfriendly as he tilted his head toward the man next to him. "This is Brody King."

With a lean, fit build, Brody looked more like a runner than body builder. Short dark hair and a thick, well-groomed beard matched the man's fierce, intense demeanor. As did the set of dark brown eyes that were laser-focused on her.

"Thanks for coming."

The man said nothing. Just a slight, almost indiscernible tip of his chin.

Okaaay...

"You good?" Christian looked to Parker.

With his hand still pressed lightly against her back, Parker turned to her, his eyes passing the question to her. She nodded, hating how touched she felt by his taking the time to check with her first.

Letting his gaze linger with hers a moment longer, he turned back to Christian and said, "We're ready if you are."

The other man scoffed, his lips curving into a sideways smirk. "Brother, we've just been waiting on you."

Quinn watched as he and Brody headed toward an impressive looking, totally blacked out SUV waiting a few spots away. She and Parker followed, his hovering oddly comforting as he walked closely beside her.

And that warm, protective hand remained in place the entire way.

6

_____

THE NEXT MORNING...

"SO LET ME GET THIS STRAIGHT. YOU LITERALLY FLY TO THIS woman's rescue, meet her in some random parking lot where, instead of thanking you, she clocks you...you spent the *night* with her at an apartment Delta Team provided, and you *still* don't know her real name?"

Parker grinned at Sydnee's obvious disapproval of his handling of last night's events. "She didn't clock me," he corrected. "It was a slap, and it didn't hurt."

Surprised him, sure. Confused him, absolutely. Turned him on a little...

We're not going to discuss that.

"I don't care if it didn't hurt." Sydnee blew out a breath. "The woman should have thrown herself at your feet for even showing up in the first place. I mean, how do you even know she's telling the truth about the masked man in the first place?"

"I've got that covered, Syd. Trust me."

"It's not you I don't trust."

Warmth spread through Parker's chest. Sydnee had always been protective of him, as he'd been with her.

"I know what you're thinking, Syd. But I promise, I've got this under control."

"Really? Because I'm thinking you've lost your damn mind."

Chuckling, he stood in the apartment's modest kitchen, willing the coffee to brew faster. "Look. I get what you're saying, and if the situation were reversed, I'd be saying the same things right back to you. But you weren't there, Syd. You didn't see how scared she was."

"Was that before or after she hit you?"

"I'm serious." He ran a hand down his face, wishing the motion could erase the terror he'd seen in those amazing eyes when she'd first woken in that car. "And before you say she could've been faking, I don't know anyone who's that good of an actor."

And he personally knew several in the business.

"The whole thing just seems fishy." His worried friend continued. "And how the heck have you not asked for her real name yet? That would've been the *first* thing out of my mouth."

Yeah, that had definitely been at the top of his things to ask last night. But then he'd seen her in that car, looking so scared and vulnerable, and suddenly all that mattered was doing whatever he could do to take it all away.

So he'd introduced himself, first. The thought being if she realized who he really was, she'd feel better. Safe.

Yeah, and how'd that work out for you, eh, Collins?

"Again, I have it covered," Parker assured her.

"I sure hope so." A soft sigh filled his ear. "I wish Ash was home. I'd make him go to Chicago and stay with you."

He rolled his eyes and grabbed two ceramic mugs from the cabinet above the gurgling coffee pot. "I get that I'm not a super soldier like the man you're about to marry, but I do know how to handle myself." *More than you know.* "The only reason I called him in the first place was to make sure Jinx had plenty of protection."

"Just remember to protect yourself, too, Park. If not for yourself, do it for those of us who love you."

A broad smile lifted the corners of his mouth as a fist squeezed his heart. "Love you, too, Syd. I'll call soon."

"Promise?"

"Cross my heart."

Ending the call with the sister he never had, Parker grabbed the newly filled pot and slid one of the mugs close. He'd just started pouring when he heard...

"Hey."

The unexpected rasp pulled Parker's attention to the room's arched doorway on his left. Jinx stood in its center, the morning sunlight behind her creating a glow befitting an angel.

And that's exactly what she looked like. A beautiful, blonde, uncertain angel he couldn't stop staring at.

He was still staring into those intelligent, guarded eyes when a splash of burning liquid landed on his hand.

Parker hissed in a breath, reflexively pulling his left hand away from the overflowing mug. "Shit!" He sat the pot back into its cradle and flailed his injured hand.

"Oh, crap!" Alarm filled Jinx's eyes as she raced toward the sink. Shoving the faucet handle all the way to cold, she grabbed his wrist and pulled him so the injured area was directly beneath the steady stream. "Stay just like that. I'll get some ice."

Before he could tell her it wasn't that bad, she'd already

snatched up a folded dishtowel from the counter next to the sink and was at the freezer, filling the center of the towel with ice.

"Here." The focused woman turned off the water and used one corner of the towel to pat his skin dry. With the gentlest of touches, Jinx gathered the towel's edges and pressed the makeshift icepack over the reddened area. "How's that?"

"Perfect." But his eyes weren't on his hand.

Neither were his thoughts.

All Parker could focus on was how the blue-eyed beauty had stolen his breath for the second time in as many days. The first had been last night, when he'd gotten his first real look at her. But this time...

She's even more beautiful in the morning.

He inwardly smiled when he realized she was wearing the black hoodie, jeans, and black lace-up boots he'd purchased for her last night. On the drive to the safehouse, he'd made an online order at a nearby big-box store that had curbside pick-up service, one of Hunt's other guys picked it up and delivered it later.

It hadn't been much. The outfit she had on now, something comfortable to sleep in, a few toiletries, a new bra and panties set...

That last one had been a guess, but she was wearing them, so he must've done okay on the sizes.

How do you know she's wearing them? Maybe she's a commando kinda girl.

"I didn't mean to startle you." Jinx brought those stunning eyes to his.

Parker schooled his expression, praying she couldn't somehow sense his most recent thoughts.

"It's okay." He didn't dare admit to the real reason for the spill. "I should have been paying better attention."

Their gazes held, the flakes of greens and blues in her eyes more vibrant in the light of day. Jesus, he'd never seen anything like them. Like two precious gemstones, their value incalculable.

But then she broke it off, her tone sounding almost too casual when she asked, "Was that Christian on the phone?"

She heard you tell Syd you loved her, and now she's wondering if you're trying to play her.

Having silently vowed never to lie to this woman again, he shook his head and answered honestly. "That was Sydnee Blake. We grew up together."

"Oh." She shrugged. "I was just curious. I thought maybe the guys found Oreo."

Her tone was breezy, as if it hadn't mattered to her one way or the other. Parker knew better.

"No sign of Oreo yet, but cats are resourceful, and they love to hide. I'm sure she'll show up soon." He watched her closely as he added, "Syd's like my little sister, Jinx. She's also engaged to the same man who arranged for Delta's help with all of this."

"Oh." The guarded woman blinked a few times. "That was really nice of him."

Does she even realize she sounds relieved?

"I'm not with anyone, Jinx." He tilted his head, thwarting her attempts at breaking eye contact. "I told you that before, remember?"

"I know." A bit defensive. "You're obviously free to see whoever you want. It's not like you and I are...together. I only asked about the phone call because I thought it might be—"

"Hunt," Parker finished for her. "Yeah, I got that."

An adorable blush filled her cheeks as she jutted her chin, her shoulders becoming stiff. Glancing back down to their hands, Jinx motioned for him to take control of the towel.

"I, uh...I guess you can probably take it from here."

Unable to tear his eyes away, Parker blindly moved to grab the gathered material. His hand landed on hers in the process.

The tiny hitch of breath filled the otherwise silent room. Her gaze returned, the expanding pupils and slight parting of her lips giving away the woman's reaction to his touch.

She feels it, too. Good to know.

It was his turn to blink. Heart kicking against his ribs, he lifted his hand so she could remove hers. The void her touch left took him instantly off guard.

He shouldn't feel this strongly about her. Especially when, as Sydnee had so vehemently pointed out minutes earlier, he still didn't know her name.

I'll know it soon, sweetheart. Very, very soon.

"So." Parker went back to the sink, setting the unneeded towel in the stainless-steel cavern. "You sleep okay?"

"Not really."

Her blatant honesty had him turning his head. Walking toward him, Jinx stopped about a foot away from him, her lower back resting against the counter's edge.

Cleaning up the spilled coffee, he forced himself to focus on what needed to be done, rather than her. "The place we're staying at tonight will be more comfortable." He tossed a wad of soiled paper towels in the trash. "Clothes fit okay?"

"Yeah." She nodded, giving her outfit a quick glance. "Perfect, actually. Thank you. And I will pay you back as soon as I get my wallet."

"Told you last night, it's my treat."

"And I appreciate that, but I'm still paying you back."

His lips twitched as he filled the second mug. The woman knew he was a billionaire, but still insisted on paying him back for a bill that cost less than two hundred dollars.

A vast difference from the other women who'd come in and out of his life. Apart from Sydnee, of course.

"Hunt called a few minutes ago," he shared. "Said he and King were at your place, and there were definite signs of a struggle."

"Because there was one." She sighed. "Did they say whether they found my purse and tablet?"

"They'd only just gotten there, but I told him to call if he had any issues."

When they'd gotten here last night, Jinx had given Hunt her address, along with her keys and a list of things she wanted from her place. On that list had been several clothing items, but Parker had shut down that idea.

It was probably overkill, but given what he knew about technology—and the classified work he sometimes did for the government that very few people knew about—he wasn't taking the chance of her being tracked.

Hence the new outfit she had on now.

The purse, wallet, and tablet she'd requested would be easy enough to check. Clothes, however, had too many places a tiny chip could be hidden or sewn into, it would take forever to do a thorough check. Thankfully when he'd explained all that to Jinx last night, she'd agreed.

Parker had to admit, he'd fully expected her to balk and throw a fit. Lord knows, the women he'd dated in past would have. But not Jinx.

Are you really that surprised? She's nothing like those other women.

"Coffee?" He pointed to the carafe.

She nodded with an emphatic, "Yes, please."

With a quick pour, he held it out for her, his entire body tensing when her fingertips brushed against his.

"Thanks." Jinx brought the mug to her lips and took a careful sip.

The moan she released—eyes closed and all—sent a rush of arousal racing though him. Quickly, before she opened her eyes again, Parker made a quick adjustment and faced the cabinets fully.

Replacing the erotic images her moan had created, he prayed for strength and broached a subject sure to vanquish the electric charge pulsing through the air...

"You had a hell of a night last night, and I knew you were exhausted." He fixed a second, appropriately filled cup of coffee for himself. "But you've had at least a little rest, and you're getting well-caffeinated, so..." He turned to face her. "You wanna tell me your real name now, or should we wait for the guys to get back with your wallet?"

Becoming intently focused on the steaming cup in her hands, Jinx's golden locks, which he could now see had a few strands of brown lowlights scattered throughout, fell like a curtain around her face.

Can't hide from me that easily, sweetheart.

"You could wait." She lifted her head and brought her gaze back to his. "But my wallet won't tell you what you want to know."

It took Parker a second to process what her words meant.

She isn't just keeping her real name from me. She doesn't want anyone to know who she is.

"You've been using an alias." It wasn't a question. "Other than Jinx, I mean."

The scant nod confirmed his suspicions. "For the past three years."

"What happened three years ago?"

"It really started *six* years ago." She looked back down at her coffee, took a sip, and turned to leave the room. "And if I'm going to do this, I should probably sit."

Well, that's not a great sign.

Following her into the living room, Parker took the recliner while Jinx sat at the far end of the couch. Placing the mug onto the end table beside her, she curled her legs up on the cushion and grabbed a throw pillow to hug.

"The short of it is, I have really bad taste in men."

He chuckled. "Gonna need a little more than that, sweetheart."

Holding his stare for a stretch, she took a deep breath and let it out slowly. "His name is Justin Reynolds, and he's an inmate at FCI. It's a federal prison in Pekin, which is about two-and-a-half hours southwest of here."

"What's he in for?"

"The official charge was 'accessing a computer to defraud and obtain value'."

Parker settled back in his chair and exhaled. "So he's a hacker."

"He was." She swallowed hard. "As was I."

It was a revelation Parker had already suspected, but he was pleased she'd offered the admission willingly.

Maybe she trusts me more than she thinks.

"What does Justin have to do with you using an alias? Or more importantly, how is he tied to what happened last night?"

"I was with Justin the night he was arrested." Jinx licked her lips nervously. "In fact, I'm the reason he got arrested."

"You?" Parker frowned. "How was that your fault?"

"I should really back up a step." She shifted in her seat. "The hacking I used to do... It was little stuff. Illegal, yes, but everything I did was to help people. I know I still shouldn't have done it, but I was young and dumb. Thought doing something wrong for the right reasons made it okay."

Having had his fair share of young and dumb days, that was something he could relate to.

"Anyway," she continued. "Justin was it for me. Or at least I thought so at the time. He was handsome and charming...and he spoke my language, you know?" Jinx released a humorless chuckle. "There wasn't anything I wouldn't do for him back then. Including agreeing to help him hack into a major credit card company, make duplicate cards from their active accounts, and use those to teach the company a lesson about targeting vulnerable, desperate people."

"Christ, Jinx." He sat up straighter. "You realize, you could've been sent away for like twenty years for something like that?"

"I know. Trust me, I know." She shook her head, clearly disgusted with herself for having agreed to such an asinine plan. "Justin told me this sob story about his parents, and how they'd had to declare bankruptcy, losing everything because of their credit card debt. So, like an idiot, I agreed to help make the public more aware of how those companies set up people, like his parents, for financial failure with all their hidden fees, massive interest rates, etc. But before you tell me again how stupid of a plan it was, I was already planning to do a dummy hack."

It was a term he was very familiar with. "So you were

going to go through the motions and make it look as though everything was working according to plan—"

"When in reality, it would only appear that way on screen," she finished for him. "Exactly."

"What about after? Your boyfriend would've figured it out the first time he used one of the fake cards."

"I figured I'd explain it away with some higher-level code speak he wouldn't understand. It wasn't the perfect plan, but I figured it would at least buy me some time to talk him out of the idea altogether." She swallowed. "I just needed to buy enough time to convince him making some grand societal statement wasn't worth the risk to himself...or me."

Parker studied her closely, and it didn't take long to understand. "That's how they got to you, isn't it? They hung your future over your head until you agreed to help them."

"Mine and Justin's, both." Her blonde hair moved up and down the tops of her shoulders as she nodded. "A woman approached me a few days before it all went down. Showed me her I.D. and said she was an agent with Chicago's FBI Cybercrimes Division. She had pictures of me and of Justin, as well as this other guy named Monty Dunne. I didn't know all the details at the time, but Monty was a suspect in several high-profile cybercrimes. The Feds could never get enough to catch him, but when they found out about Justin and his plan, they knew that was their chance."

"Let me guess. The Feds wanted to use Justin to get to Dunne—"

"And they used me to get to Justin." She finished his thought once more. "They hid a tiny camera in my hat and fitted me with a wire. If they got what they needed, I wouldn't be charged for my role in the scheme. And as long as Justin agreed to testify against Monty, they promised a lesser sentence."

"You said this was six years go. Why is Justin still in prison?"

From what she'd told him, he should've been out a few years ago.

"Because during their investigation, the federal prosecutor found other crimes Justin had committed. Things I didn't know about."

"Like what?"

"Fraud...extortion..." Her expression turned sad, and damn if that didn't hurt him to see. "He would've only been in for two years with the deal I helped get for him. But then they discovered these other things Justin had done...things I *never* would have supported...and they decided to make an example out of him."

"That's on him, Jinx. Not you."

"Quinn."

"I'm sorry?"

"Quinn Wilder. That's my real name." Those enchanting eyes stared back into his. "I figure you've more than earned the right to know it."

Ah...finally.

Parker's mouth spread into a slow grin. The wait was over. He had both the face and the name, and there wasn't a damn thing wrong with either one.

"Quinn." He held her gaze. "I like it."

"Thanks." A tiny smile graced her gorgeous face a breath before it fell. "And you're right. Justin made his bed, and any guilt I felt vanished the second he told the Feds the credit card hack was my idea."

Asshole. "I suppose it's a good thing you wore the wire."

"Right?"

A stretch of silence passed as they both became lost in their own thoughts. When Quinn spoke up again, her voice was flat, almost wooden.

"I think Justin sent that man to my house last night."

Parker could tell she absolutely believed that. He didn't patronize or mansplain how Justin couldn't have possibly sent someone to attack her from prison. Shit like that happened every damn day.

He knew it, and apparently so did she.

"What makes you think it's him?"

A flash of fear twitched behind her eyes, but it vanished. "Someone's been leaving me notes. *Miss me? I'm coming for you. You're not as smart as you think you are.* Oh, and my personal favorite...*You'll pay for what you did.*" She frowned. "He knows it was me. That I was the reason the Feds made their case. Hell, they showed him the video footage from the camera I was wearing. And since he's the only person I've ever helped send to prison, I'm pretty confident it's him. It has to be."

Every protective instinct Parker possessed flared to life. "Did you call the police?"

"No." She shook her head.

"Why the hell not?"

"Because I knew they weren't going to find anything."

"How could you possibly—"

"I accessed the security footage from the places where I was when the notes were left."

"Accessed." He tilted his head. "You mean you hacked into those systems."

"Wouldn't you, if you were me?"

Parker grinned, not missing the fact that she'd used his own words from last night against him. "Damn straight, I would have."

Relief softened her features. "Thanks for that."

"You find anything in your search?"

"I recorded it, so when I get my tablet back, I'll show you. But no." She shook her head. "The guy's there, but he's always wearing all black, including gloves and a black hat pulled down low." Quinn raked a frustrated hand through her hair. "He had to have been watching me for a while, too."

Parker's chest tightened. "What makes you say that?"

"He knew exactly where the cameras were. The grocery store...my gym...my front door... The guy always walks out of the frame and never returns. Not on foot, a car...nothing. And he never shows enough for facial rec when he is being recorded. Trust me, I tried."

I just bet you did, sweetheart.

"You think the guy who left the notes is the same one who broke into your place?"

"Yes." The answer was resolute. "The measurements I took from one of the recordings match up with the intruder's frame and build."

Damn, she was good. "Why now?" Parker thought to ask. "If Justin went to prison six years ago, why wait until now? And if you've been using an alias, how did he find you?"

"Those are the million-dollar questions." She shrugged. "And I don't have the answer to either one other than he's scheduled to be released in six months. Maybe he thought he'd play with me a bit before making his final move once he's freed."

He refused to think about what the man's end game might be.

"You said you work freelance tech support, right? Is there any way you could've been tracked through that somehow?"

"I don't see how," she answered honestly. "The freelance work I do is all under my alias, and it's remote. I work out of my townhome, running security checks and tech support for several companies around the city."

"Impressive."

"Says the billionaire." One corner of her kissable lips lifted. "I really am sorry I hit you, by the way. I don't know what came over me. I swear, I've never hit anyone before."

"Guess that makes me special." He smiled.

Quinn didn't. Instead, she stared back at him as if he were a puzzle she was desperately trying to solve. "Why did you really come here?"

"What do you mean?"

"I mean, you're...*you*. You're literally one of the richest people in the world, so I'm guessing this sort of thing isn't common practice."

Parker scooted himself to the edge of the cushioned leather, resting his elbows on his knees. With his hands linked loosely together, he turned his expression serious. "This is a first for me, I'll admit. But my money doesn't define who I am, Quinn. You asked why I'm here, and there's only one answer. You."

"But why?" She dropped her legs over the couch's edge and sat up straight. "You don't know me, Parker. Hell, you learned my name all of two minutes ago."

"You're wrong. I *do* know you. Quinn...Jinx...the name doesn't matter. You're my friend, and you needed help. It's as simple as that."

"Parker..."

"I lied about what I did for a living, because I knew it would only be a matter of time before you put it all together, and I didn't want—"

"What?" Quinn frowned. "You didn't want what?"

"I didn't want to ruin what we had." He swallowed again, his eyes searching hers for any signs that he was scaring her off. When he saw none, Parker continued, "It may sound hard to believe, but the highlights of my weeks this past year were the nights I got to talk to you. Online, over the phone... it didn't matter. Those were the few moments when I could be myself. The *real* me, not the one you've seen in the press. So yeah." He sat back. "I didn't want to fuck that up, so I lied."

"I can understand that." She nodded sincerely. "Really, I can. It's why I was so quick to agree to no real names when we first partnered up on the game. I mean, I just admitted to using an alias, for crying out loud. But I never lied to you, Parker. I may not have told you my name, and I may have been vague with some of the things I shared, but *everything* I told you was true. And after Justin and...well, pretty much everyone else in my life before him...I just find it really hard to trust people. So I think that's why I reacted so poorly yesterday. Not that it's an excuse."

"No, I get it." Parker nodded. "I also know it didn't make a whole lot of sense for me to insist on anonymity online and then try to talk you into meeting me in person. But the lie was already out there, and the more time I spent talking to you, the more I wanted to know about you. So I figured it was worth the risk to meet face-to-face."

"And now we have."

"Now we have." He nodded. "And I hope, when you look into my eyes, you can see I'm telling the truth. The stuff with my job was the only thing I ever lied about. Everything else —the way my parents cared more about their image and their two-faced friends than me, not getting my first girlfriend until I was eighteen because I was a total nerd all through high school...it was all the God's honest truth."

Another tense silence filled the air around them. It went on so long, Parker was sure his explanation had fallen on deaf ears. But...

"I know I'm probably not what you expected." Quinn shook her head with a sad huff of a breath. "Someone like you... Between my not-so-savory background and the way I treated you yesterday, it would be completely understandable if you wanted to walk out that door and never look back."

Not a chance in hell.

There was something she needed to know. Something Parker needed to make very, very clear.

With his eyes lasered on hers, he stared at the most intriguing woman he'd ever known and said, "Sweetheart, the only way I'm walking out that door is if you're with me."

7

QUINN STOOD ON THE OBSCENELY LARGE DECK OVERLOOKING the Atlantic. With the warm sea air blowing past, she wondered how in the world she'd gotten here.

Not to Parker's mansion on the beach. She very distinctly remembered the flight here.

She could still hear his cocky little quip when they'd arrived at the small airstrip not far from the apartment where they'd stayed the night before. A large, private jet had come into view through Quinn's window. Confused as to why they were there, she'd looked to Parker with an unspoken question, to which he'd replied...

Oh, yeah. There's one other thing I forgot to tell you. I didn't drive two hours to find you. I flew.

That last bit had been preceded by a flash of a smile that had made her heart race and her belly tingle. And that jet...

Quinn had never flown anywhere before, so she wasn't

quite sure what to expect. But a top-of-the-line luxury jet with room for up to nineteen passengers, a full galley kitchen capable of preparing just about any meal imaginable, two bathrooms, multiple flat-screen TV's, and an electric fireplace was definitely *not* it.

After less than two hours in the air, they landed at another small airstrip near Chesapeake Beach. From there, she was driven in the fanciest car she'd ever seen to where she was now.

I can't believe I'm standing on the deck of a mansion beach house owned by the world-famous Parker Collins.

Once again, the question of how she got here rang loudly through her mind.

Private security teams. Fancy jets and ridiculously fast sports cars. Mansions on the beach.... These things didn't exist in her world.

"Thought I'd find you out here."

Quinn turned to see Parker walking through the opened, folding glass doors behind her. The same intense, butterfly-inducing attraction she felt every time she looked at him filled her tingling belly.

Dressed in a cream-colored sweater, faded-in-all-the-right-spots jeans, and the same weathered boots he'd had on before, the man was positively breathtaking.

"The view is incredible." She finally found her voice.

You talking about the ocean behind you, or the man standing in front of you?

Before she could fully mull over the internal question, Parker crossed the distance between them, stopping inches from where she stood. His short, blond-brown hair was still damp from a recent shower, and a subtle breeze carried with it an arousing scent of fresh soap and something she could only describe as earthy and masculine.

"It's my favorite spot in the whole house." His captivating voice resonated within her as he handed her one of the two bottles of beer she'd only just noticed. "This is where I come when I need to think."

"I can see why." Quinn took the offered beverage and forced herself to look back out at the ocean. "I could stay here forever."

Realizing the inadvertent implication of her statement, she swung her gaze back to his. "I mean, if I were you. Not that I expected to stay here forever. That wasn't—"

"I know what you meant, Quinn." Amusement penetrated his hypnotic stare. "And yeah." He took a healthy swig from his chilled bottle and swallowed. "I'd stay out here forever, too, if I could."

God, I love the way he says my name.

"Why don't you?" The question was meant to be flippant. "I mean, I'm pretty sure you could retire today and not have to give up a single bit of this." She looked around.

"I've considered it, believe it or not."

"Really?" Her eyes flew back up to his. "I was just kidding."

"I'm not." Parker walked over to one of several wooden-slatted lounge chairs. Sitting down, he spun his body around and stretched his long, toned legs out before him.

Choosing the one next to his, Quinn mimicked his movements. "You'd really give up the gaming business?"

His serious gaze followed her. "I'd give it all up, if it was for the right reasons."

"Those would have to be some damn good reasons." She took a small sip. "Of course, that's coming from someone who's never had money."

"Tell me more."

"What?" Quinn frowned, not quite understanding what he meant by that.

"I want to know more about you. Where you grew up, what your childhood was like...who your parents are..." Parker's throat worked with another swallow. "I want to know who you are, Quinn. The *real* you."

"Uh...no. You really don't." She took a long pull from her bottle to buy herself some time.

"I really do."

May as well get this part out of the way. Let him see it all now, so he knows exactly the kind of person he was associating himself with.

"Okay, fine." She sat up, swinging her legs back around and planting her canvas shoes on the deck's smooth surface. "But just remember...I warned you."

"Duly noted."

Quinn almost felt sorry for the guy. Here he was, using his wealth and connections to help a friend in need...and he had no idea what kind of person that friend truly was.

"I grew up in Chicago's south side." She looked away, unable to look him in the eyes as she shared a past she'd tried so hard to escape. "My so-called parents were both worthless human beings who cared more about quick-buck schemes and finding their next fix than making sure their only child had clean clothes and a full belly." Resentment churned inside her gut, but she pushed it aside. "The only time I saw a view like this was on T.V., and *that* was only if my parents managed to actually pay the bill."

"That must've been rough."

Though she didn't want to—she really, *really* didn't—Quinn braced herself for the pity she knew was coming and made eye-contact with the sexy man again. Only...

It's not there.

Sympathy. Anger. A sadness she didn't understand.

Those were the emotions reflected back at her from Parker's fixed expression. But not even a sliver of the pity she'd been sure she'd find. Still, her usual defense of sarcasm fell from her lips before she could stop it.

"It wasn't so bad," she lied. "I mean, who wouldn't love growing up in a run-down row house with a leaky ceiling, bars on the windows, and crack pipes and burned spoons as centerpieces?"

An awkward silence swirled around them with the blowing breeze, his knowing stare almost too much for her to handle. But Quinn kept on, knowing if he didn't hear it from her, he'd probably just look it all up anyway.

"By the time I was a senior in high school, my dad was in prison, and my mom had split." She shrugged as if those major life events hadn't been devastating to a teenage girl. "I crashed on friends' couches until I graduated. After that, I worked three part-time jobs just so I could afford an apartment that was even shittier than the crack house."

Smooth, Quinn. You're a real class act.

Tucking some wayward strands behind one ear, Quinn looked away with another swig, suddenly wishing she could be more refined like the women he usually associated himself with.

A leopard can't change its spots, Quinnie. You'll never be anything more than this. May as well accept that now.

Hearing her mother's demeaning voice, she pushed herself to her feet and walked over to the deck's glass wall. With her forearms resting on the smooth railing, she looked out over the water wishing like hell she'd been born someone else.

Someone worthy of the life she'd always dreamed of. Worthy of a man like the one currently sitting behind her.

Not that she should be worried about that right now.

There were so many other, bigger things she should be focused on. The least of which being whether a man like Parker Collins could ever be interested in someone like her.

Never going to happen. No sense pretending otherwise.

"Anyway, I saved up enough money and finally bought my first computer. That's when I really discovered my fascination with technology...and hacking." The bittersweet memory felt like a lifetime ago. "Three years later, I met Justin."

Parker finally spoke up from his seat behind her, an unmistakable anger tightening his deep voice. "I bet the charming asshole said and did all the right things, too."

"Oh, yeah." Quinn nodded. "And like an idiot, I fell for it hook, line, and sinker." Pinpricks of tears burned at the corners of her eyes, but she blinked them back and focused on the slow, tranquil roll of the waves. "My mom always used to say the women in our family were jinxed when it came to men. That we weren't worthy of the kind of life others had. That we weren't worthy of true love." A humorless laugh had her shoulders shaking. "Turns out she was right." *About everything.*

"The fuck she was."

The growled declaration had her spinning back around, nearly dropping her half-drank bottle of beer in the process. She'd been so lost in her own pity-party, she hadn't realized he'd gotten up from his chair.

But there he was, standing less than a foot in front of her. And the look in his eyes...

"Your mother was a miserable bitch," Parker announced bluntly. "I may not have known her personally, but I've known plenty like her. Sad, pathetic human beings who'd rather spend their lives wasted and sponging off others, rather than doing the work to get clean and make something of themselves. And God forbid anyone close to them find even the slightest modicum of happiness or success."

Quinn blinked, the man's unapologetic assessment of her mother impressively accurate. "She couldn't stand it when something good happened to me." A fact that still stung more than it should. "If I'd get an A on a test, she'd tell me school was a waste of time. If a boy asked me out, she'd hand me a condom and tell me to stop and get the morning-after pill at the twenty-four-hour drugstore down the block."

"Like I said." A muscle in his strong jaw twitched. "Your mother was a bitch."

Parker's image blurred behind a well of tears, but she willed them not to fall as she whispered, "Why are you being so nice to me?"

A corner of his tempting lips curved. "Using a derogatory term to describe one's parent typically isn't considered to be an act of kindness."

"Yes, well. I think it's safe to say, I'm not your typical kind of girl." Quinn chuckled, loving how, even now, the man could still make her smile.

"No." Parker stepped closer. So close, the toes of his boots nearly touching hers. "You're most definitely not."

The nervous smile faded with the sudden racing of her pounding heart. Palms sweaty, Quinn's mouth became impossibly dry as she stood there, staring up into a set of eyes she wanted to lose herself in.

She parted her lips—to say what, she wasn't sure—but for the life of her, she couldn't seem to formulate a verbal response.

"You were right about something else," Parker broke through the tense silence.

"I-I was?" Quinn stammered back, hating how uncontrollable her reaction to this man was.

He nodded, his eyes never leaving hers as one of his strong hands rose slowly toward her. With an electric touch searing into her temple, he gently tucked some blowing strands behind her ear.

"You said you probably weren't what I expected, and you were right." His palm rested against the side of her neck, his thumb caressing the curve of her jaw. "You're so much more."

Oh, my.

"Parker..." His whispered name became lost in the blowing breeze. She started to say something more. To ask what he was doing. But her next words never made it past her lips.

Because his mouth was already there.

Parker pressed his lips to hers in a soft, gentle kiss. It was tentative, almost chaste in nature, and yet it was deepest, most incredible physical connection she'd ever experienced.

And it scared the ever-loving crap out of her.

Quinn sucked in a breath as she took a step back, the sudden, swift motion cutting the moment short.

Taken aback by her unexpected reaction, Parker's brows shot up even as he uttered a mumbled curse beneath his breath. "I'm sorry."

She shook her head, refusing to let him take the blame for something she'd been fully invested in, herself. "It's my fault. I never should have—"

"Stop." Parker lowered his hand with a terse shake of his head. "I get that your used to shouldering everyone else's blame, but this is on me. I kissed you, sweetheart. Not the other way around."

"But I kissed you back." And damn if part of her—a gigantic, aching part of her—didn't want to do it again.

"I brought you here to protect you. Not take advantage of you."

"You didn't—"

"I did, but I promise; I won't touch you like that again." Heat darkened his eyes as he added a low, "Not unless you ask me to."

Quinn's breath was momentarily lost as she thought about what he'd just said...and what it meant.

He made the first move. Next one's on you.

"Parker, I—"

His phone rang, interrupting what she'd been about to say.

"Sorry. I need to check that." He pulled his phone from his pocket and looked at the screen. "It's my friend, Asher Cross," he shared unnecessarily. "He's part of Charlie Team, which is another branch of the same RISC security firm Delta works for. Only Charlie Team's in Richmond, instead of Chicago."

The man's rambling made her smile, which in turn eased some of the awkward tension between them. "You should probably answer it then, right?"

"What?" Parker looked at the still-ringing phone in his hand. "Oh. Right." With a swipe of his thumb, he put the device to his ear. "Hey, Ash. Give me just a second." Covering the speaker with his hand, he told her, "Make yourself at home. I won't be long."

Quinn watched as he turned and walked away. His steps were purposeful as he crossed the deck before disappearing through the enormous, folding glass doors.

It wasn't until he was out of eyesight that she felt like she could finally, truly breathe.

Spinning back around, she kept her face toward the ocean, just in case he was still watching her from somewhere inside. Expelling a forceful rush of air, her mind worked to make sense of what had just happened.

Parker Collins just kissed you. That's what happened!

Not only that, he'd actually seemed to *enjoy* it. And what he'd said after…

Not unless you ask me to.

They were the sexiest, most arousing words a man had ever spoken to her.

Quinn lifted a hand to her mouth, her fingertips lingering where his lips had just been. God, she was tempted. And it would be so easy.

The lust she'd seen reflected in his eyes those last seconds before his mouth had touched hers were a dead giveaway. He was physically attracted to her, that much was obvious. And she would have to be blind not to feel the same about him.

But good sex didn't equal love. In fact, in her experience, it often messed everything up.

So no, she couldn't—*wouldn't*—allow herself to fall into that same trap again. Handsome, smooth-talking men were trouble. At least in her world, they were.

You're not in your world anymore. You're in his.

The amazing view and luxurious, multi-million-dollar mansion both stark reminders of that very point. This *was* Parker's world, and she had no place in it.

Something she'd do well to remember.

8

"HEY, ASH." Parker made his way past his living room and into his private office down the hall. "What's up?"

"You tell me," Asher Cross, Sydnee's fiancé and Charlie Team's sniper challenged.

Glancing out his window at the enigma that was Quinn Wilder, he tried like hell to remember a time when a simple kiss had knocked him on his ass like the one they'd just shared. But he couldn't because it had never happened.

Not until now. Not until her.

"Dude, you still there?"

Though it pained him to do it, Parker tore his focus from Quinn and went to his desk. "Yeah. Sorry. Things are a little...crazy here, right now."

"So I've heard."

"Wait." He pulled out his rolling chair and sat down. "You're calling, so does that mean you guys are already back home?"

"Landed in Richmond about an hour ago."

"Damn. Guess that was a quick in-and-out job."

"Literally." The other man snorted. "Caught the dumbass with his pants down."

"Bet that made for an awkward takedown."

"Syd's washing my field clothes on the sanitize cycle as we speak."

Parker laughed. "Bet she got a kick out of that story."

"Never gonna live it down, that's for sure." Ash sighed. "Okay, man. I've let you stall long enough. What's going on with your girl?"

"She's not my girl." *But damn, I sure wish she was.* "But she's definitely in trouble."

"You got a target yet?"

"Not a solid one, no."

"So what do you know?"

Over the next few minutes, Parker filled his friend in on everything he knew up to this point. Quinn's real name, her account of the attack in her home last night, the video surveillance she'd accessed with her impressive hacking skills—videos he'd watched multiple times during their short flight back from Chicago.

The rage he'd felt toward the faceless bastard who'd been terrorizing her was still there, simmering just below the surface.

"What about Hunt and his guys? They find anything useful when they went to her house?"

"Just evidence backing up her story about the intruder. Hunt sent me pics of the scene, but it wasn't much to go on.

The images flipped through his mind like the small, vintage viewfinder toy he'd had as a kid.

An overturned bar stool in the kitchen. *Click.* A forgotten bottle lying on the floor next to a puddle of spilled wine. *Click.* Shards of shattered crystal. *Click.* An opened man door leading out to her garage. *Click.*

But it was the mangled garage door he couldn't seem to get out of his head.

When he imagined Quinn literally running for her life... so fucking terrified she'd smashed her car into the garage door in her efforts to get away...

Parker realized for the first time what it felt like to want to kill.

No, that wasn't true. When Sydnee had been taken, he'd been more than ready to take out the bastard responsible. And he would have, too, if Asher hadn't beat him to it. But this felt different.

It *was* different.

Because this wasn't about a woman who was like his sister. This was about Quinn.

A woman he barely knew, yet was so innately connected to, he could barely think straight when she was around. Someone who, twenty-four-hours ago, was a faceless voice on the other end of the phone.

And yet, as inexplicable as it was—as deranged it might make him seem—Quinn Wilder had somehow become his priority.

Identifying and stopping the person who'd targeted her was his number one goal. Aside from that, nothing else mattered.

Not his gaming company. Not Homeland or the CIA. Only that.

Only her.

Speaking of Homeland...

"I put a call into Ryker earlier. He's pulling everything he can find on Quinn's ex and anyone he might be associated with that could possibly be involved."

Jason Ryker was an agent with the powerful government agency. Not only was the well-connected man in charge of a covert team of specialists, but he was also the official senior government handler for the entire RISC organization.

Alpha, Bravo, Charlie, and now Delta... Ryker had called upon their services in the name of Uncle Sam on multiple occasions.

For Parker, it was his behind-the-scenes and highly classified work he sometimes did for Homeland—and the CIA —that had brought him into Ryker's circle. And the man owed him.

"Tell me you didn't make that call in front of the woman."

"The woman has a name," Parker bit back. "And give me a little credit, would you? I waited until Quinn excused herself to the jet's bathroom so she wouldn't over hear."

"Sorry." Asher sounded as if he really was. "Guess Sydnee's overprotective nature when it comes to you is rubbing off on me."

"Aww..." He crooned. "I love you, too, Ash."

"Don't push it, asshole. But seriously, why didn't you just look that shit up yourself? It's not like you don't have the skills."

Oh, he had them, all right.

"I was with Quinn, remember? She only went to the bathroom once, and she was in there less than two minutes."

"Dude. I've been on your jet before, remember? It's a freakin' Linear 100E. Pretty sure you could've found some privacy if you'd really wanted it."

His jet *was* extremely spacious. And yeah, there was a private bedroom and private restroom at the back—two-person shower, included. But...

"It was Quinn's first time flying," Parker explained. "She

was understandably nervous, and I didn't want to leave her alone so I could sneak off to dig up shit on her ex."

That's not the only reason you refused to leave her side the entire flight.

There was a slight pause before Asher said, "All right. As long as you're good, I guess I'll get off of here and let Syd know all is well in the world of Parker Collins."

Parker huffed out a breathy chuckle. "Whatever. I know you called because you love me. Not that I blame you. I mean, I'm smart, rich, fit, and good-looking as fuck. What's not to love?"

A low curse and then, "I'm hanging up now."

He laughed even harder. "Hey, but seriously, man. If you could let Syd know you actually spoke to me yourself, that would be great."

"Uh...okaaay..."

"That way she'll know for sure I'm not chained up somewhere and being held captive by some crazed woman who plans to chop me up into little pieces and eat me with a side of fava beans and a nice Chianti."

When he made an exaggerated sipping sound, Asher groaned.

"You really are like a twelve-year-old, you know that?"

"Hey. Your fiancée still loves me."

"Yeah, yeah. As long as you remember she's *mine*."

Though there was no real need, Parker quickly reassured the other man. "No worries there, brother. The love I have for Syd is purely familial. Trust me."

"Oh, I do trust you. If I didn't, you'd already be dead."

Parker laughed again, knowing the former Special Ops sniper meant every word. Another quick glance out the window revealed an empty space where Quinn had been standing before.

"I need to go. Give Syd a big hug from me. I'll let you know what I hear back from Ryker."

"Sounds good. And, not to sound like my gorgeous fiancée, but...be careful. Until you know more about this wom...er...*Quinn*, you need to watch your back."

The man's sincere words tugged at Parker's heart. "Don't worry, brother. I've got this."

"I'm sure you do."

Ending the call, Parker sat back in his chair and grinned. A year ago, Asher wouldn't have pissed on him if he were on fire. Now the man was about to be the closest thing to a brother-in-law he'd ever have.

And though he wasn't quite ready to admit that to Ash, there wasn't another man out there Parker would rather see Syd settle down with.

A low dinging sound came from the closed laptop in front of him. Reaching out, Parker opened it as he rolled himself closer. The screen lit up, and in the center was a notification for a new email.

Clicking the small rectangle, the image morphed and grew into an encrypted email requiring a special password. One assigned to Parker when he'd first been approached about a classified collaboration with Homeland.

His pulse spiked with hope that it was what he'd been waiting for.

He typed in the code he'd memorized long ago and hit enter. Immediately, the image changed, and multiple windows opened at once. With a quick scan, he confirmed they were the files he'd requested from Ryker.

Parker enlarged the first one and began reading it over.

Everything the government could find on Justin Reynolds was there. His birth certificate, kindergarten graduation certificate, the name of the shrink his parents took him to when he was twelve, the notes from the few visits he attended—Parker wasn't even going to ask how Ryker managed to get that—and more.

But the most interesting intel he came across were a few layers down...

Here we go.

One click of a finger, and he had access to every statement Justin had made to the authorities, both written and recorded.

After a quick speed-reading session, he learned that the man who'd portrayed himself off as a bleeding heart Casanova was nothing more than a selfish, narcissistic asshole who didn't give two shits about Quinn.

He never had.

In Reynolds' own words, the dickhead had been introduced to her through a mutual hacking friend at a party they'd both attended. He'd seen her around, knew about her tech talent...so when another guy at the party got a little too handsy, Reynolds was more than happy to jump in and save the day.

The smooth-talking dick played to her insecurities, and little-by-little, he began grooming her for his end game...the credit card hack.

Parker pulled his Bluetooth earpieces from his other pocket. Securing one in place, he made sure it was connected to his laptop before clicking open the first interrogation video.

He pushed play.

During his initial interview, a very angry, very panicked Reynolds blamed the whole thing on Quinn. Said she came to *him* with the idea. That *she* was the one who'd done everything to put the plan into motion.

She wrote the code. She got the equipment from "some guy named Monty"...all of it.

The more Parker watched, the angrier he got. At one point, he was ready to jump through the screen and choke the lying bastard out. But then he watched the next video... and found himself smiling.

Because in *that* one, the attractive agent in charge shut the lies down quickly. Within the first two minutes, she'd provided irrefutable proof that *Justin* was the man with the plan.

A voice recording—courtesy of a protected federal source—had Reynolds on tape, running his mouth about this brilliant idea of his, and how he'd conned a "clueless bitch with badass skills" into doing the heavy lifting.

Pictures showed Reynolds meeting with Monty Dunne, AKA "some Monty guy". In others, he could be seen checking out the same equipment that had been seized the night of his arrest. And there were more...

Him shaking hands with Monty. Loading the equipment into his piece of shit car. Hauling it into the abandoned business where he was ultimately arrested.

It was at that point in the video when Reynolds read over and signed the agreement stating he would testify against Dunne in exchange for a two-year sentence in a minimum security prison for possession of stolen property —the idiot either didn't realize or didn't care that the computer equipment he'd gotten from Dunne was hot—as well as his part in the credit card hack.

After the Fed left the room and it was just Reynolds and his lawyer in the room.

"I know that bitch made a deal with them," he seethed.

His middle-aged, balding lawyer stood and clasped his

briefcase closed. "I can't speak about any deal Miss Wilder may or may not have made with the FBI, Justin."

"Doesn't matter, anyway. I knew it was Quinn before they ever showed me the recording she made that night. You wanna know *how* I know it was her?"

"Justin—"

"She wasn't surprised!" He raised his voice. "I saw it in her eyes when those assholes busted into the place. Quinn was scared...but she wasn't surprised. She *knew* they were coming, which is probably why she tried to talk me out of it right at the end."

"Again. I have no knowledge of anything Miss Wilder—"

"It doesn't fucking matter." Reynolds sat back in the metal folding chair. "I'm going to get out in a couple of years. Less with good behavior. And when I do, I'm going to find her."

"You really shouldn't make threats, Justin," his lawyer warned. "Even in jest. If anyone hears you saying things like that, they'll—"

"What? Send me to prison? I'm already going away, dumbass!"

It was at that point when the lawyer turned and left the room. But that didn't keep Reynolds from running his mouth.

And it was this next part that had the hair on the back of Parker's head standing on end.

With the door closed—and no one else to listen—the entitled prick turned his cold, rage-filled eyes to the surveillance camera mounted in one corner of the room. With a low, controlled voice, he uttered almost word-for-word the same threatening phrases written on the notes Quinn had told him about...

"You're not as smart as you think you are, Quinn. I'm

going to come for you when I get out. And when I find you, you're going to pay for what you did."

I think Justin sent that man to my house tonight.

She was convinced Reynolds was the one behind her attacks, and while the son of a bitch was still locked safely away at the prison in Pekin—a confirmation that had been included on that first page of Ryker's email—Parker had to agree.

After seeing that video, there wasn't a doubt in his mind that Justin Reynolds was involved in this up to his eyeballs.

Now he just had to prove it.

9

THREE DAYS LATER...

QUINN STOOD IN FRONT OF PARKER'S REFRIGERATOR TRYING to decide what she wanted to eat. Normally, she wouldn't be so forward in her endeavors—especially not in a house like this.

But it had been three days, and he'd made it very clear on several occasions that she should make herself at home. And if she was at her home right now, she'd most likely be staring in her refrigerator trying to figure out what to eat.

You're hungry, all right. But it isn't for food.

As it had countless times since the heart-stuttering moment, the memory from their one shared kiss filled her mind's eye. If she closed her eyes, she could almost feel him there.

His lips on her lips. The warmth of his gentle, masculine hand against her cheek. The flames of desire from his heated gaze searing into hers.

But thanks to her deep-seated issues with men, the

unexpected moment hadn't lasted long. But the after-effects...

I can't get it out of my mind.

Even now, her heart thundered with desire and her body ached with a need she didn't want to possess.

Parker, however, apparently hadn't had *any* issues forgetting about the barely-there kiss. In fact, the man had pretty much been avoiding her ever since.

For the past three days, the confusing man had spent most of his time holed up in his office—working with the door shut. On the rare occasions Quinn *had* seen him, he'd been distant. Almost distracted.

When asked if everything was okay, Parker had quickly assured her he was fine. Claimed he was just working hard to find out more about her intruder and Justin's presumed involvement, while also keeping up with his responsibilities with his company.

The explanation sounded more than plausible, especially considering her intruder and Justin were the only reasons she was even here. And yeah, the guy ran a billion-dollar business, which probably took up a big chunk of his days.

But despite those irrefutable facts—and that she wasn't even supposed to care in the first place—Quinn couldn't help but feel as though her rejection of his advances had somehow shifted things between them.

And yet, he'd still made sure she had everything she needed.

That first night, his personal chef had arrived to deliver a variety of pre-cooked meals, all packaged neatly and labeled accordingly. Parker also had a handful of outfits delivered—swimsuit, shoes, and undergarments included—so she didn't have to wear the same jeans and white crewneck during the undetermined duration of her stay.

All fitting her perfectly, of course.

While Parker hid himself away, Quinn spent her days searching for even the tiniest of clues hidden in the footage of the man who'd left her the notes. After hacking into the Pekin prison's system, she accessed the facility's visitation log and inmate phone records.

Starting with this time last year, Quinn went through the visitor's log first, using a meticulous eye as she wrote down the name of anyone who'd gone to see Justin in the last twelve months. When she was done with that, she moved on, jotting down every number listed on Justin's incoming and outgoing calls.

One-by-one, she'd begun going through every name on that list. Every number. Looking for any and every connection that might give her a lead. When one didn't pan out, she'd move to the next. And the next.

And the next.

Every straw she could grasp, Quinn would hold onto with an unbreakable grip. But with each new reach she'd made, a newer, more devastating dead end had been there to greet her.

Eventually the frustration would become too much, and she'd retire upstairs, to the bedroom Parker had arranged for her to use. One of eight, it was bigger than her own bedroom, living room, and kitchen combined. And it was so perfectly put together it looked like something that belonged in a magazine.

Or a museum.

In a canvas of what she could only describe as modern rustic, the room was a combination of soft, muted colors, sleek lines, and wooden beams. Wall-to-ceiling windows provided a panoramic view of the sand and water below, and there was a beautiful stone fireplace in one corner.

The king-sized bed was centered on the wall to her left, its black metal canopy frame rising high toward the peaked ceiling. The bedding felt like it cost more than her car, and the en-suite bathroom with its built-in vanity and free-standing soaking tub looked as if it were created specifically with a woman in mind.

Even now, three days into her impromptu visit to Casa de Parker, Quinn tried hard not to think of the others who'd been here before her. In fact, for the last three nights, she'd lain in that bed, lost in a sea of silk and the fluffiest of cottons while doing her damnedest to think of anything else.

And then she'd kick herself for letting his sexual past matter in the first place.

It didn't matter. It couldn't.

I won't touch you like that again. Not unless you ask me to.

Quinn shut the refrigerator door much harder than necessary, the glass condiment jars inside rattling noisily together with her efforts to push the unwanted memory away. She needed to forget about eating and figure out who was after her.

The sooner she did that, the faster Parker could fly her back to Chicago in his fancy jet, and she could leave the prince of gaming—and his beach front castle—behind.

Ready to march into the man's office and demand he share what he'd found on Justin so far, she huffed out a breath and spun around.

"What's the matter?" Parker stared down at her. "Don't see anything you want?"

Hand flying to her chest, Quinn's racing heart pounded against her palm as the tiny cry of surprise escaped. Doing her best to ignore his question's double entendre, she willed her pulse to steady and her lungs to slow their movements.

"Damn it, Parker!" she barked. "You scared the crap out of me."

"Sorry."

He didn't look it in the slightest.

In fact, the man seemed to get better looking as the days passed. Aside from the slightly dark circles under his eyes from lack of sleep, his typical attire of a t-shirt and jeans showcased his sculpted chest, toned, sinewy arms, narrow waist, and strong thighs.

Too bad he isn't turning around. You could watch him walk away again, just like every other time he left the room.

"What are you doing here?" Quinn asked a smidge too loudly.

Brows arching, Parker looked both ways before guessing, "I live here?"

With her lungs filling to capacity, Quinn's naturally straight teeth clamped down onto her bottom lip to keep from spewing a nasty retort. It wasn't this man's fault her overactive—and highly neglected—hormones were out of control.

Or is it?

Ignoring the meddling voice in her head, she forced a softer, more cordial expression. "What I meant to say was, why did you sneak up on me like that?"

"I don't sneak, sweetheart." The blues in his eyes smoldered. "I walk, jog...run. I've even been known to stalk across a room on occasion. But nope." He shook his head. "No sneaking."

How? How was it possible for a man to be so astonishingly charming and maddening all at the same damn time?

"I came in here to see if you were hungry."

Sure am, but not for—

"I could eat." She cut her own thoughts off.

"Good."

Something in his eyes changed then. There was a look of mischief there, and suddenly Quinn became very, *very* nervous.

"Why?" She eyed him closely, her eyes narrowing with suspicion. "What are you planning to do?"

"Not me. You."

"Me?" A deep furrow. "What am *I* going to do?"

"You'll see."

It was all he gave before turning around and walking out of the kitchen, heading straight for the home's front entrance. Too busy racing around the end of the large island to catch up to him to notice his perfect ass, Quinn padded barefoot across the tiled floor.

"Parker wait!" The balls of her feet took the brunt of her rushed steps. "You can't just say something like that and leave."

"I'm not leaving."

Uh...it sure *looked* like he was leaving.

He grabbed the knobs on both of his solid wood, double-doors and pulled.

It was still early, which meant the home's wide front steps were shaded. As was the small group of men and women standing on the first few.

"Where would you like us, Mr. Collins?" one of the gentlemen asked.

Parker smiled with a polite, "The Great Room will be fine, Harold."

Still standing a bit too closely, Quinn reminded Parker, "You said I was going to do something?"

He turned that lust-triggering smile her way. "You, sweetheart, are about to have a day you'll never forget."

Quinn opened her mouth to ask what he meant by that, but he was already stepping aside so the trove of people could enter.

The scent of fresh fruit, pastries, and an assortment of hot breakfast items filled her nostrils as they were carried past. A handful of women sped by holding what looked to be some sort of fancy tool cases.

Still unable to comprehend what was happening, Quinn stood wide-eyed as the remaining six—three men, three women—entered Parker's home. Perfectly poised and dressed for success, they rolled a wheeled clothing rack filled to the max with a colorful array of designer garments.

Several shoe boxes were stacked neatly on the racks' flat, carpeted bottom.

"Parker, what is all that stuff for?"

He shut the doors and faced her once more. "You, Quinn." Those eyes locked onto hers like magnets. "It's all for you."

And he wasn't exaggerating.

Almost instantly, she became the subject of focus for every man and woman there—minus Parker. While he once again disappeared behind that office door, she was transported into a world she'd never known.

First, she was whisked away to the kitchen where a custom brunch buffet filled with a selection of sweet and savory goodness awaited. Champagne, included.

Once she finished eating, Quinn was taken to the Great Room, where one corner had been transformed into her personal nail salon. Not one to worry about such things, she tried her best to object, but the ladies weren't having it.

Before she really knew what was happening, Quinn

found herself sitting in a portable mani-pedi chair, her feet promptly submerged in a well of soothing warm water. With one woman at her feet and the other sitting to her right, Quinn spent the next forty-five minutes getting her fingernails professionally trimmed, filed, buffed, and painted.

While her hands were otherwise occupied, she was introduced to her very first pedicure experience. It was relaxing. Moan-inducing, even. And...man oh, man, did it tickle.

Between the sudden bursts of giggles and occasional jerks of her feet, it was a wonder the poor girl taking care of her hadn't given up and walked away. Lucky for Quinn, the other woman had the patience of a saint.

Feeling more relaxed than she could ever remember, she was transferred to the next station. And the next.

Facial treatment, hair, makeup... Quinn was treated with the best by the best. Or at least that's what Jaque—the man who'd washed, trimmed, and styled her hair—had told her.

Everyone was kind, professional, and overly accomodating, and the whole experience was surprisingly enjoyable. But by the time lunch came, everything seemed to change.

Treated to a light meal of gourmet crackers, an assortment of cheeses and grapes, and strawberries as big as her fist, Quinn was halfway through her first bite of strawberry when the first tendrils of doubt began to sink in.

You don't belong here.

The thought struck without warning but was nevertheless true. This was Parker's world. Not hers.

She didn't do spa days or fancy champagne brunches. Quinn never worried about the condition of her cuticles or which shade of red went best with her skin tone. Only that her nails were kept clean and short, so she could easily type.

And there was certainly no entourage of people waiting

on standby to do her makeup and hair. Or a team of fashionistas waiting in the wings to change her entire look.

That's it. Parker knows I don't fit in here, so he designed this entire day to change that. To change me.

But Quinn didn't want to change who she was. Not for Parker. Not for anyone.

I can't do this.

She dropped the half-eaten strawberry onto the square ceramic plate. Square with a sleek, curved design, even *that* was too sophisticated for someone like her.

"I can't do this." She shook her head, uttering the words aloud that time.

"No worries." One of the attentive ladies appeared. "If you're not hungry, we can begin trying on clothes." With a snap of her fingers, the nearest rack was immediately pushed across the room to where they stood.

"No, I meant—"

"Don't worry, Miss Quinn." The other woman cut her off. "All you have to do is try these on and say yay or nay. If you like it, it's yours. If not, we'll return it to the boutique once we leave."

She removed the first garment off the rack. Slipping the gorgeous red pant suit off the hanger, she held it out for her with a smile. "You can just change here. Trust me, it's nothing we haven't seen before." When Quinn's eyes slid to the four men in the room, the other woman added, "Oh, don't worry about them. You're not exactly their type."

Gay. Right. Got it.

"I don't want to try anything on." Her breaths became shallow as full-blown anxiety fought to take over.

"Here." The pushy woman shoved the red garment into Quinn's hands. "I think this will look wonderful on you."

Damn it, she's not listening!

"I just said I don't want to—"

"Trust me. With those eyes and that hair, red is definitely going to be your—"

"Stop!" The entire room stopped and stared as Quinn's shouted voice echoed throughout the open space.

Taking a breath, she did her best to calm her racing heart and ease the discomfort building inside her. When she felt like she could speak without screaming, she tried getting her point across without sounding like a crazed woman.

"Please, just..." She raised her palms in front of her. "Stop."

The woman before her blinked but quickly composed herself and smiled. "If the selection we have here isn't to your liking, we have plenty more where this came from."

"It's not the clothes." Quinn handed the pantsuit back to the confused woman. "I mean, it is, but that's not the only—"

"Is there a problem?"

The deep, interrupting voice had all eyes turning to her right. Face twisted with concern, Parker assessed the room as he came to a stop beside her.

"Yes." Quinn met his gaze. "This. This is the problem."

The skin between his brows bunched together with a quick glance around. "Which part?"

"All of it!" Her arms flew out to her sides, hands slapping loudly against her leggings-covered thighs as they fell.

Expression fixed, the man in charge kept his eyes on hers as he told the others, "Give us the room." When the others began hastily packing up their things, he added a steely, "Leave it. I'll arrange for it all to be delivered to you later today." Parker looked away, but only long enough to offer the others a parting, "Thank you."

Those intense eyes slid right back to hers.

Without another word, the small group vanished as quickly as they'd appeared. And suddenly, Quinn was very, *very* aware that she and Parker were alone.

"What's wrong, Quinn?" His gaze searched hers for an answer. "Did something happen?" The lines on his forehead vanished. "Was someone inappropriate with you? If that's it, tell me who, and I'll handle it."

The way he'd said that last part, it almost sounded...

Protective.

It also made her think he wasn't talking about simply letting someone go. Something that—right or wrong— made her inner girly girl smile.

But on the outside, Quinn was already shaking her head. "No." She rushed to assure him. "Of course not. Everyone was really nice and very professional."

Because he pays them to be.

"Okay. Well, if the staff isn't the issue, then wha—"

"It's me." She stared up at him. "*I'm* the issue here, Parker. Not them."

The frown he still wore appeared to be etched in stone. "I don't understand."

He genuinely doesn't get it.

No, he didn't. So Quinn tried to explain. "Personal chefs, mani-pedi spa days, designer clothes... That's you, Parker. But this isn't me."

"That's okay."

"No." She smiled sadly. "It's not."

Needing space to breathe, she stepped around him and walked to the center of the impressive entryway. Following her with only his eyes, Parker shoved his hands into his jeans and remained where he stood.

"Talk to me, Quinn. What's really going on here?"

She turned and faced him once more. With her arms hugging her center, Quinn did her best to make him understand.

"Look, I get that, for you, this is all completely normal. But for someone like me..." She sighed. "It doesn't matter how much makeup I wear or what the label on my clothes reads, I'm always going to be this, Parker." A truth that left her gut tightening and her heart heavy. "I'll always be the girl who grew up in run-down row house in the south side with parents who worried more about getting high than they did their own kid. You can't change that. You can't change *me*." She swallowed. "No matter how much you might want to."

"Change you?" A flash of anger crossed over his handsome face as he yanked his hands free and marched toward her. "Is that what you think? That this was my attempt to somehow make you into something you're not?"

"Wasn't it?"

"No." A muscle at the side of his jaw bulged; his wounded eyes remaining laser focused on her. "It wasn't."

Quinn blinked. "If that's true, why bring in the hair patrol and the fashion police? I mean, I liked *Pretty Woman* as much as the next girl, but this isn't Rodeo Drive, and clearly I'm no Julia Roberts."

Parker's lips twitched, his footsteps faltering half a beat as he stalked toward her. When he stopped inches in front of where she stood, he explained.

"This wasn't about me trying to change you, Quinn. In fact..." Heat filled his stare as he blatantly let it fall the length of her body. "There isn't a single fucking thing I'd change about you."

Quinn's lower belly tingled, her core aching with a

sudden rush of arousal. But she did her best to ignore it because she still had to know, "Then what was all of that?"

"*That*, was my lame attempt at surprising you with what I *thought* would make you happy."

"Why?" It wasn't his job to make her happy.

Fairly certain he'd excel at the job if you'd just let him.

Blocking out the meddlesome thought, she schooled her expression and waited for his response.

"You've been working non-stop these last three days, trying to find a connection between Justin and the man who came after you."

"So have you."

"Yes, but I've also had other shit that required my attention. All important things, but still. I feel bad about not getting to spend more time with you."

Parker's expression softened as he rested his hands low on his narrow hips, another wave of desire splashing into her without warning.

Damn, there was just something about that manly, alpha stance that sent her pulse racing. Or maybe it was just *this* man.

But what got to Quinn even more was the sincerity in his words. The truth reflected in his eyes. He hadn't been avoiding her intentionally, nor was he upset with her for cutting their one and only kiss short.

He feels guilty about leaving you alone.

"So you arranged for me to have my very own whirlwind day of shopping and overindulgence to make up for it." Her shoulders fell as her own contriteness set in.

"Thought it might be nice for you to get a break from the prison's phone records and visitor logs." He shrugged. "Guess I was wrong."

The confusion and hurt in the man's eyes clawed away at the walls she'd built around her heart.

"It *was* nice, Park." Tears pricked the corners of Quinn's eyes as her arms fell back to her sides. "It was thoughtful and sweet, and... Instead of thanking you, I turned into a royal bitch."

"Don't." Parker's gaze sharpened, his tone becoming deep and unwavering. "Don't call yourself that."

"Why not? It's true. You did this wonderful thing for me, and I..." She swiped a tear away before it could fall. "I ruined it." Just like she ruined everything else that might possibly make her happy.

"You didn't ruin a damn thing, sweetheart. This one's on me. I guess I just thought...I mean, most of the women I know would *kill* for that kind of attention."

"Not to mention the Louis Vuittons."

"Those, too." A soft chuckle had his lips curling into the first real smile she'd seen since her moment of overreaction, but fell with a slight shake of his head. "I should've known better than to think you'd care about designer clothes and champagne brunches."

"Why should you have known that?"

"Because you're nothing like those other women." He lifted his hand as if to reach for her but stopped mid-rise.

He said he wouldn't touch you again, remember? Not unless you ask.

Focusing on his most recent statement, Quinn responded with a jutted, "No. I'm not."

"That's not a bad thing, Quinn." Another twitch of his lips. "Trust me."

"You sure about that?"

Parker nodded. "The women the world sees me with are nothing more than accessories. And before you claw my eyes out"—he raised a defensive hand—"that's all I am to them, too."

"What do you mean?"

"They weren't my girlfriends. Very few made it past the first date. And on the off chance that happened, it never lasted more than a couple months."

"Because you got bored?"

"No, Quinn." His blue stare was uncompromising. "Because *they* did."

Wait. Did he just say...

"The women got bored? Why?" She looked at their current surroundings. "*How?*"

"Because, unlike you, those types of women thrive on attention. They have this voracious need to be seen. To be coveted. And the only way to fulfil that need is to constantly be in the public eye."

"Which happens when you start dating someone rich and famous," Quinn surmised. "But they had that with you, right?"

"Not as much as they thought. And definitely not as much as they wanted." Parker licked his lips. "The thing about me, Quinn, is I'm actually a homebody."

A barked laugh filled the two-story entryway. "I'm sorry." She covered her mouth as a show of remorse. "I thought that was a joke. You know, because there are a lot of pictures of you out on the town with gorgeous women."

"No joke, sweetheart. I go out when my brand requires it, but that's it. Think about it." His entrancing gaze bore into hers, his deep voice soft and without a trace of anger or frustration. "How could I have spent so many nights playing games and talking with you if I was always out at parties, or restaurants, or clubs like those rags claim? How could we have happened if I'd been home with another woman?"

"We've...happened?" Quinn's heart slammed against her ribs.

"You know what I mean." A tiny smirk. "I'm not the man portrayed on the news. Yes, my company is important to me, but it's not everything. And sure, the money comes in handy at times, but it's true what they say."

"Which is?"

Solemn eyes stared back into hers. "It's really fucking lonely at the top."

"I'm sorry." She really was. "I had no idea."

"Most people don't," he scoffed. "Let me put it like this. You've had people judge you for your upbringing, yes? Back in your old hacker days?"

Quinn nodded but remained quiet.

"Well, I've spent my entire life around people who only want to use me for my money and fame. And contrary to what the world thinks, I didn't design that first game in hopes of becoming a billionaire. There wasn't some grand plan designed with private jets and mansions on the beach in mind."

"Yet here you are."

"Yeah, but only by pure dumb luck." Parker chuckled. "I was nineteen and in college. Wasn't into the whole fraternity scene, and I had no interest in joining all the cool clubs they had to offer."

"Let me guess. Because you're a homebody?"

"Now you're getting it." He graced her with another real smile that made her heart skip. "Anyway, at night...while my roommate was chugging from kegs and tossing his cookies... I would sit in our dorm, enjoying the peace and quiet and playing the latest and best video game available. Eventually I got bored with the ones that were on the market, so I started using my nights to research and code." Another shrug. "I took the best parts of all the games out there and combined them to make one totally kickass game. I didn't copy those others, of course. Just used them as inspiration. But I did it for myself, Quinn. Not for this." He motioned around them.

"So how'd *this* happen?

"My roommate's girlfriend broke up with him." When she arched a questioning brow, Parker offered a better, more thorough explanation. "Shawn, my roommate at MIT, had just been dumped and was too depressed to go out. I got sick of him moping around, so I tossed him a controller and told him how to play. Turns out, Shawn's uncle was this bigwig with one of the top gaming producers, and when Shawn told him about my design, his uncle asked to meet with me."

"And the rest is history."

"Pretty much." But his expression turned serious. "I meant what I said, Quinn. I'm no more like the guy you see trending online than you're like the women who use my name to climb the social ladder. I think that's why we clicked so easily with that first conversation." He paused before asking, "Do you remember that very first night you and I played together? I made a questionable kill, and you called me out on it."

"I remember."

"That was the moment I knew."

Another kick of her heart. "Knew what?"

"That you were real." Parker's hot breath feathered against her forehead as he spoke. "I'm so fucking sick of fake smiles and pretend friends. I can't stand being in a room full of elbow-rubbers and parasitic users. And I don't think... No, I *know*." He hesitated, swallowing hard before continuing, "I don't want that to be my life anymore, Quinn."

"So what *do* you want?" Quinn's question was barely a whisper.

She held her breath and waited for Parker's answer.

The breath-stealing man's piercing stare interlocked with hers as he closed the final distance between them. With the tips of his shoes nearly touching her perfectly manicured toes, his next words brought down a giant chunk of her already crumbling walls.

"I want someone who wants me for who I am, not what I have. Someone who cares more about me than my bank account. And I want to find someone who sees me and not a bunch of dollar signs." He brought his hand to her face again, pausing a hair's breadth away from her skin. "I want *real*, Quinn." Parker swallowed. "I want..."

"Me, too." His image blurred behind a wall of unshed tears. "I want that, too." And because he'd put the ball in her court that first day, Quinn wrapped her hand around his thick wrist, and brought his palm the rest of the way. "Touch me, Parker." She rose onto her tiptoes and brushed her lips against his. "I'm asking you to touch me."

And he did.

10

———

PARKER SLAMMED his mouth to Quinn's. He didn't go slow. Didn't take his time testing the waters. He just...took.

Touch me, Parker. I'm asking you to touch me.

For days, he'd been praying to hear those exact words. And at night he'd dreamed she had.

Working nearly around the clock to find something that would lead him to the man who'd broken into Quinn's home had helped. As had the multitude of phone calls, emails, and texts he received on a daily basis pertaining to his company.

I don't want that to be my life anymore.

Parker didn't know what had come over him. He'd been thinking of selling for a while now, but before today, he'd never spoken the declaration out loud. Not to himself or Sydnee.

Only her.

Quinn released a soft, throaty moan as she framed his face with both hands. Following her lead—because she was one hundred percent in charge, whether she knew it or not

—he bent down, pulled her into his arms, and lifted her off her feet.

She gasped, her hands flying reflexively to his shoulders to keep from falling backward as her long, toned legs locking around him with ease.

I'll never let you fall, sweetheart. Fucking. Never.

Deepening the kiss, the strokes of Parker's tongue grew feverish with need. "Bed or couch?" He panted after finally coming up for air.

Because they were damn sure headed to one or the other.

"Bed," Quinn responded without hesitation. "More room to maneuver."

"Always knew you were a smart woman." The low rumble of his laughter was lost in their kiss, his words intermittently broken by the touch of their lips as he began walking them through the foyer and toward the hallway.

If she wanted room to maneuver, his California king would do the trick.

Parker held his precious cargo tight against his body as he moved. Keeping the occasional eye out to avoid running them into a wall—or tripping over one of the three accent tables his interior decorator had insisted "made" the narrow space—his focus was split between keeping Quinn safe and relishing in the feel of her in his arms.

Lips against his. Covered breasts pressing against his chest. And the heat from her core…

It was right there, radiating from behind those thin, tempting-as-hell leggings. Even now, fully clothed, Parker could feel how much she wanted him. And suddenly, he couldn't get to his bedroom fast enough.

Can't. Fucking. Wait!

They reached the end of the hall. With one hand

holding Quinn close and the other cupping the back of her head, he continued to kiss, nibble, and taste as he lifted a foot and pushed open the partially ajar double-door.

Parker stepped into the master suite. Using that same foot to kick the door shut behind him, he made his way across the open space to the awaiting bed centered on the wall to his right.

His footfalls were silenced as the soles of his boots landed on the plush rug beneath the bed. The woman in his arms opened her eyes. He watched and waited, his own insecurities rising to the surface as he prayed history wasn't about to repeat itself.

It won't. She's different than the others, remember?

She was, but even with her held tightly in his arms, Parker couldn't keep those intrusive thoughts from weaving their way in.

The women he'd brought to his home in the past—and he could count on one hand the times that had happened—this was the moment when things would change. And it was always the same.

Things would be going great. They'd heat up and move into the privacy of his bedroom. He'd shut the door and get them here, and then... they'd start to look around.

Like clockwork, they'd grow wide-eyed and slack-jawed, spending the next several minutes going on and on about the windows and view. They'd move on to the expensive light fixture centered above his massive bed...and the corner fireplace.

Even the area rug protecting the tile from the bed's frame interested them more than Parker.

And almost as if he could set his watch to it, they'd always, *always* make a comment about how much it all must've cost.

But Quinn didn't look at any of those things.

Not the sizeable room or wall of floor-to-ceiling windows. She didn't turn toward the impressive fireplace or ridiculously large flat-screen, nor the luxurious chaise with the million-dollar view.

The woman in his arms—the woman in *this* moment—only had eyes for him.

Mystified, Parker whispered, "Where have you been?"

He hadn't meant to say the words aloud, but from the softening in Quinn's eyes, there was no need for regrets.

"I'm here now." A slow rake of her fingertips against his scalp. "So the only real question is what are you going to do about it?"

He wasn't sure who moved first. All Parker knew was one second he was lost in her, and the next they were ripping each other's clothes off.

She pushed and tore at his t-shirt, the two of them working together to pull it up over his head. He tossed it aside, uncaring of where it landed as she brazenly reached for his belt.

Slipping the expensive leather free of its clasp, Parker started for the button on his jeans...but she was already there.

Hands met, and fingers fumbled. She yanked his button free before pulling down the metal zipper. His thumbs dipped between her waistband and skin.

Quinn shoved his jeans down the length of his legs, stopping only long enough for him to toe off his shoes and kick them to the side. Parker slid the stretchy material over her hips and ass, pulling it free from her adorable bare feet, one leg at a time.

Reaching down, he made quick work his jeans, which had been haphazardly abandoned down around his ankles.

With the rough denim gone, the only thing left for him to take off were his dark boot socks.

One flew one direction, the other...who knew?

Parker didn't bother to check because he didn't care. The only thing on his mind was the mouthwatering beauty before him. And she was wearing nothing but a simple, lacy white bra and panty set.

I've died and gone to Heaven.

Making a silent vow to go slower next time, his palms were met with satin and lace when he wrapped his hands around her hips and pulled her body flush with his. A small, throaty gasp escaped her parted lips.

Lips swollen and red from his kisses.

There was probably something he should say. Some grand, romantic soliloquy that a woman like Quinn deserved. But for the life of him, Parker couldn't manage even the simplest of words.

She didn't seem to have that problem.

"What's the matter, stud? Change your mind?"

An arched brow almost hid the uncertainty clouding her unbridled need, the sliver of doubt peeking through tightening his chest. Almost.

Parker shook his head and set the record straight. "I haven't been this sure about anything in a long damn time." Then, because there couldn't be any doubts, he turned the tables and asked, "What about you?" He left one hand in place while running the backs of his knuckles down along her flushed cheek. "You tell me to stop; this ends now."

He held his breath, his expectant stare watching hers with precision. As hard as it would be—and right now, he was hard as a fucking iron pipe—he'd walk away. If he so much as suspected she wasn't one hundred percent in this with him, Parker would drop his hands, put his clothes back on, and leave her be.

Lucky for him, Quinn was all in.

Rather than answer with words, she began a slow, torturous slide of her palms up over the swell of his pecs. Delicate fingertips traced the lines of his collarbones before making a sensual u-turn up the sides of his neck.

A throaty groan broke through the silence, his reaction to the simple touch heightened by his body's unexpected sensitivity. The corners of her lips twitched, the vixen fully aware of the effect she was having.

Paybacks, sweetheart. There will be paybacks.

Parker's pulse grew stronger. His heart beat faster. And the aching pressure in his swollen cock made him want to toss her down onto the bed, spread her legs, and drive himself balls-deep inside her.

She wants to touch you, dickhead. Let. Her. Touch.

Quinn cupped both cheeks, her thumbs caressing the slight stubble there. With a slight rise onto her toes, she feathered her lips across his. "Make love to me, Parker." A breathy plea. "Please."

And that's exactly what he did.

Bringing his hands to her shoulders, the ends of her hair swirled into the air as he spun her around. With her back to his front, Parker took a moment to give silent praise to God for creating such a magnificent creature.

Toned and sculpted muscles kept her spine straight and her shoulders back. Despite her request, he couldn't keep from running a fingertip down the center of her spine. Starting at her bra's back clasp, he traced the dip separating a set of strong, feminine muscles.

Quinn shivered beneath his touch, the movement activating a million tiny little bumps along her otherwise perfect skin. And when Parker reached the delicate lace at the top of her panties, he barely resisted the urge to pull them down.

Instead, he continued on his path, teasing her with the lightest of touches. Following the covered seam of her perfect, heart-shaped ass, he continued lower. Watching her every breath, Parker dipped lower, pausing when his hand met the backs of her upper thighs.

Leaning in, Parker brought his lips to Quinn's ear. "Open for me, sweetheart." A whispered order.

Another shiver rolled through her, but she did as he asked and widened her stance. Smiling, he pulled her delicate lobe between his teeth before dropping a tiny kiss there. "Good girl."

"Parker…" she whispered his name like a prayer.

It was a prayer he was about to answer.

Reaching down between her legs from behind, Parker cupped her sex and groaned. Despite the silky scrap of satin there, Quinn's hot, wet arousal burned against his palm.

Fuuuuck…

A raspy whimper broke the silence, and he knew just how she felt.

Aching. Salacious. Wanton. Parker felt all those things… and more. And he knew there was only one cure.

"I know what you need, baby," he rumbled. "You just have to let me give it to you."

Eyes closed, Quinn let her head fall back onto his shoulder. "I'm yours, Parker." She panted. "Whatever you want… I'm yours."

Desperation met with lust, their combined need overriding everything—including space and time. Just like in that dark Chicago parking lot, nothing else existed. Only them.

Make love to me, Parker. Please.

The replay of the best request he'd ever heard had him pulling back. Removing the hand from between her legs, he reached up for the small metal claps at the center of her back. With a quick motion, Parker freed the two halves before sliding the thin straps from her shoulders.

The delicate garment fell to the floor next to their feet.

He moved closer, that first feeling of skin-on-skin nearly making his eyes roll back into his head. Reaching around, Parker filled his hands with a set of breasts he'd swear were made solely with him in mind, and Quinn's sharp intake of air combined with his primal moan.

"Parker, please..."

"I know, sweetheart." He kneaded the firm, perky globes. "I've got you."

With plans to return to them later, he let his hands fall. A wicked smirk she couldn't see lifted his lips. Placing a palm in the center of her back, he gave a gentle push, guiding her upper body forward.

"Put your hands on the bed."

"Yes, Sir." She flashed a devilish grin of her own from over her shoulder before obeying the low-spoken order.

Good girl.

Parker had never been a big talker in bed. He sure as hell never considered himself a Dom or participated in any sort of BDSM play. But this...

The unexpected dynamic was a huge fucking turn-on. More importantly, Quinn seemed to be enjoying it every bit as much as he was.

Playful teases and light commands. Heated glances and whispered, lascivious promises. A willing, consenting partner who trusted him, despite a past filled with nothing but disappointment from the ones she loved.

Yeah, this—with *this* woman—was definitely something he could get used to.

That's it, sweetheart. Keep trusting me, and I'll show you what real love is supposed to feel like.

Parker removed his hand from her back and straightened his spine. The tips of his fingers disappeared behind the delicate lining of her panties. He paused a fraction of a second...

He slid them down.

Though it was torture, he kept his focus on his current task, carefully lowering the scrap of material all the way to her ankles. One by one, he guided her feet off the floor just enough to remove the panties before dropping them on top of her discarded bra.

Then he began to explore.

Starting with short, soft kisses, Parker left them in slow, even intervals as he moved. Up the length of her calf. Behind her knee. The back of her thigh.

While he was giving such close attention to that leg, he ran a gentle hand up the curves and planes of the other. And when his lips found the bottom swell of her rear, Quinn released a breathy moan that nearly brought him to his knees.

Speaking of knees...

Parker dropped to his, grateful he'd gone with the plush rug, rather than the fancier, more expensive oriental kind his decorator had wanted. From this position, his face was perfectly aligned with the heart of his desire.

Christ Almighty.

Her sweet, musky scent was intoxicating. Parker's weeping cock bobbed, but he pulled upon strength he never knew he possessed and took his time.

Though they'd started out all hot and heavy, her

request for him to make love to her had changed everything. It wasn't lost on him that many people—men and
women, alike—used "making love" interchangeably with
"fucking".

Not Parker. Not with this woman.

He may not know her entire sexual history, but one
thing was clear. Quinn Wilder had never been with a man
who'd treated her the way she deserved or given her the
kind of love she craved.

I crave it, too, Quinn. But only with you.

Ready to give her the pleasure she'd been missing,
Parker lifted a hand to the opened space between her thighs.
Moving it higher, his fingers found her drenched with
arousal. And with a playful nibble to the curve of her cheek,
he slid his middle finger deep into her molten core.

"Ah!" Quinn cried out in pleasure; her inner muscles
tightening voraciously around his thrusting digit.

Holy God.

If she felt this good on his hand, he could only imagine
what it was going to feel like once he finally got himself fully
inside her.

Parker moved his finger in and out slowly. Soft wetness
met muscles of velvet, and when he sensed she needed
more, he added a second finger.

Time seemed endless as he moved in even, unhurried
motions. Push and pull. In and out.

Wanting to keep her guessing, he'd occasionally remove
his fingers completely before running them teasingly along
her wet, swollen slit. Back and forth, he'd alternate from
pleasuring her both inside and out.

Over and over, he became lost, both the act and his position erotic as hell.

Quinn pushed herself against his hand, a low mewling

sound filling the room as she begged, "Please, Parker. I need..."

She didn't finish the thought, but he didn't need her to.

"I've got you, Quinn." His fingers were pistons now, drawing out as much pleasure as he could possibly give as they pushed in and out of her soaked pussy. "Do you trust me?"

He already knew the answer, even if she didn't. Even so, Parker held his breath, hoping like hell he'd hear—

"Yes."

Her answer was low. Breathy. And it was all he needed to know.

Parker removed his fingers in one fluid motion. Quinn gasped, her disappointed gaze finding his from over her shoulder. But before she could, he was on his feet, had her spun around, and was guiding her down onto the center of the mattress.

Standing straight, he didn't even try to look away from the beauty before him. Couldn't even if he wanted to. And he most definitely did *not* want to.

Holy fuck. She's the most beautiful thing I've ever seen.

With her blonde hair splayed out to the sides and those bedroom eyes staring up into his, she was a vision. *His* vision. The one he'd fantasized about more nights than he'd ever admit.

Only reality blew every one of the imaginary images his hungry mind had created.

"You gonna stand there and stare, or are you planning on joining me?" One of her brows arched playfully.

Parker's lips curved into crooked smile as he gave her nude body a blatant once-over. "Just enjoying the view."

"Bet you'd enjoy it a whole lot more if you were down here with me."

The aching in Parker's dick grew painful. He wasn't quite ready to use them, but the need to protect this woman in every way possible had him moving to his nightstand. Pulling the top drawer open, he removed a box of condoms and tossed them onto the bed.

"Brand new, huh?" Quinn noticed the box's unopened flaps.

"Companies send me all kinds of things hoping to sign me as a spokesperson." The mattress dipped below his weight. "I get tested every year per my insurance policy, and my most recent was nearly two months ago. I'm clean, but I still want to protect you."

"I'm clean, too, but that's good to know. And...condom companies?" Her breasts jiggled with a rough, sexy laugh. "Really?"

Wearing nothing but a grin, he knelt between the small gap in her half-opened legs. "Like I said. All kinds of things."

A low swishing sound reached his ears when she shook her head against the plush comforter. "That's crazy."

"Oh, that's nothing. But definitely a story for another day."

"Mmm, yes." Quinn nodded in a moaned agreement. "Definitely."

She moved to give him more space to—as she'd so eloquently put it—maneuver. But he held her legs still.

"I meant what I said earlier, Quinn." He stared down at her, praying she could see the truth in his eyes. "I have a past, sure. We both do. But other than a few photo ops, I haven't been with a woman in nearly a year."

"A *year?*"

He could see the wheels turning. Knew what she was probably thinking. And she'd be right.

"I haven't slept with anyone since you and I started talking," he confessed.

A flash of surprise and confusion crossed over her. "Really? I mean, neither have I, but that's different."

"Why?"

"Uh...because I'm not *you*."

"The women in my past all showed me a lot of what I don't want. But you, Quinn Wilder..." His thumbs caressed her skin as his eyes remained locked with hers. "You were the first one to show me what I *do* want."

"Parker..." Her beautiful eyes softened with emotion.

"We can talk later. Right now, there's something else I want to do."

He gently nudged her legs, his throbbing dick twitching with joy when she voluntarily spread them wide. Leaning down, he inhaled her hypnotizing scent. His mouth watering with anticipation.

"What do you want to do?" Her question came out half-spoken, half-whispered.

Looking up at her from between her splayed thighs, Parker licked his lips and said, "I want to taste you."

11

———

"PARKER!" Quinn cried out as his mouth found her.

Eyes squeezed shut, the back of her head pushed against the mattress as the talented man began feasting on her sex.

Oh. My. God!

She couldn't think. Could barely *breathe* for the overwhelming sensations rolling through her...

Pleasure.

Confusion.

Desire.

Lust.

Quinn felt all those things, plus one particular emotion she refused to acknowledge. Once she did—the minute she so much as *thought* it—it became real. And when that happened...

I get hurt.

But rather than let old ghosts haunt this otherwise perfect moment, she laid back, relaxed her body, and let him have his fill.

"Jesus, Quinn." Parker spoke between licks and nips. "Never tasted...anything...like you."

Her heart flipped, her inner muscles flexing as Parker swiped the tip of his tongue directly over her sensitive entrance. She gasped again, her body much more reactive to this man's touch than anyone else from her past.

Because it's him.

Parker teased her with his tongue slowly, first up one side and down the other. For the next several minutes—Quinn had no idea how much time had passed—he licked and laved and tasted to his heart's content.

And when he was finished with that, he found her clit.

Flicking her swollen nub with the tip of his tongue, she nearly shot right off the mattress. His light caress was teasing in nature, but she was already so primed from his earlier performance, Quinn knew it wouldn't take much to push her off the edge.

And she desperately wanted to fall.

"Please," she begged shamelessly. Again.

If begging is what it takes—

Parker filled her body with a finger. First one, then another. With his lips and tongue still working her clit with perfection, he began moving his hand to a matching rhythm.

"Oh, yeah," Quinn crooned. "God, that feels so good." Had anything ever felt better?

Nope. Not even close.

"You ready to fly, sweetheart?" That rhythm never faltered.

She opened her eyes and looked down. Her insides tightened and another rush of arousal flooded her when she found him staring up at her from between her legs.

His red, swollen lips glistened and his hand continued to move. But the way Parker was looking at her...

He's like a tiger about to pounce.

Quinn nodded her head against the soft blankets. Oh yeah. She was ready.

With a sinful smile curling those same lips, Parker didn't say another word. Instead, he lowered his head, took her in his mouth, and lifted her into Heaven.

"Oh!" she cried out yet again.

She'd never been so vocal in bed before. Of course, she'd never had sex with Parker Collins before, either.

He moved his hand faster. Pushed his fingers in and out with a stronger force. Quinn writhed and panted, her fists still gripping the blankets as if they were her lifeline. But the truth was, it was him. *He* was her lifeline.

And I never want to let go.

Before that thought could fully sink in, the telltale tingling began to spread across her lower back. Her insides quivered and her legs began to shake.

At the same time, Parker began moving his tongue in small, tight circles against her clit. And when he added just the right amount of pressure...

"Parker!" Quinn shouted his name as an explosion of pleasure burst through every cell in her body. Muscles stiff, she arched her back high as a low, keening sound filled her ears.

It took her a minute—or maybe a few more—to realize the sound was coming from her.

"Holy crap." Her body felt like jello as the final remnants of her powerful orgasm began to fade. "That was—"

"Fucking amazing," Parker growled.

The warmth from his sculpted body radiated into her as he crawled his way up over her. Though she was still coming down from the delicious high this man had created, the feel of his long, hard cock pressing against her created shivers of anticipation.

Peeling her heavy-lidded eyes open, she looked up to find his staring back at her.

"God, you're beautiful." He added to his initial thought, his deep timbre sounding almost wistful as he ran the back of his knuckles down along her cheek. "So perfect."

When he looked at her like that, she could almost believe it.

"I'm not perfect." Quinn shook her head. "Far from it."

"All right, then. Perfect for me."

"Parker..."

"I'm not asking for anything here, Quinn. Not yet, anyway." Another sly smirk. "For now, I'm just happy you're here. Wish it had happened under different circumstances, of course, but I—"

She kissed him. Hard and fast. Thoroughly and without restraint. And the entire time her lips were on his, Quinn prayed he could feel the words she couldn't bring herself to say.

Breaking the kiss too soon, Parker ordered a low, "Don't move" before pushing himself up to his knees.

Reaching for the box of condoms, he made quick work of the thin cardboard. Pulling out the strand of foil packets just far enough to rip one free, he shoved the rest back inside and tossed the box aside.

And that entire time, her greedy stare was soaking in the glorious view.

Strong neck and a sculpted chest. Toned, well-defined biceps and sinewy forearms. A sculpted chest and six-pack abs. And then there was his lower half.

Well, hello there!

Long, thick, and impossibly hard, Parker's erection was levels above impressive. Quinn's inner muscles flexed, her fingers twitching with the urge to reach for him. Her mouth watered as she imagined returning the same pleasure for him that he'd just bestowed upon her.

But he'd asked her not to move, and she really, really wanted to feel him inside her. So she stayed still and waited.

Next time, Park. Next time, you're mine.

Using his teeth, he ripped the silver square open. Removing the protective sheath from its packet, Parker set the torn foil with the other items before expertly rolling the thin barrier down over himself.

With a slightly hitched breath, he brought his gaze back to hers and grinned. "Don't think I'm gonna last long this first time."

"That's okay. Just means there will be an encore later, right?"

He lowered himself over her once more, his kiss as thorough as their last. "Sweetheart, you can have as many encores as you want."

Quinn smiled, her hand sliding between their bodies with purpose. Hot and full, Parker hissed in a sharp breath when she wrapped her fingers around him. Wishing there wasn't anything between them but understanding—and appreciating—his desire to protect, she lined his hot tip to her wet entrance.

Parker didn't ask if she was ready because there was no need. She was already lifting her hips toward him, and he was already sliding inside.

Oh, my!

With her earlier climax, Quinn's body only needed a few gentle tries before it became fuller than ever before. They moaned in unison, their primal connection powerful in its fruition.

"Jesus, Quinn." Parker stared down at her in awe, his voice rough with sex. "Holy hell, you feel—"

"—so good," she finished for him.

He started to move.

Rolling his hips back, he nearly severed their connection completely before rocking forward again. Every time he repeated the delectable motion, Quinn felt another piece of her wall start to fall.

Not because Parker was good in bed, which he was. Not because he'd flown to her rescue, which he had. And it wasn't because he'd surprised her with a fancy-schmansy in-home day of pampering and designer clothes.

No, those carefully built walls of hers were being chipped away by the man's protective nature, generous heart, and sweet words. All traits she'd known he possessed before she ever saw his face or felt his touch.

Speaking of touch...

Quinn reached down, filling her hands with his firm ass. Flexing beneath her palms, she held on tight as their bodies rocked together at a pace designed especially for this moment.

Each stroke filled her to the brim as Parker ground his hips against hers. Beneath him, Quinn met him thrust for glorious thrust, and soon the room became filled with the symphony of their lovemaking.

And that's exactly what it was.

This wasn't just sex for sex's sake. The man moving inside her wasn't simply fucking her because he could. No, this was more than that.

So much more.

Minutes passed unnoticed as they learned and explored with reckless abandon. Blankets and sheets were twisted and pulled, their naked forms becoming a tangled web of limbs as their movements hastened.

Quinn wasn't sure of the exact moment it happened, but

somehow, she found herself on top with Parker smiling up at her from the mattress below. She moved her hips forward, her eyes never leaving his as she began the best ride of her life.

"Oh, yeah." Parker's fingers dug into the skin at her hips, his firm grip helping anchor her body to his. "Ah, fuck, Quinn."

God, she loved hearing him say her name. Her *real* name. And the way he was saying it now...

He's close.

Rotating her hips just slightly, she moved forward and back. Up and down.

Such a perfect match, she couldn't help but feel as if they'd been made for each other. As if their entire lives had been designed for this exact moment. A quest for the ultimate pleasure.

And for the second time today, that same, exquisite pleasure was beginning to build again.

Well, this is new.

Quinn had read about women having multiple orgasms but had never personally experienced them. Of course, this man was unlike any she'd ever known, so...

She closed her eyes, let her head fall back, and gave herself over to him.

Panting hard with his efforts, Parker reached up and found her clit. "So close." He began rubbing the swollen bud with the pads of his fingers. "Want you there...first."

"Ah!" Her entire body jolted, her inner muscles squeezing around him.

If asked two minutes prior, she would have said another climax so soon after her first was out of the question. But this man continued to surprise her in every other way, why should sex be any different?

Those fingers moved in fast, tight circles now, her body sliding up and down his throbbing shaft. And before long, her entire lower half trembled and quaked.

"There you go." His encouraging words were breathless. "That's it, sweetheart. Let it all go, baby. Just...let...it...*go!*"

Soft cries of pleasure mixed with deep grunts and guttural moans. Parker's movements became jerky and uneven as he found his own release in the midst of her own.

Quinn continued sliding herself up and down his spent length, her body a piston as she drew out every molecule of pleasure for the man who'd given her the same. By the time their movements slowed and their breaths calmed, Parker's gorgeous, sculpted face was the epitome of primal male satisfaction.

Her entire upper body fell against his. Hot and sweaty, their heaving breaths moved in tandem as they took a moment to get their bearings.

Cheek resting against his chiseled pecs, her whispered confession brought the comfortable silence to an end. "I never knew it could be like that."

"Neither did I." He leaned up, his lips pressing against the top of her head in a sweet, lingering kiss.

Parker's voice was deep and rough. Satisfied.

I did that.

A lazy, slightly-smug grin spread across Quinn's lips as she lifted her head and brought her heavy gaze to his. "I mean it, Park. That was..."

Wonderful? Incredible? Mind-blowing?

There wasn't a description worthy of what they'd just shared. Apparently the man still buried inside her agreed.

"I know, sweetheart." Another heart-melting kiss to her hair. "Trust me, I know."

It could be a line. Weightless platitudes meant to

appease her in those first few moments spent in after-sex limbo. But Quinn didn't think so.

After all, wasn't this usually the time when the guy would make some excuse as to why he needed to leave? Early morning shift at work, can't sleep with anyone else in their bed...was up late the night before caring for a sick parent...

She'd heard them all.

But Parker wasn't saying any of those things. He wasn't rushing to kick her out of his bed. And sex with him wasn't, well, all about him.

He'd been generous with his attention. Unhurried in his efforts to please her. And unlike the few men she'd been with in the past, he'd made sure she was taken care of first— twice, even—before worrying about his own desires and needs.

So no, Quinn didn't believe Parker was like any of those men. She just prayed she was right.

The man flew halfway across the country to find you, Q. He brought you into his home without so much as a second thought, and he's been working tirelessly to find the man who broke into your home. What more does he have to do to prove he's not like Justin...or your dad?

Hating to do it, Quinn pushed herself up, her breath stuttering as he slid from her sensitive flesh. Falling to the mattress beside him, she reveled in the stolen moment.

Without a word, Parker leaned over, kissing her lovingly before disappeared behind a set of double doors across the room to her left. Lost in a sea of sated bliss, Quinn almost missed the sound of running water coming from behind those partially closed doors.

Shower.

The sound of soft footfalls had her lids peeling open, her breath catching at what she saw. Or rather, what she *felt*.

Moving across the room at a leisurely pace, Parker was the very definition of male beauty. But it was the emotions radiating from his handsome face that had her lungs freezing and her heart swelling.

Peace. Happiness. And if she let herself believe it...love.

Quinn found all those things and more reflected in his gorgeous eyes, but that was crazy, right? One round of wonderful, incredible, soul-filling sex did not equal love.

And even if she wanted to go down that road again—a thought that was as terrifying as it was enticing—it was way, *way* too soon for that.

Is it, though?

Quinn considered the unspoken question as Parker closed the final distance between him and the bed. They'd only just met, yet she'd known him for nearly a year. He may not have revealed his real name or what he did for a living, but she knew those things now.

Those and so much more.

Likewise, she'd only recently given him her real name and the seedy details of her regretful past, but he knew those things now. The good, the bad, the embarrassingly ugly—Parker knew it all. And for reasons she may never understand, the sexy-as-sin man was still here.

He was here, and he was naked, and...

He's looking at me as if I hung the moon.

Justin had given her similar glances during their time together. And in those moments, Quinn had blindly accepted the façade. Looking back, however, the signs of his deceit had always been there.

She just hadn't wanted to see them.

It had been the same with the handful of others she'd

been stupid enough to let in. The few men who'd come before and after Justin...her dad... They'd all had that same misleading air about them. But not this man.

Not Parker.

Hard as she try, Quinn couldn't find so much as a sliver of deception in his contented gaze. No hidden agenda or devious plan peeking out from behind the green and brown specs in his spellbinding eyes. No pity. Just...

Love.

The incessant thought returned with vigor. But this time, rather than explaining it away like before, Quinn took a breath.

When she did, when she opened her mind and heart to the possibility, the world as she'd known it changed.

Cliché as it seemed, with that one shared look—that one private, intimate moment in time—everything became surprisingly clear.

She wasn't that young girl living in squalor with worthless parents and no money to her name. She also wasn't the same idealistic fool who'd let her daddy issues influence her choices.

That girl, that same young, naïve woman...they didn't exist.

Not anymore.

Those lost, pathetic souls had been replaced by a woman who was finally beginning to see her worth. A woman who, after years of hiding from her mistakes and letting the ghosts of her past take charge, was finally starting to feel whole again.

There isn't a single fucking thing I'd change about you.

Parker's earlier sentiment, while genuine, hadn't been the root of her defining moment. The revelation hadn't come because Parker had flown to her rescue or let her into his bed. But the incredible man had played a role in bringing the stunning realization to light.

Because when he looked at her as he was now, Quinn could *feel* the truth in what he was seeing...

A woman who was worthy of life. Of love. And for the first time in her subsistence, Quinn realized she was done with simply going through the motions. Finished merely existing. And this new Quinn...

She was ready to live.

12

_____

QUINN CAUGHT a glimpse of herself in the wide, full-length mirror in Parker's private bath...and smiled. She'd been doing that more and more over the past four days.

That's how long it had been since she and Parker first slept together. Four wonderful, amazing days since—upon Parker's request—she'd stopped using the guest room and had moved her things in here.

With him.

They'd continued their search for a lead in her case, but so far, their exhausted efforts had produced squat. Quinn was also trying hard not to worry about Oreo, the stray that became so much more.

Christian and Brody had checked in periodically, but so far there'd been no sign of her adopted pet. The good news was, they hadn't found signs of foul play where the cat was concerned, so Quinn's hope was the furry creature had gotten to safety and was just waiting for her to return.

I'm not so sure I want to go back.

A small huff of breath left her lungs as she thought about the weight of that one, simple thought. Less than a week ago, it wouldn't have even been a question. But after four blissful days working—and playing—with Parker, Quinn was beginning to reconsider all sorts of things.

It wasn't about the money. She couldn't care less about that. It was about the man, himself.

The sweet, sexy, talented man with a heart as big as his bank account...and a brain that turned her on as much as his sculpted body.

Although there were a few perks that came with Parker's life that Quinn admittedly enjoyed. His sailboat being one of them.

He'd surprised her three days ago with an afternoon on the sea. She'd never been on a sailboat before, let alone one on the ocean. But it was an incredible day.

Blue skies, sun on her skin. The rhythmic motion of the ocean's gentle waves. And when it had gotten dark, they'd made love on the top deck.

Under the light of a thousand stars.

Luckily Parker knew just where to go to avoid the paparazzi. When they did come upon the occasional boat, she'd either hide her face until they passed, or they'd been far enough away the concern was pretty much non-existent.

An image from that night flashed before her.

Parker with his back on the blanketed deck. Quinn riding him much like she had their first time. The gentle laps of water as it met the boat's smooth hull combining with their cries of passion... All getting lost in the gentle sea breeze.

She smiled at the memory, her greedy body shivering with need. It was as if she couldn't get enough.

It'll never be enough. Not with him.

Quinn locked the memory away for safe keeping while giving herself a final once-over before officially starting the day. Dressed in a cream-colored knit tank, distressed jeans, and black boots, she felt sort of...pretty.

The clothes were courtesy of Parker, but only after securing his promise to let her pay him back. As much as she hated him making the purchases in the first place, Quinn also understood the concern.

If whoever had targeted her was tracking her credit card activity, one swipe, tap, or insert would alert them to her location instantly. Neither she nor Parker were willing to take that risk.

Flipping off the light as she passed by, Quinn made her way to the home's gourmet kitchen. Every morning since staying here, a deliciously prepared breakfast dish of some sort had awaited.

Eggs, bacon, waffles, pastries... Everything Parker's inconspicuous chef had created had tasted phenomenal. And it had been made special just for them.

Okay, so maybe not all *parts of this lifestyle are bad.*

Assuming this morning was no different, she continued on her current path. But halfway between the open foyer and stainless steel haven, Quinn stopped dead in her tracks.

Standing with his back to her, Parker had one hip leaning against the shiny silver island. His head was bent forward, and from the way his arms were held, he appeared to be texting someone.

And he was wearing a suit.

For a man of his stature, it wasn't exactly a novel idea. Except every day since she'd first met him, Parker had worn jeans and T's. Or, during their many, many toe-curling encores, nothing at all.

Never a suit.

Quinn slid her focus to the top of the giant, chef-worthy island. Per routine, the breakfast she'd been looking forward to had been delivered and was waiting, a place setting left neatly in the spot that Parker had started referring to as "her" seat. But when she shifted to "his" seat, she found it empty.

Resuming her steps, she took in the entire scene as she walked toward him. When she noticed the computer bag and small rolling suitcase resting on the floor next to him, she understood.

He's leaving.

Parker turned around, the smile lighting up his face when he saw her momentarily tampering her disappointment.

"Hey, you." He turned and pulled her in for a kiss.

"Hey, yourself." Quinn looked down at his bags and back up to him. "Going somewhere?"

A whisp of a shadow crossed over him, but it was gone before she could even be sure it was really there.

He gave her a regrettable nod. "There's a fire I have to put out, and apparently I can't do it from here."

"What kind of fire?"

"Nothing you need to worry about." Parker's lips pressed against her forehead before he released his hold and stepped around her. Bending down to grab his bags, he added, "I'm on the board of several philanthropic organizations, and something's come up that needs my attention."

"How long will you be gone?"

"A day." He straightened and faced her with a wink. "Less if I'm lucky."

Pretty sure I'm the lucky one.

Countless orgasms notwithstanding, that crooked smile of his left her heart warm and her body aching for more.

"But don't worry." He spoke as he walked toward his front entrance. "I'm not leaving you here alone."

My protector.

"I'm safe here, Parker." Quinn followed closely. "I mean, it's not like whoever's after me would think to look for me here. Besides, you just said you'll be gone a day at the most."

"I'm not leaving you alone." He let go of the suitcase's retractable handle to open one of the two large doors. "Not until we catch the son of a bitch."

With the luggage in tow once again, Parker stepped over the threshold. It's tiny wheels bouncing as they maneuvered themselves across the bump.

"I get that you're worried, Park." The morning breeze made its way through a few strands of her hair. "And I appreciate it. I really do, but—"

Quinn cut her own words short as she noticed the car that had just pulled up to the house and parked. Unlike the black Cadillac waiting to drive Parker to his private hanger across town, this was a big, dark gray truck that looked like it could take on a tank.

A man who looked to be around Parker's age stepped out from behind the wheel. Tall. Good looking. Short dark hair and muscular build.

Ah, you must be my babysitter.

The passenger door opened, but instead of the equally built man Quinn had expected, a woman appeared. A beautiful, petite brunette with bouncy curls and striking blue eyes.

Dressed in a pair of cute jean capris, a white flowing blouse, and thin brown sandals Quinn found adorable, the woman's eyes held a suspicious gaze when they landed on her. But when the stranger turned in Parker's direction, those same eyes softened with a genuine smile.

"Hey, Park." She went right in for a hug.

He reciprocated the gesture, pulling the woman close with his own sweet smile.

An unexpected jolt of pure jealousy left Quinn's gut tight and her stomach churning. She'd never been the jealous type. Not ever. But seeing this man—her man—holding another woman so closely...

She so much as thinks about making a move on him I'll—

"Hey, Syd." Parker let the woman go and reached for Quinn's hand.

Syd.

The name rolled through her brain as she slid her palm against Parker's. She'd heard him say it before, but for the life of her, Quinn couldn't remember when or why.

Syd...Syd...Syd...

Then it hit her.

This woman wasn't trying to move in on Parker. This was Sydnee. The woman he'd been talking to on the phone that morning at the safehouse. If she remembered correctly, Parker had told her Sydnee was a doctor, and she was married to...

Quinn looked at the man still waiting patiently in the wings. Studying his physique with a closer eye, she realized he wasn't just fit. He was also on high alert.

Feet firmly planted shoulder-width apart. Hands clasped tightly in front of him. Eyes that were hidden behind a dark pair of sleek sunglasses yet were constantly taking in their surroundings.

He's the sniper.

Misplaced jealousy gone, Quinn's shoulders relaxed with understanding. These were Parker's friends. His happily *engaged* friends.

Aaaand...now she felt like a big jerk.

Down girl.

"Quinn, this is Dr. Sydnee Blake." Parker introduced her to the woman in question. "She's the friend I told you about."

"The one you grew up with." Quinn held out her hand and smiled. "Hi. I'm Quinn."

Those blue eyes stared right through her.

"Sydnee." Her grip was firm. "Nice to meet you."

Something about that stare said otherwise.

"You, too."

Sydnee held their shared grip a little longer than was socially acceptable, and Quinn couldn't help but feel as though she were being sized up. Not that she could blame the gorgeous doctor.

If the roles were reversed, Quinn would absolutely do the same.

"And this ugly guy right here is Asher Cross." Parker finished the introductions. "Sydnee's fiancé and all-around badass."

The far-from-ugly man slid his glasses to the top of his head. Like his fiancée, Asher's dark eyes crossed over her with an assessing glance before he offered her his hand. But his didn't hold quite the same amount of suspicion.

"Nice to meet you, Quinn." Another firm shake. "I'm assuming Park's told you why we're here."

"Actually, I only just found out about his charity problem a few minutes before you got here. But yeah. Park told me about the charity emergency and that he didn't want me to be left alone. Just in case."

The two men shared a look Quinn didn't understand before Asher glanced over at Sydnee and grinned. "Well, I don't normally bring my fiancée along with me on jobs like this, but Syd insisted on meeting you. And since, like you said, this is just a precautionary step, anyway—"

"I thought it would give us a chance to get to know each other a little bit." The other woman finished for him. Her delicate shoulders stiffened ever-so-slightly when she took in the way Parker was still holding Quinn's hand.

"Sure." Quinn smiled, not bothering to deny Sydnee's claim. "I mean, yeah. I'd like that."

Surprisingly, she meant it.

For all the fleeting animosity she'd felt upon Sydnee's arrival, the bottom line was this woman cared about Parker. Not in a romantic, threatening way. But as a friend.

The pretty doctor cared so much, in fact, she'd talked her former Special Forces fiancé into bringing her along on his bodyguard duty just so she could check Quinn out. Presumably to make sure Parker's new love interest wasn't bringing trouble to his doorstep.

How could she be mad about that?

"Well, as much as I'd rather hang out here with all of you, I really do have to go."

With another quick hug from Sydnee and a shake of Asher's hand, Parker turned to Quinn and motioned toward the brick drive. "Walk me to the car?"

Nodding, Quinn walked hand-in-hand with the sexy man down the wide steps and to the Caddy. Before they'd even reached the bottom step, a man she hadn't seen before was out of the car and waiting near the back passenger door.

"Mr. Collins." The suited man opened the door for Parker. But he didn't get in.

"Give us a minute, Max."

"Sure thing, Mr. Collins." Making quick work of the bags, the man named Max closed the trunk lid and returned to his rightful place behind the wheel.

Standing beside the opened back door, Quinn ignored

his friends who were watching them intently from the home's elaborate front stoop.

"At least you won't have to be gone long." She offered him a small smile.

"I hate leaving you at all."

Warmth spread through her chest, but she placed her free hand on his. "I'll be fine, Park. Again, who in their right mind would think to find me here?"

"Right-minded people aren't the ones I'm worried about, sweetheart."

The look in his eyes was different than she'd seen before. No, that wasn't true. Quinn remembered seeing it back in Chicago when she'd first told him about her intruder.

Parker's expression had turned dark. Almost lethal. And while his face didn't show a single sign of that hardened protector now, there was *something* hiding in the depths of his eyes.

Quit borrowing trouble, Q. You've got enough real shit to worry about without fabricating more from thin air.

"Look, I get that this is probably overkill, but..." He covered her hand with his. "You're important to me, Quinn." A bob of his throat. "I know things are crazy right now, and there's still a lot we have left to learn about one another. But I..."

"Yes?"

The quick lick of his lips was almost nervous in nature. Which made zero sense, because this was Parker.

Confident.

Fun-loving.

Insatiable.

Those were the words she'd used to describe the man in

front of her. Those and many, many more. But nervous? Not him.

Not Parker.

"I...have to go." He finally finished.

Only it wasn't what Quinn had thought he was going to say. Words that, after years of denying herself the chance—she'd hoped he'd been about to say.

It's too soon, Q. He's not ready.

Feeling silly for even thinking such things, she forced a smile and lifted her mouth to his. "Be careful, stud."

It was meant to be a short, quick peck, but Parker clearly had a better idea.

Unlinking the hands at their sides, he wrapped that arm around her waist, and pulled her body flush with his. With his other hand, he cupped her cheek and took the kiss deeper.

And by the time he pulled away, Quinn realized it didn't matter if he said the words to her.

Because she was already there.

"I'll be back as soon as I can." A rumbled promise.

"I'll be here."

As if he couldn't help himself, Parker leaned down and took her mouth a final time. And this kiss was full of a promise she prayed was real.

"See you soon, sweetheart."

"Stay safe."

"Always." With a wink and a smirk, he folded himself into the back seat and closed the door.

Quinn watched as the black car disappeared through the property's protective gate and around the corner, taking the man she was—for better or worse—falling more and more in love with.

. . .

AN HOUR LATER, QUINN, ASHER, AND SYDNEE WERE gathered together in, what Parker had coined The Great Room. She had to admit, those first few minutes alone with the intimidating woman had been tense. But that all changed after Quinn opened up to them over lunch.

And boy, oh boy, did she open up.

In a very un-Quinn like moment, she'd spilled her guts about everything over a meal Parker had arranged for them to have before he left. Well, she hadn't told them *everything.*

But minus the intimate moments between her and Parker, Quinn did tell his two friends the rest. Her past with Justin. How she and Parker first became friends. What happened to her the night she'd called him for help.

All of it.

By the time she was done, any semblance of animosity or mistrust between the two women was gone. A very important step, as far as she was concerned.

Parker had made it clear early on how important Sydnee was to him. And after hearing him describe her as the sister he never had—and seeing the way she and Asher were together—Quinn knew their relationship was as platonic as he'd claimed.

Just one more sign that he truly was a trustworthy man. A man with some pretty great friends.

"*Please* tell me Parker didn't do that to you." Sydnee's pretty blue eyes widened with disbelief upon hearing about his well-intended spa-day debacle.

Quinn swallowed her most recent sip and chuckled. "Trust me, I wish I could." She pointed to her right. "The mani-pedi station was over there, and the facial and makeup areas were over there." Another point in a different corner of the room. "And that entire space was filled with like six racks of designer clothes and shoes."

The other woman groaned as her curls hit the cushion behind her. "Lord save us from well-meaning men."

Beside her Asher took a swig of his bottled water and shrugged. "I don't know what y'all are complaining about. Sounds to me like the guy was just trying to do something nice."

"It *was* nice," Quinn rushed to explain. "But it was also just...a bit overwhelming. Especially for someone who grew up with nothing."

"I grew up with money, and it would have been too much for me." Sydnee snorted. "I swear, that man has the biggest heart of anyone I know." A quick glance in her fiance's direction. "Present company excluded, of course."

"Of course." Asher rolled his dark eyes but followed the move with a smirk and a kiss.

Quinn smiled even as a heaviness fell across her chest, and it took her a minute to realize what she was feeling.

I miss him.

The man had been gone less than two hours, and already she missed him. What was happening to her?

You're in love, Q. That's what's happening.

No, it wasn't happening.

It already had.

"Come on, you know what I mean." Sydnee clarified. "Park would give you the shirt off his back if he thought you needed it. And he's a freaking genius, obviously. But sometimes he can be so..."

"Clueless?" Quinn arched a brow.

The other woman raised her half-empty glass in a faux-toast and smiled. "Exactly."

Returning the gesture, Quinn brought the expensive crystal to her lips. The sweet red wine had barely danced across her tongue when it happened.

Bright, blinding light filled the room as the massive windows to Quinn's left exploded; their sharp, deadly shards carried into the room by a powerful wave of heat and flames.

Quinn—and the chair she'd been sitting in—were thrown several feet into the air. A flash of pain hit followed by an incessant ringing in her ears. From somewhere behind her, she thought she heard Asher screaming Sydnee's name, and …

Nothing.

13

PARKER HANDED HIS CELL PHONE, wallet, and keys to the officer manning the visitor intake desk at FCI—the Federal Correctional Institution located in Tazewell County.

Operated by the Federal Bureau of Prisons, the medium-security prison was an all-male inmate facility...and Justin Reynolds' home for the last six years.

Guilt threatened to deter his plan as he waited, but Parker refused to give in. Yes, he'd lied to Quinn about the charity board emergency. And yes, he'd made a solemn vow to himself never to be dishonest with her again.

But this was about more than protecting his identity on an MMO. This was about Quinn's safety. When it came to that, all bets were off.

Sorry, sweetheart. I'm doing this for you.

The decision not to tell Quinn he was coming here to see her ex had been an easy one to make. If he'd told her the truth about his plan, she would have insisted on joining him. And Parker didn't want her anywhere near that piece of shit.

Not even with an armed guard standing nearby and at the ready.

The plan was simple. He'd introduce himself to Reynolds, offer him a sizeable donation toward his upcoming re-entry into society, and make sure the other man understood the cost.

If Reynolds agreed to sign the papers Parker's attorney had drawn up as a back-up plan, Parker would wire five million dollars directly into the guy's checking account.

For Parker, it was a drop in the bucket. For a guy like Reynolds—a man who'd spent his life chasing dollar signs —the offer would be impossible to refuse.

"Right this way, Mr. Collins."

He followed the middle-aged woman through a secured door, which led into a long, tiled hallway. At the end of that hall, they went through another ID-required door. And another after that.

Typically inmates and visitors would meet in a different room, back near that very first door. But Parker wasn't going there. No, this particular visit—with this particular inmate —required privacy.

And no witnesses.

"Here we are." The officer lifted her chipped ID a final time before opening the door. "Sit tight, and I'll go get your inmate. I'd say make yourself comfortable, but..."

"Thank you." He gave her a tight smile. Alone now, Parker looked around at the dull, drab space.

Roughly ten-by-twelve, the room offered one small, rectangular window centered high on the wall to his right. In the center was a simple, stainless steel table with two metal folding chairs facing each other.

Filled with pent-up rage toward the man behind the notes and break-in, Parker was too wound up to sit.

You can't kill him, Collins. Remember that. You kill him, it'll be your ass behind bars. Who would protect Quinn if that happened?

Her face flashed before him and, despite his current surroundings, Parker smiled. He did that a lot when he thought about her. Or every time he saw her walk into a room.

When he saw her. Touched her. Tasted her.

There was a moment this morning when he'd come damn close to telling her how he really felt. But with Max nearby and Ash and Syd watching like hawks from the front steps, it hadn't felt like the most apropos time for something that big.

And the three little words perched on the tip of his tongue were really fucking big.

Aside from his mom and Sydnee, who were both family, Parker had never told a woman he loved her before. Had never even been tempted.

But with Quinn, things were different. *She* was different. And he was different around her.

He was...happy.

I need her with me always. I need her to stay forever.

While that was his long-term plan, he knew he'd have to tread lightly. If he told her he loved her too soon, she might get spooked and run. But if he let too much time pass, she may get tired of waiting and leave him anyway.

Meanwhile, the indecision of it all was driving him mad.

The woman craves honesty. You should just tell her how you feel.

The sound of a buzzer echoing from somewhere down the hall brought Parker's attention to the present. It also reminded him of where his focus should be.

Now wasn't the time for thoughts of love and happily

ever after. This was the time for action, hence his impromptu trip here.

He looked at the table but made no move toward it. Any minute now, Reynolds was going to walk through that door, and Parker wanted to be standing when he did.

Let them see you standing tall from the start, and they'll be less likely to try to intimidate or swindle.

It was a well-known tactic in the business world, and one he'd used on several occasions. Although sitting or standing, it made no difference to him.

Quinn's ex may think he has the upper hand, but Parker was about to prove him wrong.

The door to his left buzzed, followed by a loud metallic click. Rolling his shoulders back, Parker steadied his stance and prepared to meet the prick who'd been terrorizing the woman Parker loved.

And yeah, he loved Quinn. More than anything. Which was the whole reason he was here.

The door to the room opened, but instead of the face he'd expected to see, a different man stepped into the room.

"Mr. Collins." The balding, overweight man shook Parker's hand with vigor. "I'm William Pollard, the warden here at FCI. It's a pleasure to meet you."

A low nagging twinged inside his gut. "Pleasure's mine, Warden."

"Please." The man dropped his clammy hand. "Call me Bill."

"All right, Bill. And you can call me Parker." He looked at the door behind the other man. "I was actually expecting to see an inmate of yours. Justin Reynolds?"

"Yes, well...I mean, the thing is..." Bill's forehead beaded with sweat, and he wiped his palms along the front of his cheap dress pants. Clearing his throat, the nervous man finally spit out what he'd been struggling to say. "You see, that's the reason I'm here."

The nagging grew in strength as Parker gave that door a second glance. "Warden, where is Reynolds?"

When the man hesitated a second time, it became clear that there was a problem. And from the amount of endless sweat covering his shiny forehead, it was a big one.

"Mr. Collins, please. You have to understand. My prison houses over thirteen hundred inmates. The system we use to keep track of everyone is new, but every employee was thoroughly trained and knows how to work it. I can assure you, we're doing everything in our power, but—"

"Where. Is. Reynolds?" Parker stepped into the man's face. Voice low and controlled, the sharp demand cut off the warden's rambling excuse.

Breaths audible, the sweaty man stared back at him and shook his head. Fear shimmered in his round, dark eyes as Warden Pollard admitted, "We don't know."

His heart punched his ribs, the unexpected answer sending him stumbling back a step. "What the hell do you mean, you *don't know?*"

Opening the door, Pollard led him back through the maze of hallways and doors. Rushing to explain, he tripped all over himself as they walked. The man used words like intake system error, investigation, appropriate notifications...

But Parker hadn't really heard them.

He was too busy working through the massive what-the-fuck still racing through his head.

Somehow Justin Reynolds had vanished. The man—a fucking federal prisoner—had managed to escape.

Pollard opened the last door, and the two men entered the visitor intake area Parker had left minutes earlier.

Wasting no time retrieving his personal belongings, he paid no attention to the kiss-ass warden or his continued blathering of justifications.

Removing his phone, keys, and wallet from the metal bowl stationed beneath the glass partition, Parker spun on his heels and headed for the door.

"Rest assured Mr. Collins." Pollard was hot on his heels. "I will find out what happened, and those responsible will be held accountable. I've already contacted the FBI, and a BOLO has been issued for Reynolds. We will find him."

"No, Warden. I will."

"Wha...what do you mean by that? Mr. Collins, wait!"

Refusing to listen to another damn word the incompetent man spewed from behind, Parker gave the glass door a hard shove and stormed outside. Pulling his phone from his pocket, he ignored the copious number of notifications littering his lock screen and tapped Quinn's name from his contact list.

He put the phone to his ear and waited.

Come on, sweetheart. Pick up.

After an endless round of rings with no response, he put a call into Asher. Five rings later, and...

"This is Cross. You know what to do."

Goddamn it!

Refusing to give in to the irrational fear the warden's upsetting news had created—along with the fact that he couldn't get ahold of Quinn or the man he'd charged with her protection—Parker tried a third and final number.

Answer your phone, Syd. I really, really need to talk to Quinn.

Parker reached his car. Once inside, he shut the door, fired up the ignition, and had his seatbelt buckled in record time. Switching to Bluetooth, he sat his phone onto the console on his right and peeled out of the secured lot.

Secured, my ass. Can't be too damn secured if an inmate managed to walk right out the front fucking gate.

Sydnee's sweet voice filled his car's interior, but when he opened his mouth to let her know what had happened, he realized it wasn't really her.

It was her previously recorded greeting.

"Fuck!" Parker smacked a palm against his leather steering wheel. With a rough tap of the screen on his dash, he brought yet another failed attempt to an end and hung up.

Think, damn it! Think!

Working to tamper his rising fear, he was in the middle of a deep, calming breath when his phone rang to life. Seeing Asher's number on his screen, he blew out a breath of relief and answered the call.

"About time. I've been trying to reach you guys, but no one would answer their damn phones."

"I've been trying to call you, too."

Parker blinked at Asher's taut, gravelly tone. Remembering the numerous notifications he'd dismissed after leaving the prison, it was clear his friend had been one of them.

"Sorry, brother. I just left the prison, and they wouldn't let me take my phone past the entrance. Anyway...get this shit. I just found out Justin Reynolds escaped."

"Park—"

"Now I don't know how or even when." He didn't let the man speak. "The warden kept saying something about their new intake system or some bullshit. Feds are looking into it, but I wanted to give you a heads up. I'm sure the bastard's halfway to Mexico by now, but—"

"He's not in Mexico." Asher finally broke through.

The confidence in that statement had Parker frowning. "What?"

"Reynolds. He isn't in Mexico."

Parker's body tensed, his posture becoming rigid against the seat's expensive leather. "How do you know that?"

"Because I'm pretty sure he was here. Or at least someone working with him."

"Reynolds was at my house?" *What the actual fuck?* "Let me talk to Quinn."

A slight pause. "Like I said. I don't know for sure it was him. But—"

"Where's Quinn, Asher?" He wanted to talk to her. Needed to hear with his own ears that she was okay.

But Asher didn't put her on the line. Instead the man he saw as a brother brought his entire world crashing down around him.

"I'm sorry, man." Regret poured from Asher's words. "I tried to stop them, but...it all happened so fast. There was this explosion, and Syd..." His voice cracked, but he cleared it. "Syd went down. She's okay, thank God, but by the time I got to where I'd last seen Quinn, she was already..."

No. No, no, no...

"What?" Parker barked, demanding his friend finish the fucking sentence. "Quinn was what?"

"Gone." A rough exhale. "I'm so fucking sorry, Parker. They got her, man. She's gone."

14

QUINN PACED THE COLD, musty room as she tried like hell to figure a way out. It had been hours since the explosion, and she wasn't any closer to getting answers than when she first got here.

Including where *here* was.

She was in Chicago. That much, she knew. And that was only because she'd woken up just as the plane she'd been unwillingly placed onto was landing.

Her stomach clenched from the memory.

A headache had pulled her from unconsciousness, and Quinn remembered wondering why Parker had let her drink so much the night before. But as her awareness became clearer, she realized the headache wasn't from too many margaritas on Parker's deck...and it wasn't the next day.

It was the *same* day as it had been before she'd been knocked unconscious...by a freaking bomb!

Closing her eyes, Quinn ignored the tear falling down her cheek and hugged herself tight. With nothing but time on her hands, she'd learned that, if she tried hard enough...*fought* against them hard enough...she could keep the terrifying flashes from that horrific moment at bay.

Mostly.

Why is this happening?

The confusion and fear she'd felt from seeing the Willis Tower from the view out her tiny round window had nearly been her undoing. That and not knowing if Sydnee and Asher were okay.

Please let them be okay.

Once she'd regained control over her barrage of emotions, Quinn had studied her surroundings for a clue as to who had taken her and why. Though by the unexpected, all-expense-paid trip to The Windy City was a pretty big one.

You know he's behind this.

She had her suspicions, sure. But other than her, the small, private plane's cabin had been empty, and the man who'd exited the cockpit upon landing wasn't the face she'd expect.

He was, however, the man who'd broken into her home.

She'd bet her life on it.

He'd refrained from confessing, of course. Refused to talk to her at all, actually. Minus a few dickishly barked orders, that is.

But Quinn didn't need a verbal confirmation of her suspicions.

She'd recognized his body shape and size the minute he'd exited the cockpit. Remembered the way he'd stood in her kitchen with that gun in his hand, ready to do God only knows what to her.

But his eyes...those were what really solidified Quinn's conjecture that it was him. Those, and the slight muscle twitch in his left cheek when faced with the accusation that he'd been the one inside her home that night.

Oh, yeah. It was him, all right.

Not that it mattered. She still didn't have a name. His or the person who'd hired him. Still had no idea where exactly she was, or what their plans were for her.

And worst of all, Quinn had no way of letting Parker know she was okay.

He must be going crazy with worry.

She could practically see that mask he sometimes wore —the fierce protector willing to kill to keep her safe. That's how she'd come to think of it, but only as a romanticized exaggeration.

Until now.

Now, Quinn would give anything to see him burst through the doors. To come to her rescue—again—and take out anyone and everyone who blocked their path of escape.

It was a fantasy she couldn't afford to get lost in. Not if she wanted to find a way out of here for real.

Because Parker wasn't coming. Not without some way of letting him know where she was. And since she hadn't figure that out yet, Quinn knew...

I'm on my own.

The thought had no more entered her mind when the room's metal door began to open. Quinn spun around, flattening her back against the nearest wall to prevent a blind ambush.

Rough, uneven cinder blocks pushed through her knitted tank, scratching the skin below. But she ignored it, her frightened, wary gaze locked on that opening door.

Licking her lips, she had to physically work to control her rapid breaths. Her chest hurt from the racing heartbeat pounding wildly inside, and her stomach felt as if she'd swallowed a giant rock. But other than that...

I'm fine. This is fine. It's all going to be just fine.

A hysterical bubble of laughter nearly escaped, but Quinn covered her mouth to keep it at bay.

Damn it, Quinn. Focus!

With a few forceful blinks and a shake of her head, Quinn struggled to clear her wandering thoughts. Not an easy task given the headache, nausea, and struggles to keep her mind on a clear and present path.

Hey, wait a minute. That sounds an awful lot like a concussion...

Another flashbang of a memory chose that moment to make its presence known. The sensation of flying through the air. Asher's screams for the woman he was building a future with.

Fire. Smoke. Pain. And then...

Well, shit. Maybe she really did have a concussion. It would explain the sixteen-person drumline performing a massive cadence between her ears. And the violent churning in her gut.

But Quinn didn't have time to think about any of that now. Not when that door came fully open and the man behind her abduction appeared.

Wearing baggy jeans, a black hoodie, and worn sneakers, Justin Reynolds stood in the doorway with a calculating sneer.

The urge to vomit increased as her long-standing theory was confirmed. Even after being convinced her ex was the one behind everything, there'd still been a very real part of her that hoped she was wrong.

Right up until the moment Justin Reynolds walked through that door.

"Hey babe." A smug sneer curled his spiteful mouth.

Once an asshole, always an asshole.

Pushing away her mother's crackhead—albeit correct—voice, Quinn stared at a man she once thought she loved. Gone was the boyish charm and youthful smile, both erased by a system that was anything but kind.

With creases in the corners of his eyes, skin that looked uneven and pale, and a few sprigs of silver in his otherwise dark scruff, the man she'd once dreamed about looked as if he'd aged a dozen years in only half that time.

"Miss me?"

With a voice much stronger and steadier than she felt, Quinn shot a glare in the prick's direction. "Not even a little bit."

The man she never really knew feigned laughter as he moved further into the room. Strolling toward her, the soles of his shoes scraped against the decrepit room's crumbling floor as he slowly covered the distance between them.

"You're not supposed to get out for another six months." She stated the obvious. "In fact, as of this morning, your inmate status was still showing active."

"Still is." A cocky grin. "I learned a few things while I was away. Of course, I had to bide my time. Wait for the right guard to come along. When she did, I charmed my way into her pants...and one of the staff computers."

Her nausea grew. "How did you find me?" she demanded.

"Which time?"

"The first time." *You pompous ass.*

"Ah, yes. That was much easier than I thought." He smirked. "You ever hear of a guy named Victor McMahon?"

She nodded.

Of course, she'd heard of him. Her old team had helped

take the man down a year before she joined forces with the FBI. The story of that particular arrest lived on well past the initial news cycle and fanfare.

A former financial advisor and securities broker to several large companies in the Chicago area, McMahon made national headlines when he was arrested for tax evasion and insider trading.

From what Quinn had learned—from Holly and the others, as well as reports she'd accessed during her time with the Bureau—the man was a brilliant criminal mastermind who'd gotten cocky. And cocky assholes make mistakes.

Just like the one standing in front of me now.

"Yeah, you'd have to live under a rock not to know that man's name."

"What does he have to do with me?" Quinn kept the jerk on track.

"Oh, right. I guess I haven't told you that part. So funny story..." Justin smirked. "McMahon was assigned as my new cell mate when he got sent away. And with nothing to do for hours on end, my celly and I did a lot of talking. Well, I talked, mostly. But Vic...he listened."

"Still doesn't answer my question, Justin." Quinn prayed he didn't notice her trembling knees.

"I'm getting there,' he snapped. Running a hand down over his face, he appeared to regain his composure and continued. "

"Vic and I were talking one day, just shootin' the shit like we'd do, when we started to make a plan. It started as a joke, but the longer we talked, the more we realized we could actually do it."

"Do what, Justin?" Her fed-up voice filled the tiny room. "Tell me why I'm here!"

Moving lightning fast, her ex was well within her personal space, his meaty hand gripping her jaw so tight she thought it might break.

"Ah!" Quinn cried out from the pain. She tried to get free, but his hold was too strong.

"You're not in charge, this time, babe." Hatred reflected in his cold, angry eyes. "Look around you. There's no one watching this time. No suits waiting for your go-ahead to storm in here and save the day. You had your chance with that once, remember?" He brought the tip of his nose to hers. "Not this time."

"You're...h-hurting...me."

"Yeah?" That grip grew tighter. "Well, you hurt me, too, babe. You hurt me bad. Now it's my turn."

Another lingering stare...

Justin released her with a rough shove before taking several steps in the opposite direction. Quinn grunted, her body nearly tumbling to the side from the force.

With a hand to her tender jaw, she looked back at him with a sneer of her own. "I didn't hurt you, Justin. You did that all by yourself."

"You ratted me out!" Spittle flew from his mouth as he spun back around. "I'm not stupid, Quinn, although you always treated me like I was."

What? "I never—"

"I saw the tapes!" He cut her denial short. "I know you were the one who set me up."

She was aware of this, of course. She'd seen those same tapes, too. But something else Quinn knew...

"The FBI was coming after you whether I helped them or not!" The pressure in her head worsened. "Agent Manning approached me a couple days before our planned hack. They had pictures, Justin. Of you. Me. Us together."

Quinn frowned at the unpleasant memory. "But most were of you and that Monty guy."

"I've seen the pics, babe." He shook his head. "And Monty was their real target. Not me."

"I know. That's why, when they first came to me, I refused to talk unless they agreed to a deal."

"A deal." He snorted.

"I'm not talking about mine, Justin. I made one for you, too."

"For me?" This seemed to surprise him. "Well, I guess I should be thanking you then, right?"

"They had you dead to rights for your dealings with Monty. Between that and the proof they had showing the credit card hack was all your idea—all because *you* ran your mouth to a freaking FBI *informant,* by the way—you were looking at like fifteen to twenty years behind bars. I got them to agree to two."

"Yeah, well...two years came and went, babe. And I was still there."

"Because you pulled stupid shit on the side." She pushed herself off the wall to fully face him. "Those jobs... the Feds built that case because you were sloppy. So you can be pissed that I got your guaranteed conviction and sentence down to a fraction of what it would have been, but the rest...that's one hundred percent on you."

Having made her point clear, Quinn crossed her arms at her chest and waited.

A muscle in his unkempt jaw bulged as he crossed the room once more. Waiting until he was standing in almost the exact spot as before, an ugly twist to Justin's mouth formed.

"They wouldn't have been looking to make those cases

in the first place, if it hadn't been for you. And *that*"—his nostrils flared with a scathing tone—"is on you, babe."

"We were all targets, Justin." She forced a gentle tone.

"Maybe. But you're the one who turned."

"Me?" Now *that* was laughable. "Did you forget I was there that night, Justin? That I was lying next to you when you looked me right in the eye and threw my ass under the bus? You fed them so much bullshit that night I'm surprised your eyes aren't permanently brown!"

Quinn didn't see his fist flying toward her until it was too late.

A flash of pain exploded across her left temple and eye, the blow sending her straight to the floor. With her previous knock to the head, it took everything in her power to stay conscious...

And to not throw up.

But neither passing out nor vomiting were going to get her away from this maniac, so she pushed past the pain and forced her eyes to open.

"I didn't turn on you, asshole." Her eyes widened with several hard blinks, her voice strained from the near-blinding pain. "Unlike you...I was trying to keep...your ass... out of prison."

"Yeah?" Justin laughed. "And how'd that work out for me? Oh, that's right. I'm the one who's spent the last six *years* behind bars. But you...*you* went on to work with the very people who put me there."

Pushing herself back up to her feet, Quinn threw a palm against the stone wall to keep from tipping back over. "How did you..." She grimaced with pain. "How do you...know about...that?"

Holy crap, my head hurts. Who knew the son of a bitch could hit like that?

"You're not as smart as you think you are, babe." Justin used the line she'd heard a million times. "That's how I figured out where you live. With McMahon's help, of course."

"How did he—"

"Little known fact...a lot of the dickheads who were put behind bars by the Feds are the same men who have other Feds in their pockets. Maybe not enough to keep them out of jail completely...or at all. But sometimes information is all that's needed. Say, the address of a woman who worked as an FBI Cyber Crimes Technical Analyst for three years before going freelance and working from home."

"McMahon has someone in the Bureau." Quinn drew her own conclusion. "And whoever that someone is figured out I agreed to give them three years of my expertise in exchange for immunity. Since I still consult on the occasional case, my personnel files would also have had my current address." It was all coming together now. "You passed along my address to McMahon—"

"Who passed it along to the man he hired to leave you those little love notes." Justin grinned. "Nice little build-up to our long-overdue reunion, don't you think?"

Refusing to dignify that with a response, Quinn asked another question of her own. "How did you know I was staying at Parker Collins' house?"

Figuring out her past with the FBI was one thing. But that...

"Next time you decide to fuck a billionaire on his million dollar sailboat, you might want to make sure no one's around to see it."

"Wha..." She couldn't even formulate the entire word for the shock from what he'd just said.

With a roll of his eyes, Justin pulled a phone from his

pocket. A presumably encrypted and untraceable phone. "Same ol' Quinn. Still avoiding social media, huh?" He began typing something in with his thumbs before holding it up for her to see.

Ohmygod!

Bile hit the base of her throat, but by some miracle, she managed to swallow it back down. There, posted for the entire world to see, was a grainy image of her and Parker. Just as Justin had claimed, they were on his sailboat.

His handsome, lust-filled face staring lovingly at hers.

Her head tilted back, the tips of her hair reaching the middle of her back as she rode them both to ecstasy.

The tabloid site claiming to have garnered exclusive rights to the violating picture had censored the most x-rated parts, but it didn't matter. The frozen moment in time—a moment that should have been private—was already out there.

The damage was already done.

Oh, Parker. I'm so sorry.

"It was pure luck, really. Some dipshit photog was so desperate to get his big money shot, he camped out for six days straight hoping to get a pic of your new boyfriend. Nice upgrade, by the way. Though I'm not sure how someone like you snagged a rich bastard like that."

Someone like her.

Two weeks ago, a comment like that would have been a one-way ticket to the past. Not anymore.

"Who's the man who left me the notes?" Because that same man, at least in part, had destroyed Parker's home, kidnapped her, and most likely hurt Asher and Sydnee.

Tears filled Quinn's eyes, but she refused to let them fall. She wouldn't cry. Not in front of this man.

She also refused to accept that Asher and Sydnee were anything but fine.

They have to be okay. Have. To.

"Don't remember the guys' name, and I don't care," Justin answered flippantly. "I just told Vic what I wanted the notes to say, and he made it happen. Same with the other."

The other meaning the explosion and abduction.

"Why?" She was starting to feel a bit stronger.

"Why did I tell him what to put on the notes?"

Lord, Jesus. "No, Justin. Why would a guy like Victor McMahon go out of his way to help someone like you?"

What's good for the goose, you dickless bastard.

But rather than react to her little dig, the man's gaze filled with excitement. The look on his face was the same as that night, just before he was arrested. "Vic and I made a deal. He agreed to use his contacts on the outside to find you, and his contacts on the *inside* to help get us the hell out of that shithole. In return, I told him if he brought you to me, I'd make sure you helped him with a little side job he's been planning."

Everyone wants something from me. Everyone except Parker.

Refusing to think about him for fear she'd break down into a blubbering mess, Quinn kept her focus on the conversation at hand. "A little prison quid pro quo, eh, Justin?" She wasn't surprised in the least. "And what exactly is it McMahon wants me to do?"

"Huh, uh." Justin shook his head. "Me first. Then Vic."

Of course. "Fine." A wave of dizziness hit, but a momentary pause rectified it almost instantly. "What is it *you* want me to do?"

"You're going to finish what we started."

What we...

"You can't possibly be serious." The look on his face said

otherwise. "Jesus Christ, Justin. You've been out of prison all of what..." Quinn stopped because she realized she wasn't actually sure when he'd escaped.

"A week and a half tomorrow." Justin sounded so proud of that fact.

"Think about that a minute." She really hoped he would. "You're already a fugitive from the law. Why the hell would you want to risk this newfound freedom of yours for another scam?"

"Because I have nothing!" His volatile temper made another appearance. "Because of *you*, I have no home, no car...no money. But I'm not stupid, Quinn. I know my ass needs to lay low. But disappearing from the Feds takes cash. And the only way to get the amount I need in the timeframe I have is to steal it. And you're going to help me do that."

Quinn started to shake her head, but the increased throbbing reminded her it was a bad idea. "I'm not helping you steal anything."

"Uh...yeah. You are."

"I said no."

"You don't have a choice, babe."

"You can't force me to do a hack, Justin." Quinn refused to believe he could. "So whatever this grand plan of yours is, count me out."

"See? This was always our problem." His shoulders shook with a huff. "You always thought you were calling the shots. Well newsflash, babe. You weren't. Not back then, and not now."

"Fine." She went for hypotheticals. "Let's say I do help you steal money from whatever target you've chosen. What about after?"

"Easy. You help me, I hand you over to Vic. And then, I disappear into the sunset."

"And when *Vic's* done with me?"

You already know.

"That's not my problem."

Anger replaced her earlier fear. ""Nothing ever is." She ground her teeth together. "So that's it? I do your dirty work, and you hand me over to your buddy? A man you know will kill me the second I finish whatever job he needs me to do?"

There was the tiniest flash of...*something*. But it vanished with a shrug of his shoulder. "Sorry, babe. I don't have a choice."

They were the same words he'd told her six years ago. Right before he tried to throw her to the wolves.

So Quinn decided to do a little throw-back herself.

Taking a cue from Agent Manning's speech from that same night, she kept her expression neutral and her eyes on his. "There's always a choice, Justin. I just hope you make the right one here."

Those words had changed her life once. Maybe they would do the same for him.

"Too late." Justin destroyed her hope that he'd do the right thing. "It's already been made."

In an unexpected move, he raised a hand to her face. Not to hit her like before, but rather brush some hair from her eyes. But Quinn pulled back just in time to avoid the unwanted contact.

"It's not too late," she tried again. "We can leave right now. You know who Parker is, so you know what he has a shit ton of money. I know he'll help you out if I ask. He *will!* So let's go." She grabbed his hand and began pulling him toward the door. "We can call him from the car."

"We can't." Justin planted his feet and pulled her back.

Quinn's body boomeranged; her upper half jolting forward as her forward motion was abruptly reversed. With their arms stretched into one continuous line, Justin showed the first signs of real emotion since stepping into the room.

"Justin, please—"

"You don't get it!" Frustration and fear clouded the blues in his eyes. "If I don't hand you over to Vic, I'm dead."

Quinn's heart fell all the way to her feet. "And if you do, it'll be me who dies."

The look on Justin's face said it all. He'd already put her death sentence into motion.

"You know how it is with guys like Vic." His throat worked. "Jobs like this...you can't leave any loose ends behind."

"He's right."

Both Quinn and Justin turned toward the door where a tall, broad-shouldered man staring back at them. Dark, almost black hair with slivers of silver at his temples. Square jaw and long, straight nose. A frame bigger than most but solid.

And eyes that were as cold as the black coal in their centers.

Victor McMahon.

"Vic!" Justin gave a nervous laugh. "Hey, man. I was just filling Quinn in on why she's here."

"I heard." McMahon sauntered over to where she stood. With an outstretched hand, gave a proper introduction. "Victor McMahon." He waited but when she didn't return the gesture, he let that hand fall back to his side. "It's a pleasure to finally meet you, Miss Wilder."

"Eh, you can call her Quinn." Her ex nudged the formidable man's arm. "

"Let me save you some time." She tightened her gut and pushed past her fear. "I'll tell you the same thing I told

Justin. I'm not stealing anything." Quinn looked him square in the eyes when she added. "Not for anyone."

A slow, sort-of-there smile formed on McMahon's face. "Justin told me you were strong-willed."

"That's one way to put it." The other man snorted. "I also told her you don't leave loose ends. That way, at least she knows what's coming."

Jesus. There once was a time when this man had listened to her deepest, darkest secrets. A time when they'd been as close as two human beings could get.

A time when he'd told her he loved her...and she'd believed him.

Quinn learned long ago there were only two things Justin loved. Himself and money. But the way he was talking about her death...

It was as if they'd been discussing something as mundane as the weather.

"I supposed you're right." McMahon nodded his agreement to Justin's so-called thoughtfulness. "A person *should* know when death is upon them."

The words had barely left the man's lips when he reached behind his back and pulled a gun.

Quinn gasped, her heart flying right out of her chest. *Please God, no!*

This couldn't be happening. Not now. Not when she and Parker were just getting started.

"Please don't do this."

Her low plea was drowned out by Justin's dramatic, "Whoah! Easy, big guy. I'll get her to do it, I swear. Besides, if you shoot her, we got no one to do the job and get us the money."

"You misunderstand, Justin. I'm not going to shoot Miss

Wilder." He slid that gun sideways, it's barrel pointing straight at Justin's chest.

"What?" Panic left the man's eyes wide, his confusion and fear palpable. "Dude, what the fuck are you doing? Put that thing down before someone gets hurt!"

"You said it yourself. A person should see death coming."

"Nah, man. Don't do this." Justin threw a hand up as if he could stop a bullet. "You can have it all, okay? I-I'll find another way to make money. Seriously, man. You don't have to do this. You know I'd never tell anyone about this."

Quinn's heart stopped as Victor's finger curled around the trigger. Seeing the slight move as well, Justin's eyes grew wide as saucers.

"Victor, wait!" the desperate man shouted.

At the same time, Quinn heard herself screaming, "Don't!"

But their objections had come a half-second too late.

Victor McMahon had already pulled the trigger, his bullet piercing Justin's heart on impact. Quinn watched in horror as his body jerked from the impact before crumbling to the floor below.

He was dead. *Dead.* And when Victor turned that gun back on her, Quinn knew this man would eventually kill her, too.

15

"Anything?"

Parker's fingers froze over the keyboard, his chest tightening with remorse. Rather than look up at the source of the question, he simply changed the focus of his eyes from the data on the screen in front of him to the reflection of the man standing behind him.

"You should be at home. With Sydnee."

Emotionless and wooden, even to him, his voice sounded unfamiliar.

"Who do you think sent me here?" Asher grunted slightly as he sat in the chair beside him.

Here was Charlie Team's headquarters in Richmond, where he'd been for the past two days.

That's how long it had been since that fucking picture of him and Quinn on his sailboat was leaked. It was the amount of time he'd spent hiding away in this damn conference room to avoid the paparazzi.

Reporters hounding him about that damn picture.

His lawyers were handling the issue, claiming the picture was a fake. Personally, Parker didn't give a rat's ass if his face—or in this case, his entire naked body—was splashed all over every news station and social media site in existence. But Quinn's?

She didn't deserve to be violated in that way. No woman did.

And once she was back safe in his arms, he was going to find the person who took that image. He would find them, and then...

I'm going to make sure they never take another one like it ever fucking again.

Meanwhile, Quinn's location and rescue had to remain his focus. As it had been for the past two days.

Two. Fucking. Days.

Parker knew the odds of finding a kidnapped victim alive decreased after the first 48 hours. And those chances continued to decline each hour after that.

He glanced at the tiny digital clock in his computers upper righthand screen. A quick calculation told him Quinn had been gone forty-eight hours and sixteen minutes.

Ah, Christ.

The guilt from not having been there to stop those bastards was worse than death itself. The inability to find the woman he loved slowly eating him alive from the inside out. And the guilt...

One of the last things he'd said to Quinn was a lie. Good intentions or not, that couldn't be the last thing he said to her. It *couldn't.*

This is all my fucking fault.

After Asher's gut-wrenching call—and what had felt like the longest flight of his entire life—Parker had broken land speed records to get back to his house.

He could still feel the crushing devastation that first glimpse of his damaged home had caused. Even now, as he worked tirelessly to find even the smallest of clues as to where Quinn could be, the unprecedented fear from knowing how close he'd come to losing the people he loved most in this world was a clear and constant presence.

"Syd said to tell you hi and that you needed to eat something and get some sleep," Asher spoke up again. "She also said if you ignored that, I was supposed to remind you she's a doctor and she knows what she's talking about."

From his periphery, Parker could see the other man staring at him expectantly, but he kept his gaze forward. He didn't have to see the other man's face to know what was there...

Bruises and scratches. Pain and regret. And Asher wasn't the only one who'd been hurt.

A mild concussion and a small, neatly placed row of stitches at Sydnee's hairline were the worst of her injuries. And each of the few times he'd talked to his childhood friend, the persistent woman had assured him she was fine.

But nothing about this was fine. A goddamn explosion blowing his house to fucking hell wasn't fine. His friends nearly *dying* wasn't fine.

And not knowing where Quinn was or if she was okay...

I'm so sorry, sweetheart. So fucking sorry.

That was the worst part of it all. The not knowing.

Not knowing where she'd been taken. If she'd been injured like his friends. Or worse, not knowing if she was even still alive...

If they wanted her dead, they wouldn't have taken her. She was taken for a reason.

Parker ran a wary hand down his face and scruff-covered jaw. He hadn't taken the time to shave or shower. Hadn't eaten. And minus a few unintentional minutes of sleep, he hadn't taken a break to rest.

Because every time he closed his eyes, he was right back there. In his car speeding away from that fucking prison, Asher's life-altering words replaying over and over on a loop.

They took her, Parker. She's gone.

Those words had sliced straight through his soul like a razor-sharp dagger. After skidding to the stop at the shoulder of the road he'd been on, Parker had listened in horror as Asher recounted what had gone down at his house.

They'd been in the Great Room talking when a bomb took out the room's west wall. Stunned by the blast, Asher had lost consciousness for a couple minutes, but it was all the time the bastards had needed.

With Quinn gone and no immediate way to help her, Asher's attention had gone where it was needed most...to Sydnee. He'd sat with her until the ambulance came, and once he knew his fiancée was going to be okay, Ash had tried calling him.

Multiple times.

But Parker had already handed over his phone to the intake officer at FCI and was already in that room waiting for a man who never showed.

"We'll find her, Park." Asher muttered beside him. "You just have to give it some time."

In an abrupt move, Parker shoved himself to his feet and paced along the front of the spacious conference room.

Seconds later—once he felt as if he could speak without ripping his well-meaning friend's head off—he reminded Asher of the reality of the situation.

"It's been two fucking days. Two *days* that Quinn's been out there somewhere, going through only God knows what. And all we've done is sit on our asses."

"I know it seems that way now, but—"

Parker lost what little patience he'd managed to muster up. Halting his steps, he turned and finally faced his friend for the first time since the man's arrival.

"I've gone through every second of my security footage from that day. I've watched it over and over again, convincing myself that the answer is there; I just haven't found it. But all it shows is what we already know. The dark van pulling up to my gate, two masked men dressed in black disabling the electronic lock, and then blowing a fucking hole in the side of my house." With a forceful huff, he added a sardonic, "Oh, and let's not forget the climactic ending where you see one of the bastards tossing Quinn's limp body into the back of that fucking van before the sons of bitches took off!"

His voice boomed through the air on that last part, getting louder and louder as the image he described became clearer and clearer in his mind. It was one he'd remember until his dying day.

"So we keep looking," Asher offered calmly. "And we don't stop until we find her."

That plan was all well and good, but...

"She needs me, Ash." The heartbreaking words cracked, the heat that had been there replaced by a desperate whisper. "She needs me, and I can't do a fucking thing to help her. *Me.*" Another sarcastic scoff. "Some genius I am, huh?"

A painful knot filled the base of his throat as tears stung

the corners of his eyes.

"I get it, man." Asher stood and walked slowly toward him, his haunted eyes clouded by his own hellish memories. "Everything you're feeling right now? It's the same shit I felt when Syd was taken from me."

Parker opened his mouth to deny the man's claim, but his friend wouldn't allow it.

"You feel helpless," Asher challenged. "Hopeless, even. Like you've lost the very best part of you, and you're terrified you'll never get it back." He stopped a few feet away. "But I'll tell you the same thing the guys told me. You've gotta keep your head on straight and your shit together. Because you're right. Quinn *does* need you and being pissed off at the world isn't going to do a damn thing to help us find her."

He wasn't pissed off at the world. That was part of the problem.

Parker dropped his hands back to his sides, his shoulders falling under the weighted pressure of guilt and regret. "I never should have gone to that fucking prison." He blinked away another round of threatening tears. "I should have been the one home with Quinn. It should have been *me* there, not you and Syd."

If he hadn't left her, they wouldn't have gotten hurt. And maybe...maybe Quinn would still be with him.

If she'd been with me, I wouldn't have lost her.

Asher took another step in his direction. "This isn't on you, Park. I know that shit's going through your head because it went through mine, too. But what happened to Quinn...to me and Syd...that wasn't your fault."

Parker looked through the other man, hearing his words but refusing to accept their truth. "If I'd told her the truth, she would have been with me." A decision he'd regret for the rest of his life.

"Goddamn it, Collins!" Asher's angry voice brought the man back into focus. "You were trying to *protect* her. You saw an opportunity to do that and did what you thought was best."

"That's just it. I did what *I* thought was best." He smacked a hard palm against his chest. "Just like I always do."

His friend frowned. "Okay, you lost me."

"I'm Parker Fucking Collins, remember? It's *always* about me. I mean, I'm a genius with computers, so I must know what's best for everyone in every situation, right? Syd, Homeland Security, Quinn..." He shook his head in disgust. "You were right, you know?"

"About..."

"When we first met, you thought I was an arrogant asshole, and you were right." He broke eye contact with a shrug. "I was so goddamn sure my plan would solve all her problems, when really I was being a selfish prick."

So fucking selfish.

"How the hell is offering that prick Reynolds five million dollars of your own money selfish?"

"Because I wasn't doing it for her." The tortured admission came as he met the other man's gaze again. "As long as Reynolds was in her life, as long as the bastard was still *terrorizing* her, our chances of starting any sort of future were zilch. So I thought..." Parker cleared his throat and tried again. "I thought paying the guy off would fix that."

"Wanting to start a life with the woman you love isn't selfish, Parker." Asher's expression softened. "You did what any one of us would've done. Hell, we've all fucked up where our women are concerned. Or have you forgotten the shit my entire team's been through the past couple years?"

He thought about the men of Charlie Team. Of their

women. Parker thought about the pain and terror they'd all faced at one point in the recent past.

Every man on that team had come damn close to losing their soul mates. He'd been there when a few had reached their breaking points, just like him. Had seen them so worn down—so fucking *defeated*—they'd nearly given up.

But Asher was right. He and his team...they hadn't given up. Instead, they pushed harder. Worked faster. They put their fear and grief aside, doing whatever it took to get their women back.

And those same military-trained operatives were the same men working diligently to help him find *his* woman.

Quinn needs you. You can't give up on her now.

"You can't give up hope, Park." Asher parroted his thoughts. "I know it's hard as hell, but you've got to keep the faith, brother. Faith in us. In Quinn." The man put a hand to one of Parker's shoulders and squeezed. "In yourself."

Parker stared back at his friend—his brother—and nodded. Because Ash was right. This wasn't the time to give up. This was the time to fight. For Quinn...and the future he prayed they'd get the chance to create.

"Thanks, Ash." He cleared the thick emotions from his throat. "I know you're right, I just..." A rough swipe of his hand over his unusually rugged jaw. "I've checked every avenue I can think of, and I've come up empty."

"What about Ryker?" Asher referred to RISC's Homeland handler. "His team find anything that could tell us where Reynolds would be?"

No way was the timing of the attack and Reynolds' escape a coincidence.

"Nothing." The two men remained seated at Parker's makeshift work station along the conference table's front end. "CCTV caught the asshole in a beat-up car a few blocks from the prison a week ago"—the day Warden Pollard had determined to be the day of Reynolds' escape—"but they lost him a mile later."

"I'm going to assume you've checked out that footage yourself."

"I did," he admitted without remorse. "But I saw the same thing they did. It's like the asshole vanished without a trace. So at this point, it's going to take a fucking miracle to figure out where—"

As if designed by divine intervention, Parker's computer dinged with a notification. Hopeful, both men turned, their attention drawn to the small rectangular message that had popped up on his screen.

"What's that?" Asher leaned an elbow against the conference table's edge to get a closer look.

But Parker was already reaching to click the dismissed MMO notification closed. "Nothing. Just someone in the online game I sometimes play wanting to send me a PM."

He clicked his cursor on the tiny X, and the pop-up disappeared.

"You get those a lot?"

"Sometimes." He shrugged. "People will send random messages to other higher-level players, wanting to either join their team, make a supply or weapons trade. Stuff like that."

A low grunt was the only response the non-gaming man gave.

"So like I was saying..." Parker continued, "Unless Reynolds screws up and manages to show his face somewhere, I don't know how the hell we're going to find him."

"And it's not like he has credit cards we can track," Asher agreed.

When another notification popped up—from a different

username he didn't recognize—he closed it as he spoke. "Exactly. Which means we've got nothing. And that's not me being negative or feeling sorry for myself, Ash. We literally have *nothing*."

His friend refrained from useless platitudes and remained quiet, for which Parker was thankful. And over the next several seconds, neither man uttered a single word.

Because what was there to say?

Fact was, they didn't have shit to go on, and unless something dropped in their laps, Quinn was as good as dead.

I'm not giving up on you, baby. But I need some help. Something to tell me where you are. Please, Quinn. Please, if there's any way to reach me...

His computer dinged with yet another fucking MMO message request, this time from *third* unrecognizable username. Parker's back teeth ground together as he moved his cursor toward the X.

Why the hell these guys had all chosen this moment to start bombarding him with requests was a mystery, but he wanted to reach through his screen, find the dickheads, and—

His index finger froze a millisecond before clicking the mouse. Removing his hand to avoid accidentally closing out the newest request, Parker leaned in closer.

"What's the matter?" Asher asked from the seat beside him. "You know that player or something?"

He studied the username with an expert eye... MNiPDiX.

Number one man? Number one cop? Ten years on the job?

One by one, Parker ran through every possible solution for the alpha-numeric name. But the more he considered, the more time he felt he was wasting.

"Mani-Pedi?"

He looked to his left. "Huh?"

"The username." Asher pointed to the screen. "Looks like Mani Pedi. Not sure what the X is for, but... I don't know." He settled back against his chair. "Just trying to think."

Mani Pedi...X. Why the X?

Personal chefs, mani-pedi spa days, designer clothes... That's you, Parker. But this isn't me.

His heart thumped hard. Could that be it? Was the X for the user's disdain for mani pedi's?

One way to find out...

Refusing to get his hopes up, Parker grabbed the sleek mouse and opened his dashboard in the MMO the message requests had originated from. Clicking open his messages, he immediately found the first two...

PERSCH3FX and DZ1NRCTHZX

"Holy shit." The explicative came out a disbelieving whisper.

"What?" Asher sat up straighter. "You got something?"

"You're a fucking genius," he declared. "Well, maybe. At least I think..." Parker licked his lips and turned to his friend. "Okay, it may just be the desperation, so...I need to know if I'm making something out of shit that isn't really there."

"I trust that big brain of yours, Park. Especially when it comes to all this gaming stuff." Asher's dark eyes shone with sincerity. "You say it's there, it probably is. But okay." He motioned to the screen. "Show me what you've got."

Swallowing back a sudden rush of emotion from the other man's heartfelt words, Parker straightened his spine and got to work. "Like I said, it could be nothing, but..."

Keeping the story short and to the point, he told Asher about the conversation between him and Quinn the day he'd surprised her. Luckily, Parker remembered what the frustrated woman had said to him...word for feisty word.

When he was finished, he pointed out the similarities.

"Quinn said she didn't do personal chefs." Parker pointed to one of the usernames...PERSCH3FX. "She doesn't do mani pedis." Another point toward MN1PD1X. "And she told me she doesn't do designer clothes." Final username...DZ1NRCTHZX.

"Holy shit, Park." Asher's widened gaze swung to his. "You really think she found a way to communicate to you through that game?"

"That's exactly what I think." Parker's fingers flew across the keyboard.

Clicking on the username linked to the most recent request, Parker used his hacking skills to find the proof he needed. Within seconds, he had it.

"It's her, Ash." He smacked an excited fist on the table, the screens and other equipment trembling in its wake. "Hot damn, it's really *her!*"

She's alive!

His Quinn was alive, and she was trying to tell him where she was.

"How can you be so sure it's Quinn?"

"See that there?" Parker pointed to a specific sequence in the midst of countless others. "That's a 32Ipp4. It's a personal I.P. address linked to a private network." He looked at his friend. "It's *Quinn's* private network."

"People can have their own networks?"

"Oh, yeah." More clicks filled the room as Parker did what he did best.

Watching the endless trove of code scroll past, Asher asked, "What are you doing?"

"Tracking the I.P." His fingers never stopped moving. "As

long as she stays logged on, I can use it to locate the originating computer, which will give us the coordinates of where she's being held."

"Why don't you just message her back through the game?"

"Thought of that, but I don't know how she's accessing it or who might be watching her. If I message back and her screen dings or shows a pop-up like mine did, it could give her away."

Both men knew what captors could do to their hostages when they got angry, and it wasn't a risk Parker was willing to take. Not with Quinn.

Never with her.

"This might take a couple extra steps, but it's something I've done a billion times."

"Homeland?"

"Among others." Parker nodded.

Blood rushed past his ears, his heart physically hurting from the force of its beats, but he didn't dare stop. He was close. So fucking close he could *taste* it. A few more keystrokes, and...

The air left his lungs in a rush. Sitting back, he let his fingertips slip from the keyboard as he stared at the screen, hardly able to believe what he was seeing.

In spite of her being held against her will—despite having gone through God only knows what over the last two days—the brilliant, resourceful woman had found a way to guide him straight to her.

"Park?" Asher's tone was that of concern. "What's wrong? Did it not work?"

Parker shook his head, but... "It worked." He turned to his brother and smiled. "I know where she is."

16

QUINN TYPED OUT ANOTHER RANDOM, non-working code into the selected location and hit enter. The same as she had the last billion-and-one times over the last forty-eight hours.

Justin's dead. He just...killed him. Like he was nothing. Like he's going to do to you.

The numbers and letters on the screen blurred together behind a well of tears, but she blinked them away. Crying wasn't going to do anything but piss Victor off. And after what he did to Justin...

Focus, Q. Keep up the act and give Parker time to figure it out.

Thoughts of Parker threatened to bring on more tears, but the voice in her head was right. She needed to stay focused on the plan and not do anything that might draw suspicion from her captor.

A plan that she'd had to wait until now to implement because, until a couple hours ago, Victor's hired muscle had stood nearby, watching her every move. Today, however, he must have decided she could be trusted to follow instruction, because he'd moved the other man out into the hall to stand guard.

She hadn't acted right away for fear it was some sort of trick. A test that, should she fail, would mean certain death.

But as the minutes passed by, the more confident Quinn became that she was safe to move. So she'd moved *fast*.

And now there was nothing more to do than wait and pray.

This has to work. It has to.

In order for her plan to be a success, three things had to happen. Parker had to see the messages, realize what they meant, and get to her before Victor put a bullet through her heart.

The first two didn't worry her. Her man was as smart as they came. But that third one...

Please see the messages, Park. See them and come to me. Just like you did before.

Quinn looked at the tiny clock in the upper right corner. It had been an hour and a half since she'd sent the first one, and not knowing whether he'd seen any of them yet was driving her mad.

Inside only, of course. Outwardly, she'd kept the same emotionless expression she'd worn since that gun was fired and Justin took his last breath.

Victor hadn't wasted any time after that, either. He'd unceremoniously grabbed her arm and yanked her right out of that room, leaving the man he'd just killed where he lay.

After forcing her outside and into his car, the asshole had kept his gun pointed at her gut while the man from the plane drove. Several miles and turns later, Victor had ordered him to pull into the lot connected to the building they were in now.

A stark difference from where she'd originally been held, the three-story flat-roofed lodge was in relatively good condition. But from the overgrown weeds and tilted for-sale sign, the former tourist spot appeared to have been empty for quite some time.

The owners had apparently decided to keep the electricity connected, probably so it would be ready for possible showings. It was also a plausible reason Victor had chosen this particular building.

Computers required power, and for the job he'd ordered her to do, Quinn needed a bunch.

She could hardly believe it when the man had shared his reasons for going along with Justin's scheme to nab her.

Apparently when they were in prison together, Justin had gone on and on about how she'd set him up, and how he couldn't wait to get out to make her pay. But in all of Justin's ramblings, what Victor heard was that his cell mate had a connection to the hacking world.

One that could handle the job he'd been plotting ever since the judge handed down his sentence.

So—to hear Victor tell it, anyway—he'd listened patiently, pretending to care about poor Justin's bad luck and conniving girlfriend. And little by little, he planted the seeds of what would eventually become a plan to use the user.

Justin used Victor's connections in the FBI to find where she lived. They waited until they knew their plan was a go, and then Vic's guy began leaving those toying, terrifying notes.

And when Victor and Justin had everything in place on the inside—courtesy of a dirty guard with an eye for smooth-talking criminals—they managed to escape.

Hacking the system and switching your release dates. Well done, Justin. Well freaking done.

But what Justin didn't know was, the entire time he'd been using Victor to get to her...good ol' Vic had been using *him* for the same reason. Only he didn't want Quinn to steal for him.

He wanted revenge.

That's what Victor's demand entailed. Revenge against everyone and anyone who'd played a part in his arrest and conviction.

The Feds who'd made the case against him. The prosecutor who'd destroyed his own attorney in court. His own attorney for allowing himself to *be* destroyed in court. The judge who'd sentenced him to a federal prison.

Victor had a list of names, social security numbers, birth dates...everything she needed to destroy a person's life. And that wasn't all.

The final task she'd been given...the one she'd spent the last day and a half pretending to do...

Write a malicious code and sneak it into the software used by Sacred Securities—the cyber security company whose program had been used to catch Victor's illegal ways. But he didn't want to corrupt their entire mainframe, as she'd expected to hear.

He wanted her to gain access to their clientele data so he could steal information remotely. And from what she'd been able to see during her pseudo hacking the last sixteen hours —because he refused to let her rest until the job was done— Quinn surmised Victor would potentially be able to steal millions...if not billions.

All while destroying the company he blamed for his downfall.

Lord forbid anyone take responsibility for their own actions anymore.

She had to admit, it was a brilliant plan, really. One Quinn was fairly confident she could do. Not that she was going to tell Victor that.

Especially when the gun he kept reminding her he had would end her life the second she finished the job.

Gotta make the asshole think you're making progress...just at a snail's pace.

So far, she'd managed to fool the son of a bitch. But how long would that last?

The question had just rolled between her ears when the door to the room opened, and Victor walked inside. With paper cup of what smelled like fresh coffee, he kept his tone brisk as he moved toward her.

"Where are we?" He sat the steaming cup on the table in front of her.

"I'm still working on it." Quinn lifted the hot beverage to her lips, knowing it was expected. But it was dangerously hot, so she removed the plastic lid and left it uncovered to cool.

You'll sleep when it's done.

Those had been his words, but she wasn't stupid enough to think he meant them. Not in the usual sense, anyway. No, the sleep Victor had really been referring to was much more permanent.

"It's taking too long." An angry growl.

"I told you when I first started this wasn't a simple hack. It's not like this is something a bored teenager in his mommy's basement can pull off. If you want it done, you're going to have to give me time."

She'd already fucked over the other targets on his list. Savings accounts, credit scores...if she could access it, Victor wanted it destroyed.

And she'd done it. Quinn had gone against everything she ever stood for and with a few clicks of the keys, she'd ruined those people's lives. All because they'd done their jobs.

I'll make it right. If I make it out of this, the first thing I'm going to do is fix everything I've broken.

But even as she thought it, Quinn realized the silent promise was a lie. Because the first thing she was going to do —one thing she'd been *living* for—was to kiss Parker like crazy.

And *then* she'd tell him she loved him.

"It's been two fucking days!" Victor's pissed off voice echoed around her, his shooting hand reaching around to his lower back.

"Do you want it done right or not at all?" She swung her gaze to his. "Trust me, no one wants this to be over more than me. But if this job were easy, you wouldn't have needed me to do it."

"Maybe I don't need you." He brought that gun around, it's barrel pointing right at her head. "Maybe I'll find someone else to do the job instead."

"Good luck." Quinn scoffed. "There are about three other hackers in the world who could pull this off. Two are in Japan, and the other's in France. So you can shoot me and try your luck finding one of them...or you can quit hovering over me and let me do the damn work."

In actuality, there were four. But she wasn't about to put Parker on this maniac's radar.

Victor looked at the screen and back to her. "Just remember. You try to contact your boyfriend or anyone else, I'll know."

"How could I possibly do that when you blocked every route of communication possible on this thing?"

It was impressive, really. Something she guessed Justin had done in preparation of his newest master get-rich-quick plan. Lucky for her, she'd known a way around it.

Guess you weren't as smart as you thought you were, eh, Justin?

"You're right." Victor seemed momentarily convinced. With a one-eighty change in demeanor, he slid the gun back in place. "My apologies, Miss Wilder. I'll leave you to your work. And if you need anything...more coffee...food... restroom...Richard is right outside."

"Thank you," she muttered low.

She hadn't forgotten the goon was out there, but it was nice to have a face to go with the name. And what a fitting name it was.

Dick the dick.

Hiding a smirk, she tried another sip of the blistering brew, but it was still too hot to be safe.

Without another word, Victor turned to leave. He was halfway between her and the door when a loud blast shook the entire building.

The table jiggled, a splash of hot coffee burning her hand as it spilled over the jostling rim. Quinn gasped, instinctively pulling her hand to her chest, and just like that...a very specific memory of Parker filled her mind's eye.

He'd been standing in Delta Team's safe house kitchen, fixing coffee and talking on the phone. She'd stopped at the room's entrance, too entranced by the breathtaking man to look away.

Eventually, she'd managed to find her voice and had greeted him with a soft salutation. And that's when *he'd* been the one to fall under a spell.

Just as she'd done with him, Parker had stared at her from across the room. The expression on his face had been that of wonder and awe... The exact same things she'd been feeling when she'd been watching him.

Quinn could see it now. She could finally admit what,

buried in the back of her head she'd already known...that was it. That was the moment she realized she was in love.

Only she'd fought it. Tooth and nail, heart and soul... Quinn had spent those first few days denying even the slightest inkling of that fluttery feeling that had threatened to consume her.

It was like being stuck on a never-ending roller coaster, her emotions pingponging back and forth between excitement and anger. Fear and denial. And so much lust she'd nearly gone insane with need.

But then he'd surprised her with that horrible, wonderful idea. They'd talked...argued...and then...

They'd made love.

You have to make it through this, Quinn. You have to survive so you can tell him how you feel. A person deserves to know when they are loved.

"What the hell?"

Victor's alarmed voice snapped Quinn back to her current situation. The slight stinging in her reddened hand reminding her of the nearby explosion.

Parker!

Instinctively, she turned toward the door. Was it possible? Had he gotten her message? Was he here?

Hope like no other bloomed inside her chest, but...

What if it's not him? What if one of this man's enemies tracked him down, and they've come for their own revenge?

"You okay, Boss?" Dickhead Dick barged into the room.

"I'm fine. What the fuck was that?"

"Explosion. Sounded like it was coming from the west end of the building."

"Go see what it is."

"What about her?" The big jerk looked her way.

"Let me worry about that. Now go. Call as soon as you know what the fuck just happened."

"Yes, Sir."

The other man turned and left as Victor marched angrily toward her. In a flash, Quinn was back in her kitchen...and her attacker was closing in.

She focused on her periphery. There was no bottle of wine handy this time, but there was something almost as good.

Quinn's gaze shot back to the man heading in her direction. Just like in her kitchen that night, she forced her mind to clear and her breathing to calm. And when Victor was standing in the exact right spot...

In one fluid motion, she grabbed the cup and flung its steaming contents straight at the man's face.

"Ah!" Victor's hands flew to his face, his eyes squeezed tightly as he screamed and writhed in pain.

Run!

With her captor still working to regain his vision, Quinn took off in a dead sprint. When she got out into the hall, her hair flung painfully against her cheeks as she looked for a clear direction she should take.

As if God himself were listening to her thoughts, a round of gunfire came from somewhere to her left. Not one to typically run *toward* that sort of thing, she took off down the hall to her right.

"Fucking bitch!" Victor yelled after her.

She could hear the man's heavy footfalls as he began to give chase.

Quinn pushed her legs to move faster. Forced her muscles to work harder. And she was only a few yards away from the door at the very end of the hall when she was slammed into from behind.

"Ah!" She cried out, her body landing with a loud thud beneath Victor's.

Quinn hit and kicked and twisted as hard as she could, but the asshole was too big. Too strong.

Her attacker flipped her over onto her back, his eyes and face red from the second-degree burns her little gift had given him.

"I'll fucking kill you!" He raised a fist, preparing to punch her in the face.

She flinched, doing her best to brace for the pain she knew was coming. Only it never did because at the last second someone yelled...

"Let her go, McMahon!"

Quinn froze. That hadn't been Parker's voice, but it was one she recognized. One that sent a rush of relief flowing through her.

"Asher!" she screamed at the top of her lungs.

She was in the middle of thinking how thankful she was that he hadn't been killed protecting her when Victor's lightning-fast move took her completely off guard.

Yanking her up off the floor, he pulled her body in front of his. With a painful arm across her chest and a gun to her head, he began walking them backward.

"Don't come any closer, or I'll shoot!" he warned Parker's friend.

His friend who looked like a deadly killer with his all-black combat gear—including a protective vest, thigh holster, and a very large automatic rifle pointed straight in her direction.

He's not aiming at you.

"You shoot me, you can kiss your plan goodbye," Quinn reminded Victor. A second later, she heard...

"Listen to her, McMahon! You hurt her; you lose the only leverage you have!"

"Leverage that won't do me a damn bit of good if I'm dead!"

"So let's talk about this!" Asher yelled back.

But he was wasting his breath...

Victor had already reached the door she'd so desperately been trying to get to. In an awkward fumble of moves, he transferred his pistol into the other hand, held her close, and opened the door.

Quinn felt herself being pulled back again, and just before that door snicked closed, she thought she heard Parker shouting her name.

17

"*QUINN!*" Parker took off in a dead sprint down the hall.

His legs burned with his efforts, working harder and faster than he could ever remember as he ran toward the woman he loved...and Victor McMahon.

That's right, asshole. I know who you are.

Thanks to a last-minute call he'd received just before take-off. In the interest of full-disclosure—a.k.a., in the interest of covering his own ass— Warden Pollard had called with a bit of interesting news where Reynolds was concerned.

Apparently Quinn's ex wasn't the only inmate who'd escaped FCI. A second man—one Victor G. McMahon— had also been mistakenly released earlier that same day.

From the mugshot Parker had found while researching the crooked bastard on the flight here, there was no doubt in Parker's mind. McMahon was the same man currently holding the woman Parker loved hostage.

At fucking gunpoint.

From what Pollard had revealed, a female guard had come forward to confess her part in the prison break. With her guilty conscience getting the best of her, the foolish woman had spilled it all...

How her sexual relationship with Reynolds had begun a few months back. The ways the charming bastard convinced her the love he'd claimed to feel for her was real. How, after sweet-talking her pants off yet again, Reynolds had convinced her to sneak him into the guard's station so he could use the computer.

Using the lovestruck guard's login, Reynolds accessed the inmate data base and changed his and McMahon's release dates. The next morning—their release times set two hours apart to avoid looking too suspicious—both bastards had been escorted outside as free men.

Now they were here. Or at the very least, McMahon was here. And he'd just pulled Quinn through that fucking door.

Goddamnit!

Parker tried to focus on the positives. Quinn was alive and—from the sliver of a glance he'd gotten before she disappeared—she looked to be okay. But he knew better than most how quickly situations like this could turn, so he wasn't about to stop. Not now.

Not when he was this close.

His trigger finger itched as he ran, more than ready to end anyone and everyone who'd played a part in Quinn's abduction. Truth be told, McMahon would already be dead if Parker'd had a clear shot. But the way the asshole had been holding his hostage...

I couldn't take the chance. Couldn't risk hurting her.

He finally reached the door and—

"What the hell, man?" Asher caught up to him quickly. "I thought I told you to stay back."

"Just like you did when Sydnee was taken from you?" He

threw the man's past back in his face. It was a low blow, he knew. But damn it, they were wasting *time!*

Time Quinn didn't have.

Parker's palm met with the cool metal of the door's knob. He started to turn it but was forced to stop when a gloved hand covered his with a firm grip.

"Goddamn it, Collins. Wait!"

"For what?" His seething gaze darted to Asher's.

"Them, for starters." A tilt of the other man's head had showed the other members of Charlie Team heading in their direction. "Look, I get that you want Quinn safe. We all do. But you can't just blindly run into a situation without a plan of attack."

"You want a plan?" Parker challenged. "Fine. How about this? I'm going through this door, I'm going to run up those stairs, and I'm going to do whatever it takes to get her back. *That's* my fucking plan!"

"Sounds like a really shitty one to me."

Trace Winters—former Delta Force hero and leader of Charlie Team—closed in. Walking behind him were Kellan McBride, Greyson Frost, and Rhys Maddox.

Parker studied the deadly men as they came to a stop where he stood.

With his tall, muscular build, Winters was a force to be reckoned with. Given their training and lethal backgrounds, so were the others.

McBride was a former Marine, and the man's toned stature, clean-cut look, and knowing gaze showed it. Frost, on the other hand, looked intimidating as hell.

With his large, muscular build, long brown hair, and intelligent eyes, the former SEAL was as good with computers as Parker. And despite his stone-cold killer looks, the man's smile and kind demeanor gave away his gentle-giant heart.

Maddox, on the other hand...

The former Air Force Pararescuman was about the complete opposite of Frost in every way. Built more like a sculpted runner, the stoic man kept his nearly black hair short and neat. His unreadable expression typically fixed... except when talking about his fiancée.

But Parker didn't care what these guys looked like or if they ever smiled. For him, it was about what they stood for...

Protection. Safety. Justice.

Those were the things the men of RISC were about. And for them, it didn't matter that Parker wasn't an official part of Charlie Team.

These highly trained operatives hadn't hesitated to help him when asked. Neither had Hunt, Brody, or the rest of Delta Team, who were currently clearing the top two floors.

So far, there'd only been one known threat apart from McMahon. But Ash had taken the bulky bastard out shortly after they'd made entrance.

Justin Reynolds was still nowhere to be seen.

I'll find you, too, asshole.

"You should listen to Cross." Winters stared him down. "You go running up those stairs; you'll probably get your ass shot."

"I don't care." He really didn't.

"Well that's a really stupid way of thinking." Maddox looked over at him as if he'd lost his damned mind.

"Seriously, Collins. I'd listen to them if I were you." Greyson arched a brow. "I mean, have you ever been shot? 'Cuz that shit hurts like a—"

"Okay!" Parker raised a hand to stave off more reasons why he was being a dumbass. "Jesus, you've made your point, all right?" He released the knob and stepped back. "This is your show, I get it. Just...tell me what we're going to do to keep that bastard from getting away."

"According to the building's blueprints, those stairs will give us access to the second and third floors, as well as the roof." Winters' tone oozed authority. "Delta's already working to clear two and three, so we're going to head to the roof in a single-file line. And your ass stays in the *back.*"

"I don't give a shit if I'm first or last, Trace." Another honest response. "I just want to get my *ass* up those fucking stairs before that son of a bitch hurts Quinn." *Or worse.*

With a shared look of understanding, Winters used hand motions to alert the other men before they entered the stairwell and began their ascent.

Single file...with his ass in back.

Every step Parker climbed brought him closer to Quinn. They also ramped up the fear icing through his veins.

For as long as he lived—which would hopefully be longer than just the next five minutes—he'd never get the image of that bastard McMahon holding a gun to her pretty head.

It had only been a glance, a fleeting glimpse of blonde hair and wide, wild eyes. But he'd seen her.

Right before that door pulled shut, he'd *seen* her. His Quinn. His everything.

And she was fucking terrified.

You kill her; you're a dead man.

The murderous vow wasn't one Parker made lightly. Today. Tomorrow. It didn't matter.

If McMahon did the unthinkable and Quinn didn't make it out of this alive, Parker would send him to his maker without a wink of sleep being lost.

It's going to be okay. You're almost there. She's going to be okay.

Almost on cue, Asher came to an abrupt stop in front of him. Parker halted his steps, the sound of his own frantic heartbeat filling his ears as he waited for Winters' silent order to proceed.

A quick glimpse at the gun in his hands reminded him this wasn't about revenge. Did he want to be the one to end McMahon for good? Absofuckinglutely. But what he *needed* was for Quinn to survive.

Just a little longer, sweetheart. We're here, and we've got you.

Parker adjusted the tight hold he had on his Glock's textured grip. Little known fact about America's Most Eligible Bachelor...

I've been trained for the worst...by the best.

Between the time he'd spent with Asher and the guys at the team's private shooting range, and the official training he'd been given courtesy of Jason Ryker at Homeland when he first signed on as a freelance consultant, he was more than a little knowledgeable when it came to basic weaponry and combat.

He also understood the vast difference between the training he'd had, and the experience Charlie Team brought to the table. So rather than shove his way to the front of the line like he wanted to, Parker forced his lungs to move steadily as he waited for the signal to move.

Thankfully he didn't have to wait long.

Winters' raised fist pointed to the door. Silent assignments were handed out to each man, and after receiving nods of understanding from his team, Winters grabbed the metal door's long, silver handle and pushed.

Moving as one, each man let their training kick in as they made their way onto the roof. Upon their initial breach,

Winters went high and right, while Kellan swung his weapon low and to the left. With the immediate clear, both men swiftly made room for the others to go through the door.

A cool breeze slapped Parker in the face as he stepped onto the roof, the sound of slowly moving water reaching his ears. He gave the roof a panoramic sweep, the South Branch Chicago River flowing lazily along the property's edge.

When he and the teams had first arrived, he'd noticed the unique architecture, and how the building's entire southern half had been designed to hang suspended several feet over the frigid river below.

But he couldn't tell that from his current vantage point. He also couldn't see Quinn.

She's not here!

Parker's gut tightened with the thought that their target had somehow gotten away. But then...

"Fucking bitch!"

Every man there swung their attention to the right, where the building's massive ventilation system was positioned several feet away. McMahon's angry voice seemed to have come from somewhere behind it.

Gotcha, asshole.

He and the others adjusted their stances to prepare for their approach. Walking shoulder-to-shoulder this time, Parker and the members of Charlie Team covered the distance to the HVAC system with swift, purposeful steps.

This was it. Just a few more feet were all that separated him from Quinn. From his *life*. They just needed to find a clear line of sight to McMahon. Once that happened...

"Ah!" A feminine cry of pain.

Parker's foot was moving before he'd given it any

conscious thought, but a rough fist to his bicep stopped him. He shifted his gaze to his left and found Asher shaking his head.

A silent reminder to think with his brain not his heart.

Shit. The man was right. He had to play this smart.

For Quinn.

With a curt dip of his chin, Parker let his friends take the lead, and together the group of six made their way to the north side of the massive metal unit. Splitting them up evenly, Winters motioned for McBride and Frost to follow him around the east side, while Parker, Asher, and Maddox went west.

His heart raced with adrenaline and pounded with fear. But even as he acknowledged the terror growing exponentially with each new breath, Parker knew Quinn's best chance of survival were the men marching with him now.

More sounds of a struggle ensued before he heard her sweet, scrappy voice...

"So much for your little plan, eh, Vic?" Quinn taunted her captor. "I mean, look around you. Do you see a lot of options here? 'Cuz I sure don't."

Jesus Christ. "Is she *trying* to get herself killed?" he spoke only low enough for Asher to hear.

Rather than agree, Asher leaned back with an unexpected whisper of his own. "In case I forget to mention it later, I really hope you marry that woman."

Despite their current situation, Parker's lips twitched with a sideways smirk. "That's the plan, brother." Or part of it, anyway.

Get Quinn to safety. Figure out where that asshat Reynolds is and deal with him. Take her home...er...not home. It blew up, remember? A hotel. Take her to a hotel and make love to her until some of this fucking fear leaves you...

That was his new plan. And once each of those goals had been reached...

I am absolutely going to ask her to marry me.

After nearly losing her twice, there was no way in hell he was letting her get away from him again.

His friend nudged him with his elbow, giving him a questioning thumbs up.

Shaking his future plans away, Parker responded with a nod of his head and a thumb of his own. Hell yeah, he was ready. More than.

Don't worry, sweetheart. We've got you now.

Maddox and Asher straightened their spines, their weapons held steady in preparation. With his own gun held tight in his fist, Parker pushed away all thoughts of failure as he and the others cleared the southwest corner of the metal structure.

And then he saw her.

Standing too damn close to the roof's elevated edge, Victor McMahon stood as he had downstairs. With the barrel of his gun pressed against her temple and his other arm locked tightly around Quinn's chest, the son of a bitch was using her as a human shield.

Again.

He didn't dare look at her. If he did, if Parker would see the utter terror he knew she had to be feeling. He was afraid the fiery rage billowing up inside him would win.

So he kept his sights on McMahon...and that fucking gun.

"Put your weapon down and let the girl go!" Winters' barked order came from Parker's left.

Every man there had their own guns pointed directly at the piece of shit's head. Problem was the guy wasn't that much taller than Quinn.

No matter where they were standing, there wasn't a single clean shot between the six of them.

"Stay back, or I'll kill her!" McMahon yelled back.

Half a beat later, Quinn shouted for them to, "Shoot him!"

"My finger's already on this trigger," their target warned. "You shoot me, my hand will flex, and her brains will be all over this fucking roof!"

Parker refused to let the image those words painted enter his head. Instead, he kept his gun steady, and his gaze focused.

"There's nowhere to go, McMahon!" Kellan pointed out. "The only move you have is to drop that gun and let her go."

"I can't!" The panicked man shook his head wildly. "I can't go back to prison."

"It's either that or a body bag," Maddox didn't bother sugar-coating the guy's options. "Your choice."

"What the hell are you waiting for?" Quinn's angry voice traveled with the chilly breeze. "Just shoot him already!"

Parker did look at her then, his body becoming tense even as his heart filled. Her cheek and eye were bruised, the skin near her jaw reddened from what he assumed was her most recent blow. But even as he fought the urge to throw caution to the wind for the sake of revenge, he realized there was something missing.

Something he'd expected to see in her reflective gaze.

She's not scared anymore.

The fear he'd seen earlier was gone. Her heart stopping gaze no longer wide with terror or wild with hysteria. Instead Quinn's baby blues were razor sharp, their intense gaze remaining locked onto his.

She wants you to do it. She wants you to shoot McMahon.

Except he couldn't. Not without potentially shooting her

in the process. And that was something he would never, ever—

"I won't go back!" McMahon screamed as he swung his gun in Parker's direction.

At the same time, Quinn turned as much as she could to the right, jabbing her elbow backward as hard as she could while simultaneously reaching for the gun.

No!

A wild shot rang out, but no one returned fire because they *still* didn't have a clean shot. And McMahon knew it.

The guy was like a caged animal. Cornered by his prey and desperate in his search for a way out. Only this asshole wasn't looking for a way out.

Not anymore.

McMahon knew this was it for him, and from the determined look in his eyes, the prick planned to take as many of them down before he died. So he continued fighting Quinn for control of the gun.

Back and forth, the two pushed and pulled and twisted in their efforts. Shouts of harsh orders came at McMahon from all directions, but Parker didn't say a single word.

With his gun trained and his eyes laser focused, he saw only the man he was preparing to kill.

This wasn't a video game, and he wasn't sitting in the safety of his mansion on the beach. This was real life with a real bad guy. And gripped tightly in his hand was a real fucking gun.

Real gun, real bullets, asshole.

Ignoring everything else around him but his target, Parker adjusted his stance and steadied his breathing. He watched as McMahon moved this way and that, refusing to take his eyes off the dickhead for even a second.

But he should have.

If he'd been paying better attention to Quinn, he would've seen the fateful decision in her eyes. Might have had the chance to stop her. To keep her from risking it all to protect him and the others.

But he hadn't. Not until it was too late.

Parker was still standing there, weapon pointed and his trigger finger ready when Quinn turned to him. It was only a split second, so quickly he missed that first soulful glance. But the move caught his eye just in time to catch a glimpse of her sad, loving stare.

Quinn's lips parted. She mouthed the words *I love you*. Parker's heart exploded with conflicting emotions, and then...

It happened.

He was standing there—they were all just *standing* there —waiting for the first chance to safely intervene when the woman who'd somehow become his other half did the unthinkable.

In one fluid motion, Quinn turned and threw her body's entire weight against McMahon's center. The unexpected move sent the man's center of gravity spiraling, and as he stumbled back, he tried like hell to find purchase with his loafered feet.

"Quinn!" Parker's feet moved in record time across the tar-patched roof.

He didn't think about Charlie Team. He didn't think of his training or worry about getting struck by a stray bullet. He didn't think about *anything* other than getting to Quinn.

But he was too late. McMahon had already tripped over the roof's shallow ledge, and the greedy man was already falling...

And he'd taken Quinn with him.

"*No!*" Parker watched helplessly as she and the other

man flailed through the air. The oxygen in his lungs ceased to exist when he witnessed the love of his life splash forcefully into the frigid water below.

"Holy shit!" Asher came to a stop beside him. "Ah, Christ!"

Winters began barking orders, he and the others taking off for the door. Asher started to follow but stopped when he realized Parker wasn't hot on his tail.

"Collins, let's go!" The other man faced him.

"You go." He shoved his gun into his back waistband before pulling off his shoes and socks and tossing them to the side. "I'll meet you down there."

"What the hell are you—"

The disruptive sound of Velcro being ripped apart filled the space between them as he worked to remove his protective vest. "The fuck you think I'm doing? I'm going in after her."

"Are you mad? That water has to be thirty-five, forty degrees. If you're lucky."

"Exactly. Which means she has about thirty minutes before her hypothermia reaches potentially lethal levels."

And he refused to waste a single fucking second of that time arguing with his friend.

"Christ, man. Think about what you just said. If you go into that water, you'll expose yourself to that very same risk!"

"I know what I'm doing, Ash." Parker slipped the heavy vest up over his head before dropping it next to his shoes.

"Really? Because I'm pretty sure you've lost your damned mind."

No. He'd lost Quinn. And there wasn't a force strong enough to keep him from going to her.

With Asher's continued pleas falling on deaf ears, Parker walked over to ledge, climbed on top, and... He jumped.

The initial weightlessness took a second to get used to, but as gravity continued pulling him toward the water at a high rate of speed, his days of swim meets and dive competitions came rushing back with a vengeance.

As the top medal earner three straight years in high school and a year at MIT, Parker expertly gauged the distance between him and the river's surface. Best he could, he straightened his body into a tight, sleek line.

Toes pointed, chin up, arms and hands plastered to his sides.

Feet first, he hit the water with a loud, unceremonious splash. The breathtaking temps never even registered until he was completely submerged.

Kicking vigorously, Parker forced his way back to the top, his desperate screams for Quinn leaving his throat just as his mouth broke through the surface. He ignored his labored breaths and shivering bones and swung his dampened gaze in every direction.

"Quinn!" He shouted her name again.

Water splashed against his neck and chin as he kept tread, skimming the barely-moving current for any signs of life. Sheer panic threatened to stop his heart when he found none.

"Quinn!"

Ah, God. Please, don't take her. Please!

"Qui—"

"There!"

Parker spun his body through the water to face the river's bank. Filling a large chunk of the far-away grass stood Asher, his teammates, and the men of Delta Team. And they were all pointing toward something behind him.

"Behind you!" Asher shouted.

Using his arms as paddles, he spun back around in time to see Quinn's blonde hair disappear beneath the water.

No!

He began to swim in that direction, his eyes never losing sight of where he'd last seen her. Muscles burned and his lungs felt like they were on fire from the cold, but he didn't dare stop. When he got to the place Quinn had gone under, Parker didn't hesitate to do the same.

Drawing in a deep, deep breath, he closed his eyes and mouth and dipped into the deadly abyss. He opened his eyes, the dark, murky water nearly impossible to penetrate.

At first, he thought he'd lost her again. The fear of losing her damn near paralyzing in its strength. Yet he refused to give up.

Needing a breath, he pushed himself back through the surface just long enough to fill his lungs again. Parker went down again, the fierce need to save her pushing him on.

Seconds passed as his desperate search continued, and just when he was starting to consider the possibility that he'd failed...

There!

Movement to his left caught his eye. He swam toward it, the shocking image became clearer with each new stroke and kick.

McMahon was still alive. The bastard had his back to Parker and his meaty hands on Quinn. The two were struggling, each doing their best to push the other's head beneath the surface.

It was truly a fight to the death, and there could only be one winner. And he was going to make damn sure the right person came out on top.

Remembering the gun still tucked between his soaked

waistband and his lower back, Parker carefully approached McMahon from behind. The son of a bitch was so busy trying to kill Quinn, he didn't realize the new threat behind him.

He reached around with one hand, his other arm and both legs keeping his form as steady as possible while his frozen fingers wrapped around the weapon's rubbery grip.

Despite having been submerged, the weapon had been designed to fire regardless. But as Parker lifted it against the water's pressure and pointed it at the back of the man's head, a sliver of doubt almost caused him to hesitate.

Almost.

Ignoring the burning in his starving lungs, Parker did a last-second check on Quinn's position. Confident she wasn't at risk of being hit by a through-and-through, he pressed the tip of his barrel to the back of McMahon's head, curled his finger around the trigger, and squeezed.

The muffled shot bubbled out, the water around him darkening with the man's blood, brains, and bone. But Parker paid no attention to that. He was already pulling Quinn to the surface.

They broke through together, her gasps and coughs like music to his ears. If she was coughing, that meant she was breathing, and *that* meant she was still alive.

She won't be for long if you don't get her sweet ass out of this water.

So that's exactly what he did.

Though it took longer than he'd have liked, Parker eventually got them both over to the water's edge. While Delta kept watch a few feet away, the men of Charlie Team were right there waiting to pull them both to safety.

In a whirlwind of activity, he and Quinn were separated as the others rushed to their aid.

"Here." Asher wrapped a blanket around Quinn's shoulders. "The other team had these stashed in the back of their SUVs."

Shaking from head-to-toe, she pulled the thick material closed beneath her chin. "Th-thank...y-you."

"Ambulance is on the way." Winters thrust a second blanket in Parker's direction. "Hunt put in a call to their team's CPD contact." He helped reposition the welcomed sheath. "Apparently Delta Team has the same sort of agreement with their local law enforcement as we do with ours, which means we control whose names are included in the official report"—his pointed gaze bounced from Parker to Quinn, and back again—"and whose aren't."

He gave the man in charge a shaky nod. "Ap-ppreciate that."

Winters continued the after-action update, but Parker was too busy staring at his future to really listen.

Standing a few feet away, Quinn was dripping wet as Kellan and Asher hovered protectively nearby. Her lips were blue, she had a black eye and swollen jaw, and her teeth were chattering so loudly he could hear them.

And she was hands down, without a doubt, the single most beautiful thing he'd ever seen.

I almost lost her for good, this time.

Unable to keep from it a second longer, Parker ignored Winters' after-action report and shrugged the blanket from his shoulders. Letting it fall to the ground, he covered the distance between him and Quinn in four long strides.

The men standing around them continued to talk about damage control, locating Reynolds' body for confirmation with authorities, and other things he didn't care about. Right now, the only thing on Parker's mind—the only thing he could *see*—was her.

Without a word, he closed right in, framed her ice-cold face with his equally chilled palms, and slammed his mouth to hers. Eyes closed and his heart full of more emotions than he could possibly name, Parker took a precious moment to relish in the fact that she was okay.

Freezing cold and a little banged up, but Quinn was alive, and that's all that mattered.

Tasting of love and fear, river, and insurmountable relief, it was the best, most meaningful kiss of his entire existence. And when he finally, finally began to believe the truth of what he was holding—the truth of what he was feeling with his hands and lips and heart—Parker slowly pulled his lips free.

"D-don't ever...d-do something...like th-that...ag-gain." His warning gaze pierced hers as he rubbed his hands up and down her arms in rough, robust motions.

But of course, the amazing, unapologetic woman simply shrugged. "C-couldn't...let h-him...sh-shoot...y-you." Quinn's stuttered voice sounded rougher than normal as she added a mind-blowing, "I l-love...y-you."

She'd mouthed those same words to him just before vanishing over that fucking ledge. They'd meant everything to Parker, but hearing her actually *say* them...after nearly dying in that goddamn river...

"Ah, sweet-heart." Tears mixed with river water as they dropped down his already-damp cheeks. "I love y-you, t-too. So fucking much."

They met in the middle, their frozen lips sealing their declarations in a hard, desperate, grateful kiss. Seconds later, though he hated like hell to do it, Parker cut the moment short to deliver the bad news.

"McMahon is g-gone, but...w-we still haven't f-found Reynolds y-yet. He wasn't in the b-building, and—"

"J-Justin's d-dead." A dark shadow clouded her baby blues, her wet hair slapping against her cheeks with a shake of her head. "He's g-gone."

Parker frowned at the unexpected news. "Dead? H-how?"

"V-Victor...sh-shot h-him. Not h-ere. D-different p-place."

Never thought I'd be grateful for anything that bastard did, but...

"That's it, th-then." He caressed her pale cheek with his thumbs.

Quinn's head shook with an uneven nod. "It's really over."

Fucking finally.

For what felt like the first time in forever, Parker could fully breathe.

"N-never again, sweetheart." He kissed her softly. "C-can't ever l-lose you again."

"You w-won't." Her delicate chin quivered. "P-Promise."

And just like that, Parker's world righted itself once more. Only it wasn't the same world he knew before.

It was a million times better.

EPILOGUE

TWO WEEKS LATER...

"I COULD STAY LIKE THIS FOREVER." QUINN TRACED AN invisible line up and down Parker's forearm.

A warm ocean breeze swirled lazily around them as they relaxed on his back deck. With her back to his front and his strong arms wrapped loosely around her middle, she felt happier and more at peace than she could ever remember.

She also felt safe. Not only from the threat of physical harm—Parker had already proven himself a worthy protector on that front—but also safe in her heart.

His deep timbre vibrated against her back. "Well, the repairs are already finished, and the place looks as good as new, so... Yep. We could spend the rest of our lives right here, doing nothing else but this."

"Well, I wouldn't say *nothing* else." She sat up just enough to twist around and face him. "I mean we do have to eat." A playful nibble of his bottom lip.

"Oh yeah?" Parker's masculine hands squeezed the

curves of her ass as his heated gaze fell to her mouth. "What else would we need to do?"

Smiling, Quinn pretended to think. "I mean, we'd need to shower, of course. And probably communicate with the outside world on occasion. Just so Ash and Syd know we're still alive."

The comment was meant to be lighthearted, but she couldn't miss the dark curtain that fell over his gorgeous eyes from her words. Feeling like a jerk, she immediately did her best to fix it.

"Please don't do that." She cupped one side of his face when he started to look away. "Huh, uh. Look at me." When he did, Quinn held his tortured stare. "What happened to me wasn't your fault."

"Quinn—"

"No." She shook her head vehemently. "I know I've said it a thousand times in the last two weeks, but you are not responsible for what Justin or Victor did. Not the attack, the kidnapping...the river." Some nights when the memories find their way into her dreams, she could still feel the cold, dark water swallowing her whole. Even so, "I don't blame you. Not even a little bit. So you need to find a way to stop blaming yourself."

For the past two weeks, she'd caught glimpses when he didn't know she was looking. Haunted looks and tortured gazes marred his handsome face any time Parker thought about the craziness that had finally brought them together.

According to Asher, Christian's CPD contact had made good on his promise. So far, they hadn't seen her name or Parker's mentioned in connection with any of it.

Not her abduction, the activity at the abandoned lodge, the bodies of both Justin and Victor being discovered and recovered that same day...

It had all made national news, but lucky for them, *they* hadn't. Well, with the exception of the picture that jerk sold to the tabloid rag, that is.

Even then, Parker's attorneys had managed to get a cease and desist, and the image had been removed and banned from any and all news and social media outlets across the globe.

As for the explosion at Parker's home—which of course, had eventually gotten out to the public—it had been easily explained away by a fictitious gas leak. And since the house was on a stretch of secluded, private beach land, there hadn't been any up-close-and-personal witnesses to come forward and dispute the claim.

"I'll always blame myself for what happened, sweetheart." Parker tucked some hair behind her ear. "If I hadn't lied to you about where I was going..." He searched her eyes. "You don't do lies. Your words, remember?"

"Of course, I remember." It was why she'd slapped him during their first in-person meeting. "But—"

"—I lied to you about what I was doing and where I was going, and you were taken from me. You, Ash, Sydnee...you all could have been killed."

"But we weren't." She shifted herself up a little higher. "Am I happy about the fact that you hid your true agenda from me that day? No, I'm not. Would I have liked the chance to go with you? Absolutely. But Parker...whether you told me about your plan from the beginning or not, it wouldn't have mattered. Justin still wouldn't have been at FCI that day, and he and McMahon's goon still would have come after me. Maybe not here...maybe not that exact same day... But eventually, they would have seen their chance and acted on it."

"I just keep thinking about what could have happened to

you." His Adam's apple worked with a hard swallow. "What *did* happen, and I..."

Parker's voice cracked with emotion, and Quinn couldn't keep from leaning up and kissing those tight lips. When they softened beneath hers a few beats later, she pulled away and smiled. "I'm alive because of you, Parker." Her fingertips raked soft trails through the sheered hair at his temple. "I did what I did to protect you and the others. But if you hadn't jumped into that river..." It was her turn to get choked up. "You talk about me, but *you* could've been killed, too. You could have died trying to save me."

The image of him jumping off that roof still haunted her. She'd seen it happen, her heart nearly stopping from the sight. But she lost him again when Victor pushed her back under the freezing water.

It wasn't until that muffled gunshot tore through the water—until he saved her from being *murdered*—that Quinn even knew whether or not Parker had survived the fall.

"I would jump from a thousand rooftops if it meant keeping you safe. Because that's my job now, Quinn." He kissed the tip of her nose. "You're mine, and I will do whatever it takes to protect you."

If her heart felt any fuller, it would burst.

"I feel the same way about you." She smirked. "Guess we make a pretty good team after all, huh?"

"The best." He guided her body into a straddling position. "But there is one more thing I need to confess."

"Me, too."

"You?" Her surprising response furrowed his brow. "What do you have to—"

"It's not really a confession, I guess." Quinn licked her lips nervously. "I mean, I never lied about it or anything. It's just a part of my past I want you to know about."

"Okay..."

"So, you know how I helped the FBI with their case against Justin, right?"

"Yeah."

"I didn't just get immunity for my part in it." A corner of her mouth lifted slightly. "I also got a job." When Parker's expression remained unchanged, Quinn explained further. "It was all part of the same deal. As long as I helped them get the evidence they needed *and* agreed to work for them for twelve months, I'd be in the clear for creating and implementing the code in the first place. So, I agreed, and for the next three years, I worked full-time as a technical analyst for Chicago's FBI Cybercrimes Division."

"Why three years if you were only required to work the one?"

"The work I did was important. Rewarding, even. And a nice change from where I started."

"Why'd you leave?"

"I didn't." She swallowed. "Not fully, anyway. That's what I wanted to tell you." Another quick swipe of her tongue. "I'm still an official consultant for the FBI. They don't contact me very often. Just when they come across a particularly skilled hacker they aren't able to catch on their own. So anyway...that's it." Quinn filled her lungs and let the air out slowly. "Now you know everything."

He stared back at her but remained quiet. Her pulse spiked with uncertainty. Surely he wasn't mad, right?

How could he be upset that she was working with the good guys? Just because she hadn't told him yet, it was still honorable work, and—

"I'm an official consultant for Homeland Security and the CIA," Parker blurted. He blinked, but half-a-beat later, that sexy, crooked grin of his lifted those kissable lips as he added, "And I just broke about a dozen federal laws by telling you that, so unless you want me to be the one going to prison, I'd appreciate it if you didn't let on that you know. At least not until I clear it with my handlers."

Quinn stared back at him, her eyes searching his for the humor she expected to find. She *continued* staring, thinking surely he had to be kidding. He was just teasing her, right? Making light of what he could tell had made her nervous to share?

But Parker's eyes gave nothing away. Nothing other than the truth.

"You're serious." She blinked. "I thought you were just joking, but—"

"Not a joke, sweetheart." Parker chuckled. "And in the interest of full disclosure, I already knew about your stint with the FBI. But only because I came across that information when I was digging around on Reynolds." He winced back against the chair, as if he thought she was going to hit him or something.

Wouldn't be the first time.

But Quinn just smiled. "It's okay, Parker. Like I said, it wasn't like I was hiding something bad. I guess I'm just so used to keeping everything locked inside, that I..." She sighed. "I don't know. But you... I totally get why you didn't tell me what you do on the side. I mean, the threat of prison time is a pretty good motivator to keep quiet, right?"

He was quiet for a moment, those eyes of his filled with an admiration she didn't understand.

"What are the odds?" His tone was almost wistful. "Two people like us meeting the way we did. Reuniting the way we did, and then—"

"Falling in love the way we did," Quinn finished for him.

She leaned down and kissed him again, just because she could.

It was meant to be a sweet, playful kiss...but Parker had other ideas.

The man's impressive six pack flexed against her as he lifted his upper half into a sitting position. Their tongues met, Quinn swallowing his primal growl as her tank top-covered breasts pressed against his.

Frayed, faded jean shorts stretched high on her thighs as she locked her ankles behind him, and his steely bulge ground teasingly against her aching core.

She tilted her head to the side as Parker left a trail of hot, wet kisses along her racing pulse. "How much time do we have?"

"Don't care." More breathless kisses.

Quinn giggled. "Everyone's coming here soon." A low moan bubbled up from her throat when he nibbled the place where her neck and shoulders met. "We have to be ready."

"I *am* ready." Parker kissed his way back up to her lips before pulling away to meet her gaze once more. "Are you?"

The emotion she found reflected in those hazel eyes left her breath hitching, and Quinn realized he wasn't talking about the party they had planned for later that day.

"Parker?"

"I'm ready, Quinn." He ran the back of his knuckles down her cheek. "I'm ready for this. For us."

"Me, too." She smiled, her heart feeling as though it would *burst* from the love she felt for this man. "I'm ready, too."

Green and brown speckles shone in the late morning sun. "Are you sure? Because I'm a selfish bastard, sweetheart. I want it all. Marriage, kids... Or if you don't want kids, that's okay, too. We'll get a dog. Or another cat. Or a...turtle."

"A turtle?" She snickered. "Really?"

Another cat, she could understand, given how quickly Parker had taken to Oreo. Who, as luck would have it, showed back up the same day they'd flown back to her townhouse to box everything up for the move.

It had been a tearful reunion for all involved. The final missing piece of her crazy, unbelievable, far-from-traditional Cinderella story.

Last Quinn checked, the black and white ball of fur was napping in her new favorite spot—smack dab in the center of Parker's bed.

"Baby, I'll get you a damn tarantula if that's what you want." He cringed. "I won't go near the fucking thing, but if that's what will make you happy, then that's exactly what you'll get."

Crazy thing was the sweet, totally *unselfish* man meant every single word. But as she'd once told him before, she didn't need him to buy her things to make her happy.

I only need him.

Quinn was curious, though...

"What about you?" She posed the question back to its original creator.

Parker frowned. "What about me?"

"What will make you happy?"

He stared back at her, those soul-steeling eyes of his seeing and accepting every part of the person she'd become. Her past and present, her aversion to photographers and living in the public eye... None of that mattered to the man in her arms.

Which only made her love him even more.

Parting his lips, Parker started to answer. His intelligent, loving gaze making her feel as if she was the most important thing in this man's world.

Quinn waited, fully expecting him to say something sweet and sappy—because that's just the kind of man he was. Sweet, sappy, incredible...*insatiable.* But the next words that fell from his talented mouth stopped her heart mid-beat and stole her ability to breathe.

"Marry me."

"What did you just say?" The question came out all tight and strangled because seriously...she could *not* get her lungs to move.

"I said marry me, Quinn. And...shit." Parker frowned. "I don't have a ring yet. But I'll get you one. Big, small... diamonds, sapphires...whatever you want. You can even pick it out if that's what you prefer."

Ohmygod! "Parker, I—"

"I love you, Quinn." Another fast, hard kiss. "Not this house, or the money, or the cars... I love *you*." He paused, a shadow flashing over his eyes just then. "Those two days you were missing...when I couldn't find you, I thought..." He cleared his throat. "What I'm trying to say is, I know what it's like not to have you in my life, and I can't...that's not something I can..." Parker drew in a deep breath and let it out slowly. "Bottom line is, a life without you is completely unacceptable."

His fumbled attempt at proposing made her lips twitch, but Quinn rolled them inward to keep herself from laughing. While the delivery could use some fine-tuning, she understood exactly what Parker had been trying so hard to say.

Because she felt the exact same way about him.

It wasn't the fanfare one would expect from a man of his stature. There were no cameras flashing or gigantic diamonds swimming in champagne. No message written in the clouds or fireworks dancing with the stars.

But it was real.

Parker's proposal was adorable and sweet. Romantic and unplanned. In a word, it was... perfect.

Just like him.

"Since you put it that way..."Quinn brushed smiling lips against his. "I mean, far be it from me to put you into an unacceptable position."

She could feel the hard kick of his heart against hers as he held her body close to his.

"Just so we're clear." Those gorgeous eyes of his glistened with hope. "What exactly are you saying?"

With more love in her heart than she had the right to feel, Quinn stared back at the man she wanted to grow old with and said, 'Yes, Parker." Tears of joy fell from the corners of her eyes. "I'm saying yes."

His face lit up like a kid at Christmas. A beat later, Parker stood, holding her tight as he swung a leg over the chair. His lips barely left hers as he walked them inside and down the hall toward his bedroom.

"Parker!" Quinn giggled again as they crossed the threshold. "What are you...we have company coming in like—"

"Four hours." He followed her down onto the bed. An annoyed Oreo gave them both the stink-eye as she jumped from the mattress and sauntered away. "Don't worry." Parker's eyes darkened with mischief and desire. "I'll make sure you're ready in plenty of time."

Well in that case...

Quinn fisted the front of his shirt and brought his mouth to hers. With all thoughts of guests and cookouts on pause, she spent the next next two hours making sweet, glorious love to the man she was going to marry.

Her best friend.

Her protector.

Her lover.

My forever.

And from that moment on, Quinn never thought of herself as a jinx again.

PARKER STOOD JUST INSIDE THE FOLDING DOORS, STARING OUT at the small crowd gathered outside on his main deck. Taking advantage of the isolated moment, he watched as his friends talked and laughed. Some swayed to the rhythm of the upbeat music playing from the small speakers mounted near the roof.

Men on the left, women on the right...

A slow grin formed, the way they'd divided themselves up reminding him more of a junior high dance than a cookout. One he and Quinn had planned as a modest gesture of thanks to those same men. Only they weren't just men, they were heroes.

In every sense of the word.

Trace, Kellen, Asher, Greyson, Rhys... Each one of those men had put their lives on the line to save Quinn. And before her, there had been others.

So many others.

First during their time in the military, and now, with RISC. No matter what branch they'd served, or what team these men choose to serve, one thing was abundantly clear...

Parker was beyond blessed to have them in his life. Not

only because they'd played an intricate role in rescuing Quinn, but because they were his friends. His brothers.

And as far as he was concerned, the men of Charlie Team—and the women who loved them—would forever be his family.

"Hey, you."

Speaking of family...

He turned toward the raspy voice that drove him wild to see his fiancée walking toward him.

Fiancée. Damn, I really do like the sound of that.

Blonde hair blew with the whispers of the wind as eyes more beautiful than the endless ocean behind her found his. Parker's insatiable cock twitched, the zipper of his purposely gawdy pink flamingo shorts growing tight at the sight of her in that simple-yet-sexy sundress.

Of course, it wouldn't matter what she had on. He was always like this when she was around. Didn't matter that he spent every night reacquainting himself with every inch of her mouthwatering body.

Quinn appeared, and he got hard.

But who could blame him? The woman was the whole package. Brilliant, brave, sweet and sexy... And by the grace of God, she was his.

I really am one lucky son of a bitch.

"Whatcha doing hiding out in here all by yourself?"

"Not hiding." Parker pulled her in for a kiss. "Just watching."

"I know." She kissed him back. "It's kinda creepy."

Parker barked out a laugh. "God, I love you."

"I know that, too."

Her response—paired with an ornery grin—made him laugh even harder. "So what's the verdict?"

The question referred to an earlier conversation they'd

had—after the mindblowing round of afternoon sex, but before the arrival of their guests.

From over her shoulder, Quinn looked back at the group of RISC women and smiled. "I like them." Her gaze returned to his. "They're all really nice."

"Told you."

She gave her pretty eyes a teasing roll. "Yeah, yeah...you were right."

"Usually am." He winked. "So what have you learned so far?"

"Well, let's see." Quinn began listing off all the things. "Mia is an absolute doll. Emma said she and Trace want us to start coming to the annual Charlie Team Christmas parties. Taylor invited us to come see her and Greyson's house in the country, and Vanessa..." Quinn stared back at him pointedly. "That woman is a total badass. Oh, that reminds me." She snapped her fingers. "They're all planning a girls' weekend for a few months from now, and they invited me to come."

The excitement in her voice warmed his heart in all sorts of ways. "That sounds like a lot of fun."

"I thought so, too."

A few seconds of peaceful bliss passed before he asked, "So. You ready?"

He watched her closely for even the slightest inkling of doubt. But the only things he found in her softened expression were love and utter assurance.

"I'm ready." Quinn smiled.

"Alrighty, then." He linked his fingers with hers. "Shall we?"

Escorting the most incredible woman he'd ever known through the wide-open doorway, he motioned for the catering staff standing off to the side to begin. Within minutes, each of his guests had a freshly poured glass of champagne, as did Parker and Quinn.

"Can I have your attention, please?" Not a single one of his friends turned his way. "Hey!"

He looked over at Quinn to say he was going to go shut off the music, but closed his mouth when he realized she had the situation under control.

Lifting her curved thumb and middle finger to her mouth, the blonde beauty's shoulders rose with a large inhale half a second before filling the air with an ear-piercing whistle.

Everything stopped. The talking. The laughing. Even the music, though Parker wasn't sure who made *that* call. But either way, all eyes turned in their direction.

He leaned his head toward hers, muttering low so only she could hear. "Is it wrong that I am a little turned on right now?"

A crimson flush filled her cheeks, and damn if he didn't find that even sexier than the impressive whistle.

Everything she does turns you on.

Knowing his inner voice was spot on, Parker didn't even try to fight it. Instead, he cleared his throat and addressed the awaiting crowd.

"I'd like to start off by thanking you all for coming here tonight."

"You flew us here in your private jet and promised us food and beer!" Asher hollered back. "Of course we came!"

"Ash, you be nice!" Sydnee yelled at her fiancé playfully.

The entire space filled with laughter and a few other sarcastic jabs. When it quieted down, he picked up where he'd left off.

"I flew you here in my private jet and am giving you all the food and beer you can consume because I owe you." He met each man's stare. "Delta Team, too, but unfortunately they got called up for a job and couldn't make it."

"Just means more food and beer for us!" Greyson lifted his glass with a grin.

Parker laughed, but then, "Seriously, though. You guys didn't just help me save Quinn's life that day. You saved mine." Tears pricked the corners of his eyes, but he blinked them back and fought past the rush of emotions. "I don't know what I would have done if I'd lost her, and because of your team, I'll never have to find out."

A collective "Awe" came from the ladies, but the men, however, either tipped their heads or jutted their chins his way. It was that whole silent, male thing guys did when they wanted to express their feelings without having to *actually* express their feelings.

Normally Parker was the same way, but not today.

"I've met a lot of powerful men and women in my life." He eyed the entire group. "But none have been as tough or as determined as each of you. Ladies, I will forever be in awe of your courage and strength. Your tenacity and inspiring bravery."

"Here, here!" Kellan cheered, prompting a round of applause and whistles.

"And you guys..." Parker turned to the men of Charlie team, praying they could see the respect and admiration he felt for each and every man there. "You step up when you don't have to. Often when no one else can or will. You run into the fire when others turn their asses back around and run the other way. And the best part is you don't do it for fame and glory. Or money. You do it because someone needs to and because you refuse to stand aside while evil tries to destroy the innocent. So on behalf of a nation who has no idea how grateful they should be for you, I thank you."

He lifted his glass in a toast, taking only a small sip before lifting his hand in the air to let them know he wasn't quite finished.

"One more thing." He made sure they were listening before continuing. "I may have the fancy house and the private jet, but what you've found with them." He motioned to the women who owned them. "That is worth more than anything money can buy. And I know that because I finally found it, too. With Quinn. Which is why, about two hours before you guys got here, I asked her to marry me."

Several audible gasps reached them as a beaming Quinn announced, "And I said yes!"

The entire deck erupted with whoops and hollers and claps of joy, but Parker's focus was solely on the woman he was pulling into his arms.

"So this is what it feels like to be happy." She looked over at the men and women who'd all found their respective partners. "This is what it's like to have a family."

"Yeah, sweetheart." Parker used a gentle touch to guide her eyes back to his. "This is exactly what that feels like."

"Forever?"

Ah, that's an easy question to answer.

"You and me." His lips feathered across hers with a whispered, "Forever."

Not ready to say goodbye to the men of RISC?

Check out Anna's new RISC Delta Series:
CHRISTIAN (Delta Team #1)

ALSO BY ANNA BLAKELY

Charlie Team Series

Kellan

Greyson

Asher

Rhys

Parker

Marked Series

Marked For Death

Marked for Revenge

Marked for Deception

Marked for Obsession

Marked for Danger

Marked for Disaster

R.I.S.C. Series

Taking a Risk, Part One

Taking a Risk, Part Two

Beautiful Risk

Intentional Risk

Unpredictable Risk

Ultimate Risk

Targeted Risk

Savage Risk

Undeniable Risk

His Greatest Risk

Bravo Team Series

Rescuing Gracelynn

Rescuing Katherine

Rescuing Gabriella

Rescuing Ellena

Rescuing Jenna

TAC-OPS Series

Garrett's Destiny

Ethan's Obsession

WANT TO CONNECT WITH ANNA?

Newsletter signup (with FREE Bravo Team prequel novella!): BookHip.com/ZLMKFT
Join Anna's Reader Group:
www.facebook.com/groups/blakelysbunch/
Follow Anna on Amazon: amazon.com/author/annablakely
BookBub: https://www.bookbub.com/authors/anna-blakely
Author Page:
https://www.facebook.com/annablakelyromance
Instagram: https://instagram.com/annablakely
Goodreads: https://www.goodreads.com/author/show/18650841.Anna_Blakely

Made in the USA
Coppell, TX
21 April 2023

15892346R00157